UNBALANCED
MERCY

OTHER BOOKS BY J. WARREN
PUBLISHED BY REBEL SATORI PRESS

Stealing Ganymede
Silencing Orpheus
Drowning Narcissus

UNBALANCED MERCY

J. WARREN

Queer Space
New Orleans

**Published in the United States of America by
Queer Space
A Rebel Satori Imprint
www.rebelsatoripress.com**

This is a work of fiction. Names, characters, places, and incidents are the product of the author's imagination and are used fictitiously and any resemblance to actual persons, living or dead, business establishments, events, or locales is entirely coincidental. The publisher does not have any control over and does not assume any responsibility for author or third-party websites or their content.

Cover image by Sofia Sforza.

Library of Congress Control Number: 2020940209

Contents

Prologue

"Good afternoon," the impeccably well dressed man said. He wore a black fedora and underneath his houndstooth jacket he had a black satin vest on.

Dolores squinted up at him from the table. She set the books she'd been cradling down, then pushed the chair back.

"No, no," the man said, gesturing. "There's no need to get up, my dear." He pulled out a chair on the other side of the table and sat down. She fought the urge to squint again because for some reason his face seemed slightly out of focus.

"Do I know you?" Dolores asked.

"You soon will," the man said. Dolores found herself thinking that, with anyone else, this would seem creepy beyond compare. For some reason, though, she found the man charming. He leaned forward and picked up one of the books. "Lovecraft? I see," he said, as if it explained something.

"Term paper," she said, blushing and wondering why.

The man nodded, "Quite. I often re-read the master's works. I find him to be something of a comfort in these troubling times." The man sat the book back down and picked up the next one. "Ah, the quintessential examination of the nastiness in Salem so long ago." Dolores adjusted her glasses and found herself simultaneously proud of herself for selecting a book this stranger thought so highly of, and at the same time perplexed at that very feeling. The man sat the book down and picked up the last one. "And, of course, Crowley. Not an incorrect theory of the way magick works, to be sure, but certainly an…esoteric understanding."

"Who are you?" Dolores managed to whisper as she leaned forward. She had been attempting to take the book from his hand, feeling somehow exposed, as if she'd been caught doing something wrong. The man sat that book down as well, making the volumes into a neat stack.

"Shall we dispense with the fiction that this is work for a class, though?" The man didn't move, but somehow Dolores felt as if he was leaning in closer.

"What do you want?" Dolores asked.

"Ah, finally we come to the point," the man said. Though he didn't move, Dolores felt as though he had leaned in closer. "It is not what I want that matters, Dolores VanDecamp. It is what you want, and how I can help you get it." He handed her a card with his name on it and smiled. She couldn't help but feel it was the smile of a shark about to bite.

BOOK 1

"The conscience of the world is so guilty that it always assumes that people who investigate heresies must be heretics; just as if a doctor who studies leprosy must be a leper. Indeed, it is only recently that science has been allowed to study anything without reproach."

—Aleister Crowley

1. Special Agent Paul Lowe

I'm sitting at my desk, finishing up the latest paperwork. Guy who ordered a hell of a lot of fertilizer also happened to have some hits on an "alt-right" website, so ASAC Wicks tells me "go knock on his door." There I am, then, on the next flight to Wyoming. Turns out the guy is a bit of a racist jerkoff, but he's legit. Divide number of acres owned by total poundage and bingo. Just more paperwork.

Don't get me wrong, this kind of stuff isn't glamorous but it's important. I'd much rather find out the guy is just some yokel who thinks his biggest accomplishment is his skin color than a bad guy with a plan, if you see what I'm saying. After all that stuff last year, I don't mind a bit of crossing some Ts, you know?

"Paul? See you for a minute?" Director Jimenez stuck her head through the doorway and asked.

I looked up from the computer screen and, if I'm being honest, barely managed to not jump out of my seat. "Sure," I said. Then I stood up. Then I looked for my jacket which was, as always, on the back of my chair. Even as I was doing these things, I felt how separate they were. How out of it I must look to anyone watching. And they were watching—it's not every day that one of the directors comes down for a chat—normally they send for you.

I walked out into the hall sliding into my coat as I walked.

The director was standing against the opposite wall. "Walk with me," she said, turning on her heel and heading for the elevator. I caught up.

"You've been with the Bureau for how long now, Paul?" she asked, pressing the button then turning to face me.

"3 years," I said.

"3 years," she repeated, but her face showed nothing. The elevator arrived and we stepped inside. She pressed the button for the second subfloor. Almost the lowest anyone could go in the building.

The doors slid closed. We both faced forward. "Your record is fantastic, especially considering that thing last year. The church bombings," she said. "To be honest, how you handled that case made you a name people know upstairs."

I didn't know whether to say thank you or not.

When the doors opened, I expected to see endless rows of boxes and file cabinets. As far as I knew, that was all that was down this far. I was mostly right, but the director began walking along a row of cabinets and turned a sharp right at the end of the row. She walked along a path between the end of that first row and the beginning of a second set of rows. After a hundred feet or so, she turned a sharp left and we walked along another row. We crossed over another pathway between sets of filing cabinets and into another row. At the end of that row there was a wall, but also a small alcove. As we entered that alcove, I saw that there was a door on the left. The sign on the door said P I Division.

The director stopped and turned to face me.

"You gained the reputation as someone who is levelheaded, able to think through difficult situations. That's a good thing. I wish I could say your reward was that we were moving you upstairs. Unfortunately, that is not the case."

"Ma'm?" I asked.

"In just a moment, I'm going to knock on that door," she said, gesturing with her head, "and introduce you to Special Agent Miranda Burton. She is the senior agent in charge of the P I

Division."

At that moment, the door opened, and a tall woman with glasses and dark hair to her collar appeared. She had on the standard issue dark pants, light blue shirt, and navy blue suit jacket that almost all female agents wore these days.

I was in the act of asking, "P.I. Division—,"

"Paranormal investigation division," Burton said, her hand still on the door.

"Special Agent Miranda Burton, this is Special Agent Paul Lowe," the director said.

Burton stepped forward and extended her hand. I shook it out of reflex, but I still felt very confused. "Welcome aboard," Burton said.

"Paul, I'm assigning you to P.I.. Until further notice, you will work alongside Agent Burton. You can call over to the pool to ask someone to bring down any personal affects from your desk." There weren't any. She already knew that.

"Wait, I don't...I don't understand..." I started to say.

"Step in and we'll talk," Burton said, turning aside to allow me through the door.

The director was already walking away.

"Ma'am?" I asked.

She stopped and turned on her heel. "Make us proud." She then turned back and walked away.

"Paul?" Burton said and when I looked back at her, she gestured through the door.

I looked back toward the director's retreating back once more, then stepped through into the office. There were two desks loosely facing each other in a V-shape on the edges of the room, and a waist-high table in the center. It was covered with boxes, some stacked on top of one another, some not, and over that were maps and photos. Toward the back of the room was another door. One of the desks was covered in folders and books. It had a computer monitor that was at least ten years old, and a name plate that read Miranda Burton. Behind the desk on the wall was a poster that read "Hang in there" and showed a kitten barely hanging on to a branch

The other desk was completely barren, but I could see in the dust that it used to have a computer monitor and a nameplate, as well.

The door closed behind me and Burton came around to face me. She crossed her arms over her chest and waited until I'd finished surveying the room. "I'd offer you coffee, but it's on the blink. I've sent in a requisition for a new one, but who knows when that will get here." She stepped to her desk and leaned against it, arms still crossed. "Have a seat."

I walked over to the empty desk and leaned against it, crossing my arms. It was only after I'd settled into it, too late to change, that I realized I had mimicked her pose exactly. I hoped maybe she wasn't the kind of person who would notice such a thing, but her left eyebrow inched up a bit.

We weren't off to a great start.

"First off, hello," she said. "I'm Miranda. Of course, I tell everyone that, and yet ever single person I meet in this building insists on calling me Burton no matter what I say, so…"

I didn't say anything. Not out of any kind of hostility, but simply because I didn't know what to say. This wasn't my first transfer, if, indeed, that's what this was, but it was the first I'd ever had that was this unexpected.

"Do you prefer Paul?"

I nodded.

"Good. Okay. Well, I'd prefer you call me Miranda, but I'm guessing you're going to call me Burton, anyway, so there's that. I was assigned down here to P.I. about four years ago. At that time the senior agent was Abner Booth, the man who used to work that desk," she said, gesturing with her forehead, arms still crossed.

"What happened to him?"

"Agent Booth…Abner…was killed in the line three weeks ago."

"I'm sorry," I said, standing up and dropping my arms out of reflex.

"Thanks," she said.

"I…I didn't see anything about an agent's funeral in the bulletin. Did they…?"

"I asked them not to. There were a number of people that I…

Well, let's just say I was worried about who might show up. The family held a private ceremony. It was…nice."

"Still, I'm sorry to hear it."

She nodded, then looked back at me. Her eyes were the same color as dark oak, I noticed. "Thirty years with the Bureau. Ten of them down here, working P I."

"I have to say I'm more than a bit confused. What exactly is P.I.?"

"As the director said," she said, moving to the other door on the far end of the room and taking a key out of her pocket. "Paranormal investigations division."

"Wait. Wait. Wait," I said. "Like that TV show?"

She laughed bitterly. "Do you know," she said, placing the key in the lock without looking at me, "that's the exact same question I asked Abner when I was transferred down here." She shook her head and then turned the key. "Come on." She opened the door. She stepped inside and I followed.

The room inside was rectangular, about sixty feet long, and filled with three rows of the same drab filing cabinets that existed outside. Her heels echoed when she stepped. "This is where our work lives," she said. She walked to the nearest row and leaned against one of the cabinets.

"But that…that was a TV show."

"What do you think the bulk of that show was based on? Loosely, but still. There are things that the Bureau knows about the world that we can't just leave lying around for anyone who wants to file a Freedom of Information act case to find." She waited while I took it all in.

"So why did you choose me?" I asked.

She sighed. I could see she was deciding something. Then she nodded and said, "We didn't."

I waited for a moment. "I'm not sure I understand."

"Don't get me wrong, you are a fantastic agent. Your file is textbook up and comer. Thing is though, as you no doubt noticed, we didn't put the word out that there was an opening down here or anything."

"Yeah, that's what I mean," I said. "No offense, but I don't know that this is the kind of job I'd have put myself in for if I'd seen a bulletin. So, I figure this is just a routine reassignment kind of thing, that you had an in with the director and asked for me or something. You're saying that's not the case?"

She shook her head. "Again, don't get me wrong, I probably would have had I know you were out there. Thing is…the thing is that you're here because you came to my attention, that's true, but not in the way you think." She waited a moment, staring at me. Then she said, "Last week you were contacted by two people who took you with them to another location. Do you remember this happening?"

"What?" I asked.

"That's what I thought," she said. She walked past me back into the office and waited. When I stepped back through, she closed the door and locked it. "Here," she said and tossed me the key she had. I caught it. "You and I are the only ones who have the key to that storage room. Not even the Director himself has one." I put it away in my pocket. She stepped over to her desk and picked up a file. "Here," she said, opening the folder.

When I looked, I could see myself walking through the metal detector in the lobby. Two people were with me, a tall, emaciated man and a woman with very long hair. "Do you recognize either of these individuals?"

I took the folder and looked closer at the photo. "I don't."

"But you can clearly see that is you with them, yeah?" she asked.

I nodded. I couldn't explain it, but it was clear to me that I was the person in the picture.

"They knew enough to obfuscate the minds of the people around so that no one stopped them, and they wiped your memory but good, but they didn't get the cameras for some reason."

"What's going on here?" I asked.

"We—," she said, then stopped herself, shaking her head. "I believe that these were two agents of the Malleus Maleficarum. This has the hallmarks of their work. They abducted you right from this building with no one, not even you, the wiser. We need to find out what they wanted, and why specifically they wanted you. When this was brought to Director Jiminez's attention, she put in the request to transfer you to P.I. immediately."

"Why?" I asked. My hands started to shake and I tried to steady them.

"Because this room may be the only place on the planet you're safe from them," she said. "So, you see, it's provenance in a weird way. I was just starting to look for a second person to help out, and then suddenly here was a case involving a fellow agent. I didn't pick you for this job, the universe did."

I likely would have rolled my eyes at what my father would have called a "granola, hippy-dippy" cliché, but one, I was still trying to keep myself from shaking at the thought of having been abducted, and two, I could tell she was in deadly earnest.

She picked up a remote control from her desk. With a few flicks, an ancient television sitting in the corner against the wall came to life. She pressed a few buttons and the screen showed five men in what grade-school children would call "pilgrim hats" standing shoulder to shoulder with a gallows in the background. From the noose hung a young woman.

"They are called the Malleus Maleficarum. Loosely translates to 'Hammer of the Witches'," Burton said. "They began as a witch hunting institution loosely affiliated with Christian ideals, but as always, when you get a bunch of straight white men in a room together, there's no telling what manner of nonsense they get up to." The next slide clicked into place. It showed ten men and women dressed in drab gray suits. "In about 1920 or so, though, a new ideology came into vogue in their ranks—the idea of keeping an eye on the witch population—,"

"Wait," I said, "I thought study after study proved that the Salem witch incidents were wholly faked. Mass paranoia or whatever," I said.

"Those were fake. However, that doesn't mean that there weren't actually witches and other paranormal factions functioning during that time. In fact, not far from there, at that time, there was a group of—actually, let's not get sidetracked. So, the ideology of the group over time changed from ruthlessly hunting down and killing witches to allowing them to do whatever they were doing and keeping an eye on them."

"Standard FBI procedure," I whispered.

"Exactly. In fact," she said, clicking three slides ahead. The slide that appeared showed a complicated series of circles forming a grouping of Venn diagrams. "When they were left alone, these groups of people using magick began to form a kind of shadow government, a...grouping of groupings, if you will. It's gone by many different names over time, but today it is called The Conclave. Not the most awe inspiring title, if you ask me, but then neither is 'The Executive Branch.'"

"One representative from each of the great clans and also one from each of the...well...I suppose 'types' would be the best way to say it. One sorceress, one soothsayer, one blood mage, etc." she said. As she said each word, my eyes were drawn to that particular circle and how it overlapped with certain others. "It all functions quite a bit like our own version of governance, really, proving that bureaucracy, not music or dance, is the true universal language. Within that structure then are substructures that handle things like budget from taxation, or those that, for instance, handle coordinating the needs of those who have fallen on hard times, etcetera."

"Whereas many would argue that The Conclave owes its existence to the Malleus," Burton continued, "eventually Malleus was brought into The Conclave and now functions in many ways like a sort of Department of Justice for the paranormal community."

I laughed, "Like in the books about that magickal kid with the scar..."

She rolled her eyes. "At any rate, we both wind up with very similar jobs, Malleus and The P.I. division here. They try to catch cases before they wind up on my desk, though."

"Is magick somehow illegal?" I asked.

"No," Burton said. "But what people do with it sometimes is, either because they don't know the laws or because they do and just don't care. The healing stuff, the binding people from harm stuff, that's all fine. But when people start using spells and charms to bend rules and break laws, that's when we step in."

"We step in?"

She looked directly at me, quirking her head to the side.

"Do you…practice?…magick?" I asked.

"No, I'm not a witch or a wizard, a sorcerer, a mage…no."

"Then, if you don't mind my asking," I said, "how exactly do we 'step in'?"

"Ah, I see your point. It's not always easy. Most of the time, though, the sight of a nicely pressed suit, a badge, and a gun are enough to convince people to stop whatever it is they are doing. Most of the time," she said and I saw her glance at the picture of her old partner quickly.

"And in those instances when it isn't enough?"

She paused for a moment, staring at the desk. When she looked back at me her face had somehow become even more sober than it was before. "I won't lie—it can get messy. There is what the people upstairs might call a turnover rate to this job. You're not the first to suggest that walking into a fight with a magick practitioner wearing only a gun and the law as protection is not ideal."

"I was thinking knives to gunfights."

The corner of her mouth quirked. "Something like that, yeah. However, we have something many of them don't: Knowledge. You'd be surprised how many people jump into using mystic forces without knowing much about their origin or what has happened to others. It's like what people do with the terms of service agreement from Apple. The mystical version of clicking 'agree' without reading ahead. Well, unlike some hothead undergrad who tripped over an extradimensional portal, I have read the fine print. The one thing the FBI is actually good at is keeping files on things." We both smiled. "I go into a situation with some kid who has just pledged his life to a being from another dimension for the power to read minds and influence emotions and before I step out of the car I have read up on all the other cases like that. Figured out what to do before the kid even knows I'm about to knock on his door."

"What would you do in a situation like that?"

She leaned back in her chair. "In a case exactly like that in particular? Once a telepath or an empath gets their dander up, they go to guns immediately. Defenses go up and they attack quick. So the idea is to soothe them all the way until the cuffs are on. You treat a kid like that the same as you would someone hopped up on PCP or bathtub crank. You talk them down as best you can without showing your pistol. Meanwhile your partner has circled around behind them and has already drawn down. If the kid gets wise and starts to squint, they get a 'you are under arrest.'" she said. "There's only been once that I've run up on a kid strong enough to control two of us at the same time. That one…ended badly."

"Did you bring the kid in?"

"Not alive, no. Trust me, though, that's never the goal. Never. People who use magick, people who are connected to other planes of existence, what have you? They're Americans just like any of the rest of us, for the most part. They get the same protections under law that any other American gets. Habeaus Corpus, timely trial, the whole nine yards," she said. "I didn't want to put a bullet in that kid, but that one…he was already too far gone."

"Do we have access to any…I don't know…objects? Things like that?"

"Magick lamps to level the playing field? No. That stuff all gets turned over to evidence. Or, if it's real bad news, I give it to Malleus and they dispose of it."

"You trust them to do that?"

"It's a working relationship. I keep tabs on what's going on. I assume they do, too. That leads us back to your case," she said, leaned forward, took another folder from the bottom of the pile and opened it. Inside were blurry pictures of a man and a woman standing on a street. "Any recollection of either of these people?"

The woman did look a little familiar, but it was like I was looking at a yearbook photo of someone who was thirty now. "I don't know. Sort of. Who are they?"

Burton didn't seem amused, "I've asked them again and again why the wipe leaves behind residue but they don't really like to answer my questions. Interesting, though."

"What is?" I asked.

"Do you remember the fact that we just had a similar conversation about thirty minutes ago in there?" she asked, gesturing toward the door to the file room.

"No. Wait, did we?" I asked.

She nodded. "Curioser and curioser. This wipe seems to be ongoing. Any time we talk about it, once we're done, it looks like memory of the conversation immediately slides out of your head."

"Wait, you're saying that—,"

She put away the folder and I found I couldn't remember what was in it. I tried to get back to the conversation but I couldn't remember what we had been talking about.

"There is an author...she writes a lot about the supernatural. Mostly vampires. From what they've told me, she has a habit of getting into trouble. Turns out, just as many people who actually deal with the supernatural on a daily basis are fans or critics of her work as people who have no clue any of this actually goes on. They pop up and want to have long conversations with her, setting her right, mansplaining...or, I guess in this case, magesplaining, and some of them aren't so very nice about it, I hear. And every time they come to her aid, they have to clear her mind out again. Erasure after erasure and it seems like in some ways it just isn't working anymore. At any rate," she said, rolling her eyes, "I believe that these two people who walked in here and walked out with you are Malleus agents."

"Walked out with me?" I asked.

She shook her head. "Two Malleus agents walked into this very building and kidnapped someone without bothering to let me know they were coming. It was, to say the last, rude."

"But you say you've talked to them. If they were coming in here, why didn't they bother to talk to you about it?"

"Now you're starting to ask the right questions. There is a kind of...professional courtesy between this office and the Malleus. We tend to at least try to talk to one another if we think an operation might step on the others' toes, the same as we would with the DEA or ATF. These agents, though," she said, gesturing toward an open folder nearby with a picture that showed me being escorted through the metal detector with this man and this woman by my side. "These agents may be known to me. And, worse, as you asked, why not come talk to me first before simply walking you out of here. I was just about to set up a meeting when word came down from upstairs that you were being transferred." She shut off the projector and the room grew dim.

"Does anyone—,"

"Upstairs know about the fact that we have contact with an agency or, indeed, with The Conclave itself? No. And they don't want to know, either. That's been made abundantly clear."

"So—,"

"No, I don't think your transfer is something either The Conclave or Malleus itself either advocated for or outright ordered. The evidence just doesn't seem to point that way. If they were going to do that, why would they need to walk you out at all? They could just wait until you were transferred and then ask for a meeting. That's been a fairly standard procedure in the past, so I don't know why they'd deviate from it. No, whatever happened, your transfer is most likely unrelated."

"Do you think that—,"

"It's possible that these, then, were not in fact Malleus agents? That's a possibility, but a very disturbing one. It's on my list of things to look into."

"Do you always know what someone else is thinking?" I asked, speaking quickly to get it all out before she could say anything.

"No. Your line of inquiry, though, was fairly obvious." She stared into space for a minute, then said, "No offense intended."

I nodded, but, if I'm honest, a bit of offense had been taken.

"So," she said, setting the remote control for the slide machine down and crossing her arms. "That brings us to you. Not only newly assigned to P.I., but you are, in fact, your own first P.I. case. Thoughts?"

I struggled to say something. I wanted to say something, but all that happened was my mouth opened and I stared at the wall to her left.

"Precisely. You're a good agent. I've read your files. Especially about that thing with the church bombings. Brutal. But, as violent as that case was, the cases we deal with down here are going to twist you, turn you, leave you wondering what side is really up. When you get out of your depth, the best thing to do I have found is to simply say so."

"Is this the same speech you got when you joined?"

"Yes. In fact, I came down here with another agent. We were both to join Abner," she said, glancing down for just a moment. "The other agent didn't make it past the first week."

"What happened?" I asked.

"He insisted that he was alright, and that he didn't have any questions, and that he was 'good to go.' His words. I, on the other hand, was willing to ask for help, to ask for clarification when needed, and I remembered to take a pause when I felt I needed one."

"What happened to the other guy?"

"He is quite comfortable and doing fine at a hospital for the mentally disturbed. I visit him at least once a month." She leaned forward. "All of which is to say that there are a few ways we can proceed with this case, but none of them are what you might call, 'standard procedure.'"

I took a deep breath. "Two hours ago," I began, "I was just having a normal Monday. I was thinking about getting a second cup of coffee and trying to get my emails to zero pending. I'll be honest, I already miss that. But according to the director, I don't have any choice. This is my new assignment. No going back. So," I said, standing. "What do we do first?"

As if she'd been waiting for that exact sentence to happen, Burton clapped her hands against her thighs and swiveled her chair. She picked up another folder from her desk and put it between us without opening it.

"Before we can truly get started on your case," Burton said, "I have one I'm working on as we speak. I could really use your help with it. I'd like to clear this one, then move on to yours." She picked up a new folder, opened it and handed it to me. Just inside was a picture of six young people standing around a park picnic table. Four young men and two women. Hooded sweatshirts, jeans, inexpensive sneakers. Just under it was another photo of what appeared to be the same group, only here they were all in what could only be described at 19th century formal wear—velvet blazers, knit shawls, lace cravats, the works.

I thought for a second, I have a case? I let it slide, though. The morning had already been very weird.

"This merry band of young people called themselves The Order, making them approximately the three millionth group ever to do so without realizing everyone else had the same idea," she said, gesturing toward the folder. "It seems they got involved with the *real* stuff." I looked up at her.

"Not that those other forms are not valid. Far from it, in fact. But…well the best way to put it for now is that there's magick and then there's magick. There's helping your aunt's arthritis with a poultice, which is powerful, but then there's bending the dreams of the world's population to your will, and that's…well, that's a whole 'nother thing. These kids," she said, tapping the photo, "they stumbled on to the big stuff, and they stumbled on to it way too soon. It's like…teach a kid to swim and he or she has the basics they need for the deep end of the pool at the Y, but technically they also know how to swim the English Channel, right? Only, your average thirteen year old doesn't accidentally wander from one to the other. Someone goes out to try themselves against really truly deep water with dangerous currents, they tend to prepare themselves. Get a teacher. Study up. That sort of thing. If you wind up in truly dangerous water by accident—,"

"—you tend to drown," I said. She nodded.

She sat a new folder in front of me and opened it. Gruesome pictures of a badly-sliced-up body. Nothing I hadn't seen before, though. "Victim's name was Charlotte Coleridge. Twenty-three. Found just inside an alleyway. No relation of any kind to the poet."

"Would it have mattered if she had been?" I asked, trying to be funny.

Burton didn't smile. "Had there been? Yeah, maybe. 'In

Xanadu did Kubla Khan, etc.'" Burton sat down next to me and moved one of the photos so that the one below it was visible. On the victim's torso was a large slashing wound. "M E says cause of death is exsanguination. She bled out. Whatever did it had, and I'm quoting here, 'damn near surgical levels of sharpness.' And look how long the gash is."

I leaned closer. "No way a scalpel is long enough for that, or that it stays in the attacker's hand long enough to make that slash unless the victim is already down."

Burton nodded, "Good eye. Evidence says the cut is pre-mortem. All of them are, in fact."

"Very long blade, then."

"Exactly. A very long blade to be that surgically sharp. There's no way someone keeps something like that hidden unless they do all their work at home and are very good at concealing the thing while in public," Burton said. "Coroner says time of death would have been about 8 am or so."

I pull another of the photos from the stack showing the body within inches of the sidewalk. "If the attack happened right there, the attacker would have to have been very fast with a blade that large to get that many cuts before someone walked or drove past."

Burton nodded. Then she tapped her finger against the photo of the alleyway. "See the problem?" That's when I knew: this was a test. She already had all the information. She was grilling me to make sure I was up to her standards.

"Wait," I said. The alleyway wasn't by any means spotless, but there was one thing that was missing. "Where's all the blood?"

Burton leaned back in her chair. "Now you see it."

"So the victim was killed somewhere else and dumped?"

"That's the assumption the detectives were working on," Burton said.

"And it's not the case?"

Burton shook her head and crossed her arms. "No signs of rope or anything else on the wrists, no remnants of carpet fiber or cardboard fiber or even plastic from trash bags."

"You're saying you think…"

"She *was* killed right there. There's no way the attacker moved her there without something to hold in the blood after that many cuts. None. So that only leaves one other possibility," Burton said as if it was the most obvious thing in the world. "Lunch?"

It was only eleven, but I never turn down food.

She didn't say anything else on the way to the elevator. I was convinced I'd never find the office again without her, so I stuck close by. As we hit the lobby floor and walked out, I felt as though people were watching me very closely because I was with her. I also noticed that she didn't seem to notice anything at all, moving, as my dad would have said, with a purpose.

"Asia Nine okay?" she asked as we walked out the front doors. "They got a Basil Noodle that's pretty good." I stick close to her as we walked up 9th and crossed. She still hadn't said anything as we turned up E street. The wind was nice, and the chance to stretch my legs was even nicer. Still, her quiet unnerved me. We walk in and even though they've only been open ten minutes or so, they all smile and wave at her. She walked right to a table and sat before I could even ask if we should wait. I sat across from her. Before the young man can even finish saying hello, Burton ordered. "Basil Noodle with chicken and iced tea. Do you trust me?" she asked, looking at me. I nod because she was already ordering, "and Kapow on rice with pork for him. Iced tea." The guy nodded as though this is exactly what he expected to happen and walked away.

"Thing is," she said, as if the conversation never stopped, "it's not like that blood simply disappeared. Coroner says she did bleed out from her wounds."

"Miranda," a guy in a gray suit said as he and a woman in a blue suit walked past.

"Jack, Kim," Burton said.

"Okay," I asked, "so where did it all go?" The tea arrived. She dumped two pink packets into hers immediately and stirred with her straw. She looked at me pointedly, then made a production of taking a long sip of her tea through the straw. When she finished, she cocked her head to the side.

"Wait, so you're suggesting—," I started to say.

"More than suggesting. I think that this blade our attacker is using? I think it's got abilities. Properties of some sort. And I think it may be a blood drinker, or what we call 'The Bathory Effect.'"

Part of me wanted to get up and walk away from the table. I can see she has seen it in my eyes. "Don't go; you'll love the Kapow. Besides, it's on me. When was the last time someone paid for your lunch?"

It had been a while.

"Okay," I said. "So you think that maybe this thing, this blade, is mystical?"

She nodded.

"And that the blood isn't all over the place because the blade itself...what...drank it?"

She nodded without blinking.

Thing is, no part of me disagreed. A part of me thought it should for show's sake, but when I thought about it, I felt the explanation made sense. "What did the local PD decide?" I asked.

"They filed it away and shuffled it until it wasn't on anyone's active case list."

"How did it wind up on your desk?" I asked. The food arrived. She put the napkin across her lap with one hand while the other dug into the noodles with her fork. I picked up a chunk of what I assumed was the pork and blew on it.

"Danberry, Robert A, 25, two days later. Velmoor, Michael, 21, one day after that. And there's more," she said after swallowing a gulp.

She was right—the pork was really good. "How do these not all wind up alarming the PD and keeping the case from being shuffled?" I asked.

She put her hand in front of her mouth and said, "across state lines," with her mouth full. She swallowed after a moment. "All of them similar—exsanguinated, left in relatively public places, no blood at the scene, no signs of being moved." She took another big bite.

"And all of these detectives just so happened to shuffle their cases away?"

She nodded, then held up her hand in front of her mouth again. With her mouth full, she said, "Until this last one." She swallowed and took a sip of tea. "New detective very interested in crossing the T's. So he sets up a search that pings the search I already had in place and suddenly there it all was."

"How many so far?" I asked. The pork was unbelievable. The place started to fill up with other people in suits.

"If we're strict? 9. If we're a bit more loose with our definition? Could be as many as 15. There are two that are being examined closer."

"Any leads?" I asked.

She nodded. I looked down to see she was over half done with her noodles. "I think it ties in with a case that has been on the backburner for a while, but I'm not sure. We need to go talk to some folks first." I nodded and kept eating.

"Here's the interesting part," she said after a few moments. "Director shows up, takes you downstairs and plops you into P.I., a unit most people think is a myth, and you don't even blink. You, a guy who was on his way to one of the rockstar divisions— Violent Crimes, maybe even all the way to Behavioral Analysis, one of the places that gets you noticed, gets you promoted. You were on track to be one of the big boys with the big offices and yet here you are, down in the basement," she said. "And thing is, you'll pardon me for reading you, but thing is, you look content."

"Do I?" I asked.

"You do. I haven't heard you bitch about any of this. Not once." I started to say something but she held up a hand. "Oh, don't get me wrong. I can see you're skeptical. That doesn't bother me. A lot of other guys, though, they would have gotten up and walked away."

"I guess maybe, yeah. I mean, I thought about it," I said. She smiled and nodded. "I was taken off guard, I don't deny that. I didn't know what to think. But I'm coming out of shock. Other than the mention of blood drinking swords or whatever, it sounds like this is pretty standard work. Hypothesize, interview, reformulate based on data, etc."

She nodded and sat back, "Exactly. That's exactly what we do down here. So," she said, "are you in? You could still back out, you know; go to the director and say this isn't a good fit or whatever. No one would blame you for——"

"I'm in," I said.

"Good," she said and used her fork to push some of the noodles around smiling. "Good," she said again, and shoveled in a forkful.

"Who are your leads?" I asked.

"Could we get the check, please?" she said out loud to no one in particular. She finished her noodles; I, about half of my pork. She grabbed the fortune cookies, slapped down two twenties and stood, placing the napkin over the plate as if it was a shroud. I did the same and followed her back to the office.

Once the door was closed, she threw her jacket over the back of the chair behind her desk and rolled up her sleeves. She pulled another folder off the top of her filing trays.

"Covens. Lodges. Church of the New Dawning of the whatever, you get the idea. People who practice magick tend to find one another. So, this group of kids, The Order," she opens the folder up once more. "Like I said, I have reports that they got into the business of imbuing objects with power."

"Imbuing...?" I said, looking up at her.

"Asking the great god of whatever to take your house keys and make them impossible for you to lose. Asking the spirits of your ancestors to grant great luck to the person who wears this ring. That kind of thing."

I nodded.

"Problem is, there are always two kinds of consequences when people try to imbue an object with power—intended and unintended," she said. I waited. "I just heard how stupid that sounds. I mean, that's like saying 'water comes in two forms, solid and wet.'" She shook her head, "At any rate, whenever people like this decide to pour magick into an object, they bring it to life. They usually manage to fumble their way through and get it to do what they want it to do—think of it like hotwiring a car; the more experience and talent they have, the better the job turns out."

"And so," she went on, "the thing most of them don't know is that there are always things that show up in the object that they didn't intend. So for instance a case we worked last year was where a smartass kid wanted to make his car keys able to open any lock." My eyebrows shot up. She nodded. "Yeah, well, he got very lucky considering his actual skill level and it wound up able to open a few different brands. The problem was that it also had the effect of making him obsessed with puzzles, and eventually to what psychologists would call full-blown OCD. We finally caught him because he was sneaking in to young girls' houses to attempt to rape them but instead wound up going through the house straightening all their pictures and rearranging their silverware drawers. In the case of this object? We aren't a hundred percent sure, but we think that it's some kind of blade weapon designed to not only be eversharp, which is what they intended it to do, but it also wound up able to do...other things."

"Like drink blood?" I asked.

"Exactly," she said.

"Okay, I think I get it. Thing is, though, how do we go about finding this thing? Normal procedure for a missing object is profile the person you think probably has it, do a press conference of some sort, triangulate places the object was last seen, etc. Textbook. We could start by going through her life, interviewing past lovers, teachers, find out who she had grudges against. Connect the dots."

She shook her head, and said "Thing is, that could work, but not in this case—we don't have that kind of time. The...Agent... warned me that the subject knows we are actively looking for her and that some aspect of the blade is...well, it's hiding her. Keeping us from being able to use our normal methods to box her in. She's going to try to run. So, we need to find ourselves a sensitive."

"A sensitive?"

"Yeah," she said, leaning back in her chair. "A sensitive. On the street, they call them 'hounds.' As I understand it, it's not a particularly nice name to call someone in that community, but they all say it, anyway. We need one."

"What do they do?"

"Just like a police hound. We give them a kind of scent to follow, in this case, a bit of something she's worked magick upon, and then he or she—statistically almost always a she, by the way, which is interesting in and of itself—finds that scent and hopefully leads us to her."

"Okay. Where do we find something our subject has worked... uh...worked magick on?"

"Upon," she said. "We say worked magick upon. Well, that's where things get interesting. We're going to have to go find the other object that her group worked on. To get that done, we need to go talk to these kids."

"Okay. Interviews, then sensitive, then, if necessary, find object to help us find the actual object we're looking for," I said.

"You got it," she said.

"So, once we get the interviews done, how do we find a sensitive?"

"I have a friend," she said.

"That sounds mysterious," I said.

"No, just complicated. They're an ex of mine," she said.

I leaned back in my chair. "Okay," I said. I took a deep breath, then exhaled. "So, I wouldn't be doing my job if I didn't ask the dumb questions. I mean, that's why I'm here, right? The new guy? So, here goes: why's it so important that we find this thing? I mean, other than the fact that it's a supernatural weapon, and those probably shouldn't be left just floating around. Why don't these Malleus people just go scoop her up and deal with this weapon thing?" I asked.

She leaned back in her own chair. "Because I asked them to let us do it."

"Because you want the collar? That's a little flimsy, if you don't mind me saying so," I said.

"It's like this," she said, steepling her fingers in front of her. "Either we do our job here, or we sit back and record details of them doing the job. We're either an effective deterrent against people using magick to commit crime or we're just sitting here twiddling our thumbs. And they, by which I mean Malleus, are watching."

"Think of a serial killer. Any one of them will do," she said. "Got one?"

"Yeah," I said.

"Great. Now imagine how much more successful at killing that serial killer would have been if they could turn invisible, phase through solid objects, *and* it only took one cut to drain almost all the blood from the victim in seconds."

I whistled, which was odd to me because I hardly ever do it.

"Yeah. Exactly. Whoever they are, they are weak, driven by rage and jealousy, and this thing is going to wedge into them…in fact, it probably already has…then slowly but surely stoke their anger until they're not thinking very well anymore, then wedge down far enough to pop them loose. At that point, an ancient killing demon, or something to that effect, capable of who knows what will be loose in the world and as skilled as a five-star chef using the weapon it has."

"Okay," I said. "I think I get it. So, from your perspective, this is any other serial murder, it just so happens that the murder weapon is…exotic."

She nodded.

"And you don't…I mean, you know these people. I don't. But…you don't think maybe they're keeping anything from you? Professional courtesy only goes so far sometimes."

"I worried about that some, but ultimately?" she said. "I have to do what I have to do out here in the land of the normal people and try to catch a killer with whatever information I have."

"*We* have," I said.

"We have," she said.

"Okay, so this idea…taking something from the…realm of the supernatural or whatever…" I said. Burton smiled but didn't stop me. "How often does this happen?"

"Well," she said, "the good news is, not often. It's extremely difficult working. To the best of my knowledge," she said, gesturing toward the door that lead to the archives, "and I'm not bragging, but it's fairly extensive, this is rare. Even when someone knows what they're doing and is specifically trying to do it, it seems to be very hard to do. But what these kids managed…" she said, drifting off.

"That's just what I mean. Like," I said, "I can't start out fixing a bowl of cereal and suddenly find myself with toast."

"Well, it's not quite like that. It'd be more like starting out fixing a bowl of cereal and instead of pouring milk you accidentally grabbed a bottle of Jack, poured it in the bowl, and took a bite before you noticed. Even that's not a very good way to explain it. If what has happened is what I *think* has happened, what these kids were doing was already extraordinary."

"And you're thinking it was an accident?"

"I'm hoping. All the signs are pointing that direction, at least initially. Until we get a look at the thing, a legit hands-on look, we won't know," she said.

"You ever encounter anything like this before?" I asked.

"Kind of," Burton said. "Worked a case about a year back where a kid managed to wish his teddy bear alive."

"Like that movie?"

"Where do you think that guy got his idea from?" Burton said. "I wish our case turned out nice like that one did."

"It got ugly?"

She nodded. "Turns out the kid wasn't using magick, an entity from another dimension was using the kid's hurt and anger as a portal. Got into the bear and started trying to get the kid to do things. Luckily enough the kid was way more scared of going to jail than of the threats the entity made against his mom."

"That is lucky," I said.

"It seems that, one night, while the kid was with his father, before the judge pulled the dad's visitation rights, the dad had fallen asleep watching that sword and sorcery show everyone liked a few years back. Well, right after that was a rerun of some super graphic show about life in prison. The kid saw that and was scared straight for the rest of his life. Or, at least, I hope he will be. That's the idea, at any rate." Silence fell between us.

"Alright, let's call it a day," Burton said.

"But we could easily hop on the plane and get one interview in before—,"

"We could, sure, but I want to be fresh for them. I know you do, too. Go home. Get some sleep. Abner's approach was…different, you see," Burton continued. "And, since I intend to keep on using Abner's techniques, it would be best if we started on them fresh tomorrow."

"Different how?" I asked.

Burton thought about it for a minute, then said, "Malleus, ever since we found out about it in the early sixties, has always been a mystery to us. For the longest time, P.I. division was only supposed to observe and report. Standard FBI tactics. Gather info for a rainy day, you know? Abner Booth came up through that system. Once he was in charge…and now that I'm thinking about it, do you know he never told me how his first partner, the guy who trained him, died? That's strange. At any rate, once Abner was in charge, free to run this office as he saw fit, he made overtures."

"How so?" I asked.

"Well, for one, you're going to need to start meditating," Burton said.

"Excuse me?" I asked.

"Meditating. Balancing your psychic space. Cleaning your—"

"Please don't say aura."

She shrugged. I leaned my head forward and pressed my eyelids with my thumb and forefinger.

"You ever read any of the Bond novels? The real ones, by Fleming himself," she asked.

"No," I said.

"In them, much more than in any of the movies except the first one, Bond engages in spycraft. Single strand of hair across the front door to see if anyone has broken in. Specifically listening for clicks on the other end of the phone—early listening devices were a lot easier to find than they are now. That kind of thing."

"Okay," I said and stood.

"What I'm getting at is that, spies during the cold war had their things. Spycraft they engaged in as part of their job. Kept them safe. This," she said, gesturing toward the folders she had under her arm. "This is now your job. And I grant that it's unusual. And the things you need to do to keep yourself safe, well, they aren't 'usual,' either." But this," she gestured to the folders again, "this is the job. Now, you go to the director tomorrow morning first thing and you tell her you don't want this assignment, that's okay. I get it. But you come back in my office door tomorrow morning, then you're in. All the way in. It becomes *our* office door. Got it?"

I didn't say anything for a moment. She picked up a folder from the desk and flipped it open.

"Okay," I said and walked out the door.

I didn't get much sleep. My brain was spinning all night with the new world I now knew I inhabited. I couldn't help but look at everything I came across and wonder. The customers in the pizza place on the way home, were some of them using magick? The woman in the elevator, was she an agent of Malleus Maleficarum? I sat up most of the night drinking milk straight from the carton, eating pizza straight from the box, and staring blankly at the television, but I couldn't tell you what had been on.

The next morning when the alarm went off I was still on the couch. I had nodded off sitting up. My mouth was dry and my head pounding. Still, I got up, got showered and dressed and made it to the building at five 'till 8, as usual. I had to stop myself halfway back to my old desk. I hadn't been paying attention while thinking about this new situation and I'd ridden the elevator to the old floor and stopped at the old water fountain as always. It wasn't until I saw an acquaintance walk by and give me a quick smile that I saw what had happened. I turned and walked back to the elevator. I was in the middle of hoping no one I knew from this floor would see me standing there with the down button lit up.

As it turned out, I had no luck. "Paul?"

"Hey, man," I said. It was Ames. I only knew him well enough to say hello, but still—how to explain if he asked (which he almost certainly was going to do)?

"Where you off to?" he asked, gesturing toward the lit up down button.

"New assignment," I said. "Very—," I said, putting my finger to my lips, hoping it would work. In this building, the less you said about what you were doing, the more important people assumed it was.

"Ah," he said, his eyes going wide. Just then the elevator opened up.

"See you around," I said, stepping in.

"Yeah," he said as the doors slid closed. Luckily enough, the elevator was empty, a rarity at that time of the morning. I pressed for the basement.

"Good morning," I said to Burton as I opened the office door. She was already at her desk reviewing files. The laptop open on the desk near her was small and razor thin. I'd never seen anything like it. Before I could ask, though, she said, "What do you know of protection circles?"

I closed the door behind me and set my briefcase down on the desk across from her. "I'm assuming that they aren't the same thing as crop circles?"

She smiled, but I noticed that it didn't touch her eyes. "No. Protection circles. Psychic emanations that form a protective barrier between the person in the center of the circle and whatever is happening outside it." She closed the file she'd been looking at and then closed the lid on the laptop. It chimed one of the most pleasant notes I'd ever heard in my life and then the blueish glow that had surrounded it faded. Burton stood and came around the desk. "We need to make sure you can use one."

"A…protection circle? I don't…I mean, I don't know anything about magick or how to use it," I stammered.

"This you will need. There are other things, basic things that every first year practitioner gets taught. You'll need them. We'll start here, though."

"Wait," I said, leaning against the desk. "I thought you said we just kept an eye on them," I said, gesturing toward the files room.

"We do, but from time to time, that means getting much closer to what you might call 'the action' than you would otherwise be comfortable with. Things like being able to produce a protection circle might mean the difference between tracking down someone who is bringing spirits in from the outside realms and being possessed by one of those spirits which is brought in," Burton said.

"Couldn't we just call an old priest and a young priest?" I said.

"Funny," she said in a way that let me know she didn't think it was. "You're going to need to take off your shoes," she said, sliding hers off and sitting down with her legs crossed over one another.

"Wait, what?" I asked.

"In the beginning, it helps to be very comfortable. This isn't going to come easy."

"I'll just keep them on," I said.

"Paul," she said. It had the desired shocking effect. I wasn't aware she knew what my first name was until that moment. "Will you trust me on this? You trusted me enough to come back this morning—trust me on this."

I shook my head. Then I toed out of my shoes and slid my sports coat off, laying it on the desk that she'd indicated was mine. I sat down with my legs crossed just like hers.

"Are you right handed?" she asked. I nodded. "Then cross left over right."

"Okay," I said, rearranging. "Why?"

"It's a trick to get your brain to move into a different mode. Buddhist monks use it. Hands in your lap, left over right as well."

I did as she suggested.

"Okay, now that you're comfortable, close your eyes and picture yourself surrounded by a bright blue circle," Burton said.

"A what?" I asked.

"Think of it like a kind of wall between you and the world around you. A wall made of light."

"Is this standard procedure?" I asked.

"Try to get your breathing under control," Burton said.

"At some point, are you going to show me how to summon a demon?"

"Not for a little while," Burton said without opening her eyes.

"Wait, are you serious?" I asked.

"If I had my way this would be standard training at Quantico. They didn't react so well when Abner suggested it, though, so I've…

let the matter drop. Now, again. Picture yourself surrounded by a bright blue circle," Burton said.

"This seems ridiculous."

"Executives from Fortune 500 companies routinely pay upwards of fifty grand for guided meditation seminars like this. You get this one for free. Picture yourself surrounded by a bright blue circle," Burton said.

"But were you serious about the demon summoning thing?" I asked.

Burton said nothing. I closed my eyes again. I pictured myself surrounded by a bright blue circle. But then my mind wandered again. The circle disappeared and instead I remembered a particularly embarrassing nearly-sexual encounter with a young woman when I was back in high school.

"Concentration is the key. It's very easy to slip. Remember—one slip in a protection circle could cost you your life," she said.

I opened one eye to see that she still had both of hers closed. Something about her posture suggested she was at total peace. She opened her eyes.

"It's not easy, but it can be done. You just have to get used to it," Burton said.

"Okay, but of what use is this out in the field. I can't sit down and meditate for fifteen minutes while we're chasing a suspect."

"That's the thing," she said. "Eventually you get good enough to do it without having to stop and meditate."

"Wait, what does that mean? Can you do that?" I asked.

"I have gotten to the point where I can do it while running."

"You're shitting me," I said.

She shook her head and closed her eyes again. I closed mine.

It took all morning for me to be able to do it and have it remain stable. By the time we broke for lunch, I was exhausted and covered in cold sweat.

"Good," she said at last. "It's a start. We'll practice every morning from here on out and by next year you should be—"

"Next year!?" I interrupted

"I told you; none of this will come quickly or easily, but it will come," Burton said, sliding back into her shoes. She paused for a moment and looked at me.

"I need to get back to my house and shower, *again*, then I'll be back," I said, walking toward the door. The exertion had left me soaked and exhausted.

"What is it?" she asked before I got halfway there.

I stopped at the door and turned to face her. "How long did it take you to adjust when you first got here?" I asked. "Like really settle in?"

She thought for a moment. "A good two years, really, before things stopped surprising me."

I shook my head. "I'll be back," I said.

Once I'd gone home, gotten clean again, changed, microwaved the leftover pizza and made it back to work it was early afternoon. I took the elevator straight to the basement and walked in to find the office empty. She came back thirty minutes later.

"I have a few questions," I said. Things I'd been thinking about while at home and on the drive back.

"I would hope so," she said. "I'd be pretty surprised if you didn't." She sat down at her desk. She leaned back in her chair and steepled her fingers in front of her.

"So, alright, look…I came back this morning. I'm in. I have to ask, though—if there's all this…if magick really exists and people use it all the time, why have I never heard of it?" I asked.

She sat down and tilted her head to the side. "Well, the thing is that you have. You see it all the time. You've just trained yourself to think that you haven't. That you aren't seeing it."

"I don't follow."

"You, you're an observant type, right? I mean…" she said, gesturing all around us. "The FBI, right? Still, we see what fits comfortably into our perception scheme. You see a kid skateboarding and he pulls off some amazing trick and you say, 'wow, that kid is really talented,' or 'wow, that kid is really lucky.' Thing is, though, that kid may also be using magick. A pro athlete seems to heal much faster than you would with a similar injury and everyone is happy because their favorite team gets to go to the whateverbowl. They say it's because that team has the best medical staff money can buy or that the athlete just has superior genes and heals well. Sure, maybe, but maybe they also have a sorcerer on staff who worked healing on the guy." She leaned back and crossed her arms. "You see it all the time, but your way of looking at the world doesn't allow for the possibility of magick so you file it under something else."

"But does that mean that maybe I or someone else has gotten the wrong guy in a crime?"

She nodded, "it does."

The quiet stretched between us for a moment. "Then...?"

"It's one of the things we do down here. We shadow any investigations where we think that there might be magick involved."

"Has...has that ever happened to me specifically?" I asked.

She smiled a bit, "No. If it had, I don't know that the chief would have let you come down here. It has happened before that someone was transferred down here and then they found out a guy they were sure was the murderer had been framed by a wizard... that the evidence had been illusory. She didn't take it very well. That hasn't happened since, though. That was during Abner's early days."

"So no one ever finds out?"

"People work very hard to make sure that it doesn't become common knowledge. That's part of what the Malleus does. But they don't have to work as hard as you'd imagine. It's not that people are stupid, but that is part of it."

"What do you mean?"

"Herd mentality helps a lot. If thousands of people saw a real act of magick happen tomorrow there'd be no stopping it. But since it's never more than maybe a hundred, almost always far less, they can easily be dismissed as cranks, or worse, locked up for their belief. We try to keep that from happening, but sometimes..." she shrugged. "It's part of the laws that the practitioners have to follow, too. Malleus comes down pretty hard on anyone who violates that part of the agreement."

"That they have to stay under the radar?" I asked.

She nodded.

"So how do people keep someone like a card reader from being found out. Wouldn't you notice that their readings were always super accurate? Or that a particular herb shop's salve really does heal broken bones?"

She frowned. "This is part of the law that some don't agree with, but…part of what they agree to is that when serving those who are, for lack of a better term, 'normal,' practitioners have to include a…well, a built-in level of error."

"Huh?"

She stood up and walked to her desk. She took out a small tin and threw it to me. I opened the lid and inside was a powerful smelling clear jelly. "Don't touch. That's a healing gel." I sat it down on the desk beside me. She tossed me another identical tin. I opened it and the gel now had a pleasing rosy color and the smell was far less pungent. "So is that, technically. I know you can spot the differences and they're on purpose. One is the real deal. I bought it because sometimes I don't have time to get to the hospital after being shot," she held up her hand to stop my question. "The other is what that same healer keeps on the shelves in the front of the store. She markets it as a salve to heal scars, especially stretch marks after birth or weight loss surgery. It works to heal, but she's added things to it and reduced the amount of the actual working ingredients to make sure that it works like a miracle on small things like scars and crow's feet, but the other one," she gestured to the first tin, "that'll heal compound fractures in less than twenty minutes. Someday I'll tell you how I know that."

"So the Chinese market…"

"There's one legit one, the others are knockoffs for tourists. The real one is in an alley not far from here," she said. "Bono from U2 goes to the real one once a year to get the stuff that he uses on his throat."

"Huh," I said, looking at the actual healing tin.

"Here," she said, gesturing for them back. I closed them both back up and tossed them to her. She stored them in the drawer. For a second I thought about asking why she had both, but decided against it.

"Why do they agree to it?" I asked.

"I'm sorry?" she said without looking up.

"Why do they agree to it? Living underground all the time. The laws and the surveillance. Why agree?"

"Self preservation," she said without looking up.

"I don't follow. Well, I mean, I think I do, but what do you mean specifically?"

"Here's how Abner explained it to me: 'it was either this or the burnings would continue.' Like I said—this," she gestured outward toward the room, meaning everything that was currently the case. "This was the compromise. Regular everyday people, people who can't summon ancient death deities, who can't call forth the power of the element fire at will, they don't like that someone else could get the drop on them. I mean, look at the fuss the NRA kicks up with just the *idea* that the government *might* come to someone's house and try to take their guns. Now what if you told them that the lanky kid down the street, the one they have a bad feeling about, could, at any moment, say a few words and spit lightning bolts from his fingers. They'd start lynching every kid who even kind of looked like the first one, let alone what they would have already done to that poor bastard, himself. Once everyone calmed down enough to see that was the direction everything was headed, all-out war or peace, cooler heads started to try to find some middle ground. This was that middle ground, these laws. This idea of both sides having some surveillance and control methods in place. It took a while," she said, sitting down with a sigh. "People who had grown up with complete freedom weren't exactly in a hurry to get in line, if you know what I mean. Still, over time, the Malleus was able to make their case. And we were able to help them do that. Some things… some things got swept under the rug that maybe shouldn't have…I admit that. But in the long run, we have peace."

"Except for this killer we're tracking."

"Yeah. But consider this—very few of these things happen. Imagine how many more *could* happen," she said.

"How many do happen?" I asked.

"On average? We get something like this about once a year,

maybe twice if it's a bad time—major planetary alignment, supermoon, that kind of thing. Of course, a few years back was special—the damned total solar eclipse carving a pathway across the country. Even Abner said he'd never seen anything like that before."

"So things like eclipses or solar position do affect it?"

She grinned, "When people say that the veil between worlds is thinner on October 31st every year, that isn't just something they made up. Dia de los Muertos is a very real thing. Here," she said, tossing me a book that had been on her desk. *An Introduction to the Arcane* it read on the cover. "You'll need to get that read ASAP," she said, pronouncing each letter crisply.

I'd spent the whole night eating Chinese takeout and reading the book. As it turned out, many of the things that appeared in horror movies I'd seen disguised as fiction were, at least according to this particular author, true. Especially low budget horror movies from the 80s. I'd fallen asleep at the kitchen table, my forehead resting on the book. I woke up to my usual alarm going off. Less than ten seconds after I sat up in the chair and closed the book, my phone rang. I picked it up; it read "Burton."

"Hello?" I answered.

"Meet me at Dulles in about an hour. Bring your go bag," she said and then hung up.

A little under an hour later I was stepping out of a cab with my go bag in front of Burton. Somehow I'd known exactly where she'd want to meet despite the confusion of the airport. She nodded, and, saying nothing, picked up her own bag, turned, and entered.

"We're booked on the 11," she said over her shoulder.

"Time to go dig in to the case, eh?" I said. She didn't answer.

Neither of us said much during security check or waiting. Eventually the plane was in the air and once it was, I asked, "Who is our first visit?"

"Eric Fisher. Records indicate that he is currently living with Damian Reichart, who would be next on our list, so it's likely that we can get both interviews done together."

"Why these two first?"

"A hunch. Reading through the materials, their names don't come up very often. Either that's on purpose and they're both very smooth operators, or," she said, "they are the quiet ones of the group. If that's the case, they'll be best at giving us background."

"Standard procedure," I said. She nodded. I let a few moments slip by, then asked, "Got any family?"

Burton looked at me. I could tell she was deciding something. Then she said, "A sister. Younger. She's in the Air Force. Two kids, a husband, a dog…that kind of thing."

"What does she do for the Air Force?" I asked.

"I asked once but she can't tell me," Burton said, looking down at her shoes. "Whatever it is isn't exactly black ops, but it isn't far from, I gather."

"So you're both down in the basement?" I said with a bit of a grin.

Burton looked at me and nodded, "Yes. You?"

"Two brothers and a sister. All older. All of them have a bunch of kids. I eventually had to buy a calendar to put on my refrigerator just to keep track of all their birthdays. Both my brothers went into long haul trucking, but at different times. They like it, and they make a ton of money. Their wives are real close because they wound up living not far from each other. My sister is a professor at Marymount. Married one of the other professors there." I said. "Folks?" I asked.

"Still alive," Burton said. I could tell that was all I was going to get.

"My dad is, but mom passed a few years back."

"I'm sorry to hear it," Burton said.

"Thanks," I said. I decided to press my luck—if we were going to be partners, I needed to connect, to get information. "Seeing anyone?" Burton couldn't stop herself from looking stung for a second, then got control of her face. "I didn't mean…" I started but didn't know how to end that sentence so I let it trail off.

"No, it's…it's okay," she said. "No, I'm not. You?"

"Not really," I said. "I mean, there's someone I've been talking

34

to, but you know how it is. Investigations don't keep regular hours."

The rental was already hot inside when we opened the doors. Burton walked to the passenger side first, so I took it that I was driving. Like a lot of people my age, I would bet, I still looked for some sort of place to insert the key. After a moment I remembered, put my foot on the brake and pressed the green button. The engine came to life. I pulled out of the rental stand and onto the main road away from the airport. After a minute or so, I said, "We could have requested one that had the software that lets you plug your phone in and we could use the navigation…"

"We don't need it. I'll tell you when to turn," Burton said.

I laughed, "Are you that big and bad an agent, you memorize maps before we're even on the ground?"

"No," she said. "I used to live here. We're about twenty minutes out."

I turned the AC up.

"Do you remember your first time ever having to do one of these?" I asked after a few minutes of silence.

She nodded, "It was about a year before I was transferred over to work with Abner. Little girl had gone missing and the police had exhausted all their own leads. They finally admitted that it was likely she'd been taken across state lines. They called us in. First thing we had to do was, of course, re-interview all the people they'd already talked to. My partner was a guy named Blovich. Poor guy caught no end of ribbing for the name, but he was a solid investigator. We pull up to the parents' house and no sooner has he shut off the engine than the father comes out onto the porch with a shotgun in hand. Now, standard procedure is to try to de-escalate, right? Calm things down. So I start running through the talking points they give us to do that in my head. Meanwhile, Blovich just gets out of the car, calm as you please, and said, "is that a …" and he names off the exact kind of rifle it is. Make, model, etc. The man's caught so off guard that before he knows it, not only is he not shooting at us for whatever reason he thought it would be a good idea to shoot at people, but he and Blovich are talking about upcoming hunting season. Damndest thing I ever saw."

"Did the guy ever say why he went for the rifle before he even knew who you were?" I asked, obeying the navigation's order to keep left at the fork.

"Eventually, yeah. Reporters had gotten wind that we'd come in and they took our visit to him to indicate that we were suspicious he'd murdered the kid. Some stringer had come in town who wasn't familiar with the way we work. The father had gotten so mad, he swore that if he ever saw that reporter, he'd bury him. You know how tempers get in an investigation. So when we pulled up in a rental, he thought we were either more reporters or the guy come back to press his luck," Burton said.

"Wow," I said.

She laughed. "By the end of the whole thing, I think he and Blovich actually did go hunting together on some property the family owned up north. What about yours?" she asked.

"Standard thing. Farmer ordered a lot of fertilizer. We had to go out and verify it eyes-on. This was with my first partner, too. Guy named Montz. Nothing special really happened. Guy was nice. His wife offered us lemonade. We went out and looked at the stock and verified all the numbers. Gave him the standard 'don't make bombs' warning. He was shocked that the rules had changed. Said he'd just wanted to stock up in case something went wrong with the loan next year. Montz stepped in horseshit and stunk up the car all the way home. Still, as stupid as it sounds, that was the day I first really felt it."

"Felt it?" Burton asked.

"Like I was doing the work. I mean, you're doing the work pushing paper from one stack to another, sure, but until the first time you get to actually flip the badge open and say 'Special Agent' and your last name, it sort of doesn't count."

She laughed.

The address was in a new development outside of town. Brand new, quickly-thrown-together apartment complexes in the middle of large grass fields. Meant for those who want to live close enough to a large city to get what they want at odd hours, but maintain the illusion of living in the country.

We parked and walked to the door. For some reason, I expected to hear a dog, but there was none. Our knocks were met by silence for a moment, then the door opened. Behind it was a skinny young man. Red hair and glasses. Dressed in basketball shorts and a polo shirt with the logo of a very expensive designer on it.

"Hello?" the young man said.

"Eric Fisher?" Burton asked, flipping her badge open.

"Yes?" he asked stepping back a bit.

"Special Agent Miranda Burton, this is my partner, Special Agent Paul Lowe. Could we talk with you for a minute?" she asked.

His brown furrowed, "Sure."

"Hon, who is it?" came a voice from upstairs.

"It's the FBI, babe," Eric said. The sound of something falling over came to us and then the sound of footsteps coming down the stairs. The other young man was dressed similarly only with long sleeves pushed up to his elbows and brown hair.

"FBI?" he said.

"Damian Reichart?" Burton asked. He nodded.

"Good. We'd like to speak to you both. May we come in?" she asked.

"In the beginning, it was all 'do what thou wilt.' You know how it is. We were...we were into it," Eric said. Damian half smiled and put his hand on top of Eric's. "You have to understand, when... when you're a pasty little queer kid from whereverthehell, Kansas, and all you've had shoved down your throat is capital-G God all your life, to hear anything else is powerful. To hear something that makes sense, though? To hear something coming from a place that tells you that you're okay and that, even bigger, the *universe* thinks you're okay, too? That there's no judgment, only consequences for your intentions? Well..."

"Yeah," Damian said under his breath and looked away. He patted Eric's hand twice.

"So, yeah, we got deep into this stuff and we got there quickly.

"Where did you meet…" Burton glanced down at her notebook, which sparked my interest. I hadn't known her for all that long, but from what I'd come to see, she had all these names and their information memorized long before we walked in the door. Why was she playing dumb? "Amy Paulson and Vernon Reid?" I don't know if they see it, but she looked up before she said the last name. Then it hit me—she's watching reactions. It'd been a while since I had to do any of this kind of partner work. Eric's face moved a little, but it was Damian who closed his eyes and turned his face away. I saw that he was the one who knows something more than he's saying.

"We were all in that stupid lit course," Eric said, looking over at Damian. They both grinned. He looked back at Burton. "I didn't want to take it. Literature is his thing," he said, gesturing with his chin. "Still, we were newly dating and I didn't want him to know how much more I prefer a good mystery mass market paperback to anything by Audre Lorde or whoever."

"It wasn't that bad," Damian said.

"And that was the class of professor…" Burton stalled again but I can see she's looking directly at them underneath her eyelids. "…Doctor John Francis?"

They both nod and their faces go slack. "Yeah," Eric said.

"American Literature One," Damian said.

"Only he didn't waste a lot of time with all the early stuff. He called it 'the greatest hits of the 1850s.' *Scarlet Letter, Moby Dick, Walden,* that stuff," Damian said.

"As the semester goes on, though," Eric continued, "we start to notice that lots of kids are dropping out. By midterm it was pretty much just us."

"Us?" I asked.

"Amy, Vernon, Damian, me, Alex…and Delores," Damian said. Eric nodded.

"Delores Vandecamp?" Burton asked, flipping a few pages for effect.

Their faces grew tense simultaneously as they nod. She glanced at me quickly then looked back at them.

"Was there anything...anything unusual about the class?" Burton asked.

"I wouldn't know," Eric said. "I wasn't an English major."

Damian said, "I didn't notice it right away, but eventually it became pretty clear. He was...he kept asking about the supernatural."

"How so?" I asked.

"Well, like...take the *Scarlet Letter* for instance. Do you know it?" Damian asked.

I shook my head. Burton said, "It's been a while, but that's the one with the woman who comes to early America ahead of her husband but he never shows and eventually you find out she had an affair with the local preacher because he was, y'know, attractive and conflicted. She winds up having a child that is his, right?"

"Kind of. The whole thing centers around the idea that the kid acts weird and the priest never really does acknowledge that the kid is his until the very end when he might have already gone mad from being drugged by her ex-husband who does eventually show up with all this knowledge about plants and stuff," Damian said.

"Yeah. You remember, Doc went on..." Eric said.

"Doc?"

"Professor Francis. That's what he wanted us to call him. Doc," Eric said.

"He said he liked how it made him feel like a doctor from those times," Damian said.

"Go on," Burton said.

"Well, Doc made a big deal out of Hester's husband's special knowledge that he got from living with the Indians for a long time. Said he was a wizard, a male Green witch."

"A Green witch?" I asked.

"Those are the kind that know herbs, plants, medicine and stuff. They make their own soap, keep bees...that kind of thing," Eric said. I nodded and gestured for him to go on.

"Well, so, there's kind of a standard way people interpret that book and that's kind of the way you said," Damian said, gesturing toward Burton. "That the young hot priest was conflicted and lonely and here's this lonely young woman whose husband is probably dead already so they sneak out into the woods and, y'know…"

"Right," Eric said, "but Doc, he had this other idea. He kept asking us 'what if the supernatural is actually involved, here?' We kept arguing with him that Hawthorne, that's the author," Eric gestured toward me. I nodded. "That Hawthorne is working through his own conflicted Christianity, but Doc, he says, 'what if the devil was out in those woods?' There's a part where the Governor of the colony, his sister, a known witch, sees Hester and says that she knows that Hester is in the devil's book, and that she's been with him out there in the woods. Doc says to us, 'what if she's right?'"

Damian said, "In other words, Doc had this idea that maybe the devil had disguised himself as the preacher in order to lure Hester to have sex and that Pearl, that's her daughter's name, and remember the kid has been acting really weird this whole time, that Pearl is really…"

"The daughter of the devil," Eric chimed in, making his fingers wiggle and grinning ear to ear. They both laughed. I can't help but smile, too. Burton doesn't, though.

"At first we just laughed, but it kept on," Damian said. "We get to *Moby Dick* and Doc convinces us that the part where Ahab melts down anything metal on the ship to make the harpoon that will kill the whale is actually a feat of black magick. And you can kind of see that."

"I baptize you not in the name of the father but in the name of the devil," Eric said. "It's right there in the book in Latin."

"But Doc doesn't just let that sit, he says, 'remember that Ahab asks for the men to give up their razors, too. Not just metal, but metal that would have blood on it. Shaving yourself on a moving ship means constantly cutting yourself, even for someone who is good at it,' he says."

"You guys certainly do remember a lot of what he said off the top of your heads," I said.

Eric nodded, "If you'd ever met him, you'd see. He just has this way of talking. Even when he's saying something insane, it half makes sense."

Damian said, "So, when he says something like this, something that kind of half makes sense already, it has…an effect."

"By the time he got to *Walden*, he had us seriously thinking that Thoreau wasn't writing it in the diary, but the reason he moved out into the wilderness was so that he could get closer to nature, which is what he says, but Doc was convinced what he meant was…" Eric said.

"That he was taking up the practice of witchcraft and needed privacy and a place to hold circle. A place to grow his own materials that he needed. A place he could sacrifice on an altar without people seeing." Damian finished.

"And none of these would be considered in any way your standard interpretations of these books?" I asked.

Damian shook his head emphatically, "No, I'm pretty sure if anyone knew this is what he thought about these books, he'd be laughed out of the academy."

"But you didn't think it was all that ridiculous," Burton said.

They both shake their head no. "In fact," Damian said after a moment, "We found it to be more and more convincing. And that's when Vernon had the party."

"The party?" I asked.

"The get together at his house that was just for us. Those of us still in the class."

"Was Doctor Francis there?" Burton asked.

Damian shook his head no. "No. Just us. The students."

"We weren't Thelemites, by the way," Eric said.

Burton doesn't flinch, staring at them as if no one had said anything. "I'm curious—why do you feel like it's important that you tell us that?" I asked.

"I dunno. I mean, don't you guys have like a…bias or whatever… against that kind of…thing? That's what I'd heard, anyway. It's… it's just that what we were doing…it wasn't…that," Eric finished.

I didn't know what a Thelemite was. For a second I wondered if Burton would tell me, or if I should excuse myself and go look it up.

"Go on," Burton said. I noticed that she didn't answer his

question but decided to ask later. Rule number one of being a good partner—don't blow your partner's vibe while they are interviewing.

"So at that first party, that's where we all really started to get to know one another. It felt good, you know? To suddenly have a group. I mean, we all talk about how we don't need anyone and that we're perfectly happy, but when you finally have a group, it feels good," Damian said.

"And this group especially," Eric said, and patted Damian's hand.

"What does that mean?" I asked.

"All of us, we were kind of—,"

"Good students," Eric finished for Damian. "We knew it, too. For the next few semesters, we made sure we were all together in our classes and as we became close in our energy work, we became close in our mental work, too. But it was evident right off the bat. We all clicked immediately."

"Same books, same thoughts, same music, even," Damian said while Eric nodded.

"Was magick mentioned at that first meeting?" I asked.

"No," Damian said. "Vernon didn't bring it up until the second party. We all asked why he was having it at such an odd time—a Wednesday in the middle of a break week. He said it was the solstice, and when we asked it said that it was a tradition he'd kept from his house. His mom raised him Wiccan."

"But he wasn't?" Burton asked.

"No. His practice was much more...contemporary," Eric said. "And when we asked he answered all our questions honestly. Showed us his altar, his blade, etc."

I wanted to stop him and ask about these things, but I could see that nothing he'd said so far struck Burton as odd, so I didn't.

"The strange thing, like I said earlier, is that it all seemed so familiar and...I dunno...right," Damian said. "Especially to Amy and Delores. They took to it all so quickly."

"How long did it take before you were all practicing together?" Burton asked.

"Not long. Maybe a month, month and a half? We didn't mark

it on the calendar or anything, but it was as the next major event approached." Burton nodded as if she knew what that meant. I didn't say anything, making a note to ask her later.

"And what part did Doctor Francis play in all of this?" Burton asked.

"Well, that's the funny thing. He was never there at any of our meetings, never a member, but later on, when the subject came up, we all admitted that we saw him as a kind of father figure. He wasn't a part of us, but he was always looking over us. We didn't find out until much later that Doc and Vernon had had a…a thing…early on," Damian said.

"A 'thing'?" I asked.

"Doc was Vernon's academic adviser, but he told us later that they had become very close, drinking beer together, consulting each other on their writings, and eventually Vernon said that a lot of his own individual practice had come from mentoring that Doc had given him," Eric said.

"Doctor Francis was a practitioner?" Burton asked, but I can tell from her tone she isn't in the slightest bit surprised.

Eric and Damian nodded. "We never asked, but he might have been a member of some of those famous circles. There were some…hints. A big lodge somewhere back out west, maybe." Burton nodded. I made another note to ask.

"But he never attended your group's rituals?" Burton asked.

Damian shook his head, and said, "No. Somehow, though, I always got the feeling he knew what we were up to. He called us his 'all-stars.' We took every class we could from him, everything he offered. There were a few times when I was pretty sure he made up classes just to have us around."

"Classes like?" Burton asked.

"They didn't really have a set theme. We kind of wandered from text to text. To be honest, I just think he was happy to find a group of young people that he didn't hate," Damian said.

"Hate's a strong word," Eric said. "Maybe…maybe 'connected more easily with' would be better."

"Who had the idea to up things from general energy work to

producing objects?" Burton asked.

Eric, hand still on top of Damian's, looked into Damian's eyes for a moment. "Mostly Vernon's, at first. But after a bit, it was Delores."

"She got...she was pretty preoccupied with it," Damian said.

"Obsessed?" I asked.

The both nodded. Silence settled in for a moment.

"We started with all the stupid little stuff everyone starts with. Putting luck charms on some of our favorite items. Keychains, a wallet, all that stuff. We made a few abalone shells we picked up on the internet into scrying pools, stuff like that," Damian said.

"But she wanted to push it bigger. One day she shows up with a small axe. One of those ones you'd get at like a home store or something. She wanted to make it so that the blade would never go dull. We called it 'eversharp.' We read up on it and it was a difficult working, but not more than a couple of night's worth," Eric said.

"The problem?" I said, sensing it.

"The eversharp working requires blood," Eric said.

"Had you not done any work with blood up to that point?" Burton asked.

The both shook their heads no.

"Was specific blood required?" Burton asked. I wanted to break in and ask some questions of my own, but mostly because this is all so new to me.

Eric nodded, "from a deer."

"Which were not in season at the time," Damian said.

"How did you know that?" I asked. I may not know much about magick, but I can tell neither of these kids are exactly the hunting type.

"Alex. He was just as uncomfortable as we were," Eric said. "He suggested that if we waited until deer season we could probably find someone who was preparing and butchering their kill for storage in a freezer. That they'd likely have the blood we wanted."

"But that wasn't good enough," Burton said. They both shake their heads no.

"She wanted to do the working that week," Damian said.

"When we asked why, she said it was for her own protection."

"Was she worried about her safety?" I asked.

"That's the thing," Damian said. "This was the first time she'd mentioned it."

"I was convinced she was just using that as the best excuse to make us move more quickly," Eric said. "She knew if she said she felt unsafe that we'd all try to make this happen for her."

"You didn't believe she felt unsafe," Burton said.

"Not really, no," Eric said.

"And you?" Burton asked, turning toward Damian.

After a moment, he said, "Maybe." Eric rolled his eyes.

"What made you think so?" Burton asked.

"Well, Delores was…she wasn't the kind of person who stayed quiet when she felt something deeply. Not that a woman should have to, but…you know…the kind of world we live in…she made… enemies," Damian said.

"That's a pretty strong word to use," I said.

Damian nodded, "I don't mean like people who wanted to kill her or whatever, but we had all taken our turns pulling her away from a group of guys out at the bar when she got it in her mind that they needed to be taught a lesson."

"As in?" Burton asked.

"She'd get right up in their faces. She was fearless," Eric said. "One of the things I admired most is that she could get mad and get right up in someone's personal space and cuss them out without ever falling back on sexist or homophobic ideas. I mean, if I was that mad, I'm not so sure I'd be able to do that. To make someone feel low and that they needed to rethink what they were doing without having to use some of that old programming, you know?"

"She never needed to," Damian said. "But the townies around here…you know how it can be. It almost made them more mad that she never stooped to insulting their maleness or their sexuality and yet still made them feel like shit. More than one time we had to flee to the car and barely made it out of the parking lot before someone could grab her."

"But never any one person in particular causing trouble for

her?" Burton asked.

"No. Nothing like an abusive ex or any of the stuff they tell us to watch out for," Damian said.

Burton asked, "Last question. The last two items you made before the group broke up. What were they?"

Eric said, "the sword and the...the other thing."

"And what were they worked into...what were they imbued with?" Burton asked.

Eric glanced at Damian before turning back to answer, "The sword? Light. Healing. Good things. The other object...the one she kept calling Killraven?...we were trying to make it vigilant, helpful in a bad situation. By then we were way beyond just putting one working onto an object. We were..." Eric trailed off.

"We were attempting to move whole...spirits...maybe, if you want to call them that...into the objects," Damian said.

"And that last weapon...things had gotten so toxic in the group by then...it was...there was no way it could have turned out well, but we all just wanted it over by then," Eric said.

I'm thinking I should settle in because we've finally made it to the crux of what Burton wants to know when she snapped her notebook shut and stood. "Thank you," she said. "You've both been very helpful. If you think of anything else," she said and hands them a card. She's almost out the door before I catch myself and follow her.

"That ended...quickly," I said as I opened the door. She's already sliding behind the wheel.

"They don't know enough about the workings. They were lower level people. There mostly for their energy. You can tell. If we want to know about the objects, we have to talk to someone higher up," she said, starting the car and pulling into traffic the second I have my seatbelt clicked in place.

"So why did we need to talk to them?"

"One, I didn't know they were lower level until we talked to them, and two, lower level members have a better handle on social dynamics than the leaders do. Beyond how to manipulate the lower level folks, I mean. Leaders don't have time to learn about who is dating whom. We would have had to gather that information at some point. Just got lucky it was the first stop."

I waited a moment, then asked, "and a Thelemite?"

"There is no departmental bias against them."

"Okay. But...what *is* a Thelemite?" I asked.

"There's no way to define it for you quickly. It's a big concept. A way of practicing magick, but also of thinking about the world and man's place in it. At its core, it's someone who practices in a way that jives with Crowley's *The Book of the Law*, but even that is... kind of debatable. Thelemites, at least the way that I understand the practice, don't really have a central dogma...it's more about studying the concept and implications of the will."

"As in, the will to live, or the will to succeed? That kind of thing?" I asked.

"That, but more. At any rate, what he was asking about is a pejorative understanding. He was afraid that we thought he and his partner were doing the dark stuff...sex magick for enslavement, human sacrifice, that kind of thing."

"Do they *do* that?"

"No. Well, at least, not the ones who actually are Thelemite. There's always some fringe character who misunderstands something and goes off on his own path. It shows that he doesn't have a very deep understanding of what he's talking about, which is one of the ways I know these were the lower rung of the ladder folks," she said.

"So who now?" I asked.

"Lunch. Then we need to talk to Alex Caroline."

"Not Vernon Reid?" I asked.

"No. We have to have all our ducks in a row before we knock on his door," she said.

"Okay," I said. "Where does Alex Caroline live?"

"Look in the green folder," she said.

As soon as I flipped it open, I saw the address. "You're kidding."

"Nope," she said. "Never moved."

"This ought to be interesting," I said and kept reading.

"Shouldn't we…" I started to ask.

"If this were another unit, yeah. But the thing you've got to get used to," she said, "is that we're not the same as the other divisions. You'll notice the director didn't refer to us as a number. That's a part of it. We're not just off the books, we're *off the books*. Traditions, procedures, modes of thinking…all that works to bust human trafficking cases or cartel activity. But what we deal with? We have to think outside the lines." She reached in her purse with one hand while still driving, pulled out a copy of *Through the Looking Glass*, and handed it to me.

"I read this when I was a kid," I said.

"Lots of us do. You need to go back and read it as an adult," Burton said.

"Why?"

"So that you can believe six impossible things before breakfast," she said.

The door creaked open. The man who stood behind it looked shriveled, like he was a bigger man before and then everything got sucked out of him. His beard was already showing gray.

"Alex Caroline?" Burton asked, her credentials already out and open. "Special Agent Miranda Burton, this is my partner, Special Agent Paul Lowe."

He flinched. "What's this about?"

"May we come in?" Burton asked. I took a second to register the fact that, even though we were dealing with some highly odd things, Burton's procedure is by-the-book crisp.

"Sure," Alex said, stepping aside.

The floorplan was huge; open. I thought you could stuff maybe my whole apartment into this first room. There was a hallway that lead to other rooms behind. I could see why they wanted to use this place to gather.

I stayed near the door but Burton walked to the middle of the room. There was a mattress on the floor off to the side. Small tables sitting on books as their legs near the makeshift bed. Other than that, there was no furniture anywhere in the room. Sandalwood smoke drifted through the entire place.

Alex stood almost six four but slouched and wore a white robe. His hair, flat brown, curly, touched the collar. His glasses are in older frames but there were no scratches on them.

From somewhere back in the back of the house a cat mewed.

"Can I help you with something?" Alex asked.

"I was wondering if I could ask you some questions about Delores Vandecamp," Burton said.

Alex stepped back but did an admirable job of keeping his face calm. The cat, black (of course), came to the end of the hallway and sat as though waiting to talk to us. People say this all the time, but I can't shake the idea that it's watching us, listening.

"I…I haven't talked to Delores in a long time. Tea?" Alex asked, turning his back to us.

"No, thank you," Burton said.

"None for me, thanks," I said.

We followed him into the hallway, though; it's obvious he isn't stopping. I put my hand on my gun. As we passed into the hallway, the cat curled its tail around my ankle and then followed us. We enter a long, narrow kitchen just inside the hallway to the right.

"I had just started a batch," Alex said, picking up the kettle and pouring into a pristine large black mug. "It's almost like someone warned me there would be company."

He put the kettle back on the burner and turned the burner off. Then he picked up the mug with both hands and walked between Burton and me back toward the hallway. We enter a room full of rows of steel folding chairs directly across from the kitchen. He grabbed one and handed it to me. He picked up another and handed it to Burton. Then he took one for himself and walked us all back out into the front room. He opened his and flopped into it. Burton placed hers about three foot from his and I put mine just a bit back from her shoulder and then sat.

"When was the last time you talked to her?" Burton asked, her notebook already in hand, pen already moving.

"Not since the last time The Order met. That has to be, what… over a year, now?" The cat jumped into his lap and then, again, sits staring at us, perfectly still. Alex put his hand on its shoulders.

"And how would you say you know her?" Burton asked.

"We were friends. I mean, at least, that's how I felt about it. I know the others...well, they all had feelings about her from the beginning but I never saw any...well...we were friends."

Burton flipped back a few pages, then forward again and asked, "You were a part of Doctor John Francis' American Literature class, is that right?"

Alex nodded, "That's where we all met, yeah."

"And it was meeting in that course that lead to you all eventually forming a cohort?"

"We thought of ourselves like a lodge, in a sense, though we weren't Thelemites. Not strictly to the letter, at any rate," Alex said.

"How so?" Burton asked.

"It would take a long time to explain. You know how there are covens in Wicca but also those who have individual practices?" Burton nodded. "And the individual practitioners tend to be... idiosyncratic in their rituals? Imagine that, only picture a group that had idiosyncratic practices." He blew on his tea, then sipped. The cat didn't move.

"And this was the place those rituals were held?" Burton asked.

"Not at first, no. At first we were more...traditional, maybe? Or maybe just caught up in a moment. No, our first two attempts to work together we did out in a field."

"A field?" I asked.

"There's a lot of undeveloped land near the university and trails that lead back quite far if you know where to look. Especially toward the outer end of the circle drive, back near the Greek houses. To be honest, I don't think we were the only ones using those woods for rituals," Alex said and smirked at his own joke.

"Why move inside, then?" I asked.

He inhaled then exhaled heavily. "It became evident pretty quickly that we had...the right stuff. We were actually making things happen. The woods out there didn't feel...safe, maybe? We wanted a more controllable area, especially if we were all going to be naked."

"Were you working specifically in those traditions, the ones that require skyclad ritual?" Burton asked.

"Nah," Alex said, "it was just more fun that way." He laughed. The cat blinked. "So, it was at that point that Vernon revealed to us just exactly how much money he had."

"Money?" I asked.

"Is that not already in the file?" Alex asked. "Yeah, the dude was a trust fund baby. Loaded, and I mean. The next week he said he had a surprise for us and he brought us all here. He'd bought it outright and had already had people in to fix it up, make it livable."

"What had been wrong with it before?"

"Crack house. At least, we were pretty sure. Bank seized it and it sat dormant for a long time until Vernon came along. They must've thought they'd found their salvation when he rolled in with that kind of cash and took the place sight unseen. Still, it turned out to be perfect," Alex said, looking around. The cat meowed but still didn't move. "Bastee, here, came with the place."

"How so?" I asked.

Alex leaned in and kissed the cat on top of its head. "The night we moved in she was already here. Never left and we never tried to make her. We all considered it a good omen, and we made sure to set offerings for Bast on the communal altar." The cat got down from Alex's lap and curled just to his side, preening herself. "Once we all said how much we liked it, Vernon said that was good, because it was ours in perpetuity. Me, Eric and Damian all asked if we could move in…you know…save on rent. He said that sounded good to him, so as soon as the workers had the place in some kind of order, we three moved in."

"And you've been here ever since?" Burton asked.

Alex nodded. "I mean, toward the end there, when things got ugly, I found myself other places to be, couches to crash on, etc., but yeah. Until Vernon says otherwise, this is where I live. The lonely sentinel. The last Monk in the Abbey," he said, smirking and then sipping tea. "It helps to not have a lot of distractions from my work."

"What work is that?" I asked.

"You didn't see it in the other room?" he asked. "I'm working on combining certain elements of Qabalah with some elements of string theory. How certain ideas about string matricies match up almost perfectly to certain ways of thinking about the hexagrammatic matricies underlying the Sephirot. Kleene's star set, for instance."

I caught Burton's face as it moves for just a second. I looked back at him, but he didn't notice, too caught up in his own ideas.

"Did we walk across an active working without you warning us?" Burton said. I've been around her for just long enough to note the shift in tension in her voice.

"No," he said, and my shoulders relax a notch. "I wouldn't do that," he said. "None of what I was working on is active right now."

Burton paused for a moment. "Are you teaching any students right now?"

"Yes," Alex said. "But nothing like what we were doing. It's all low level stuff for retired college professors and massage therapists. Energy working to help heal a client's bad rotator cuff, how to make an herbal-working infused bath bomb for a nephew with bad ADD, that kind of thing."

"And you're registered?"

"With Malleus? Yeah. I obey the rules now that I know what they are. You don't have to worry about me," Alex said.

"You weren't registered before?" I asked.

"We didn't know," Alex said. "Like I said, when we all first got together it was…a rush. We didn't now anything about the society, the history, the laws. We were just doing whatever we felt came next. If we'd known…"

"Do you think knowing the laws, registering, educating yourselves…do you think all of that would have stopped Delores?" I asked.

Alex didn't move for a moment, then shook his head no. "No," he said. "She was headed for a bad end no matter what. We were just all so excited at the time, so happy with ourselves and what we were accomplishing none of us really paid much attention."

"Did she take the…the object…with her as soon as the working was done that night?" Burton asked.

"No," Alex said. "We had kind of made up our own rule about workings, especially big ones. When I finally did learn about Malleus, and I saw that they had almost the exact same rule, I almost laughed. No, as soon as we were done with any big making, we put it in the vault below and studied it for a bit to have a better idea of what it was we'd done. Delores and Vernon were really good at that. Sensing with objects, you know? So they'd take some time to feel out whatever we'd done and make sure there didn't seem to be any unusual aftereffects. Unintended consequences, you know?"

"Can we see the vault?" I asked.

"Sure," Alex said after a moment of hesitation. He set his mug down on a high shelf on the bookcase and then walked out. We followed him down the hall again to a door that lead to stairs. The smell is how all basements smell no matter what you do to them… ozone and cold dirt with a bit of mold. He flipped on the light and we followed him down the steps. Below is a room about half the size of the main room above. To the right was a glass and steel case that, even though somewhat worn, looked more technologically advanced and modern than anything we'd seen in the house above. He stopped halfway to it. "Here it is."

"You made this?" I asked stepping close to the glass. I reached out and almost touched it before Burton grabbed my wrist and shook her head. I put my hand in my pocket.

"We all did. It was one of our first major workings as a group. We decided that if we were going to be making objects, then our first one should be a place where those objects could be stored. Vernon called it a 'gun safe.' We all immediately got the metaphor and we created it." Burton walked a half-circle around it never once touching it while Alex talked. He goes on to say, "I honestly think it'll outlast this house. They'll find it when they come in to demolish the place. I've been thinking that might not be a great idea, though, so I've been thinking about how to dispose of the thing."

"And?" Burton asked without looking away from it.

"No ideas just yet. We did a really good job with it, I think."

Without meaning to, I'm certain, Burton nodded. "Malleus

folks know this is here?"

Alex nodded in return, "Again, Agent, I comply with the rules, now. It's registered and has been inspected. They know it's here. They count it as my property, though."

Burton turned on her heel and walked up the stairs. I waited for Alex then followed. He reached past me to shut off the light and close the door. Burton is already waiting near the front door.

"When was the last time you spoke with Eric Fisher?" Burton asked.

"It's been a while. Couple of years."

"And Vernon Reid?"

Alex looked at the floor, "I talk to Amy more than I talk to him."

"Amy Paulson?" Burton asked.

Alex nodded, "They're not together any more, but she keeps me updated on him."

"Thank you for your time," Burton said and walked out the door.

I smiled at him and followed her.

"Who's next?" I asked.

"He kept saying that he intends to follow the rules, now. It was very important to him to let us know that," she said, and clicked her seatbelt into place as she starts the car.

"Mean something?" I asked.

"Maybe," she said as she pulled the car in gear and into traffic. "Maybe. It's not unusual for these groups that spring up out of nowhere and don't register to break a rule or two without knowing it. But he seemed really interested in making sure we knew he wouldn't break any more. I think maybe he's under investigation."

"Maybe he's trying to go legit. Get registered. What does that process involve?"

"Could be," she said. "It would involve monitoring and maybe some surveillance. Remind me when we get back to the office to put in a call about him."

"Okay, so who's next?"

"If we go to Amy Paulson, she'll give us a bit more on Reid before we see him, and that could be valuable, but…" she drifted off.

"There's the chance she calls him the second we're out the door and if he doesn't want to be talked to, he rabbits. Who knows, though, maybe he wants to talk to us. Help us track Delores down and stop this thing."

She nodded.

"And from what Alex was saying, there's the chance she might be with him right now, anyway," I said.

"You hang out with your exes on the regular?" she asked.

"No, but just from the sound of it, these two had a special thing. Deeper than just the usual 'grow old with me' bit."

She goes quiet for a minute. "We could always have someone go out and snag him and bring him in while we're talking to her. Put him on ice for a bit to ruffle his feathers."

"Maybe. Problem is, we might need his cooperation, especially if it is Delores we're after. If we don't have any leverage, all we would have is his good will. And if we've already burned that, then…"

"Do you have any doubts based on what we're hearing that it *is* Delores we're after?" she asked.

I shook my head no.

"Good," she said. "We're on the same page then. Okay—let's go have ourselves a conversation with Vernon Reid."

The address turns out to be a gated community of condos. The guard has to let him know we're coming just to get us buzzed in. Not ideal. The guard gives us a parking space number to go to. As we drive through, it's everything you'd expect. Thin, beautiful people loung by the immaculate pool, spotless sidewalks, and hundred-thousand dollar sports cars in front of almost every condo. A teenager's idea of what being rich looks like? That's this place.

We pulled the car in to the space we were told to go to and get out. As soon as we step onto the curb, a slim man with dark skin and stylish hair opened the door to a condo just down the walkway.

He waved.

"Well, he isn't shooting. That's at least something," I said. We walked toward him. As we get close enough even I'm struck by how attractive he is. Think Lenny Kravitz only with even more time to work out and more money.

"Officers," he said. Even his voice was sexy.

"You might be overdoing it, Mr. Reid," Burton said, taking out her badge. I reached for mine and fumble, dropping it on the sidewalk. "Perhaps a notch or two less."

"I don't know what you're talking about," he said, smiling. I picked up my badge and showed it.

"Special Agent Burton, this is Special Agent Lowe. We'd like a few minutes of your time to talk."

"Mister Reid, have you gone through registration with Malleus?"

"Yeah," Reid said. "Of course."

"Are you currently teaching any students?" I asked. I may be new to this, but the procedure bears a striking resemblance to everything I've done before. Now that I've seen it a few times, I can at least help out, I think.

"Were you leading the ceremonies during the time before your group disbanded?" Burton asked without looking up from her notes.

"Yes," Reid said.

"No one else took the lead during the ceremonies that your group was performing during that time?" Burton asked, again without looking up.

"Nope," he said.

"So you were functioning as a de facto high priest within this particular circle of practitioners?" Burton asked.

"I guess so, yeah. I mean, we didn't vote on a leader or anything, but if there was someone who was in charge, I guess that would have been me," Reid said.

"Can I see your vouch?" Burton asked.

"My...?" he said. His hands moved as if he's about to pat his pockets.

"Your vouch? The document from a high priest or priestess

that certifies that they witnessed you completing the ceremony to be raised?"

"I…uh…I don't have that, I don't think," Reid said.

"You don't think or you know that you don't?" Burton asked.

"I…I don't."

She finally looked up from her notes. "So you were operating a group that was performing summoning and making rituals knowingly without having registered yourself as the high priest of the group, and without any vouch papers from any tradition that could show that you have had training to perform as a leader for such a group?" Burton asked.

"Do I need to get like a lawyer or something?" Reid asked looking at me.

"Answer my question, please," Burton said.

"No. I mean, I guess. I didn't know that I had to register is what I mean I guess."

Burton waited a moment, then wrote something down, longhand. She's sweating him, letting him worry a bit.

"I mean…If I was still doing that stuff, of course I'd register, but I'm not, you know?" he said, looking from me to her and back. "I quit it all."

"Only you attempted to glamour two Federal agents just this afternoon," Burton said without looking up, still writing.

"I didn't mean anything by it—I just…I mean, come on," Reid said, flashing a charming smile and shrugging.

"Are you aware that casting in any way toward a Federal agent is considered an assault?" Burton asked, looking up, her hand going still.

"Okay, look, look—I didn't mean anything by it. I mean, it was just…new people, it helps with…I mean, come on, y'know?…"

Burton leaned back in the chair and sets the pen down. She studied him for a moment. "An unregistered coven of beginners decides to start working some of the most difficult spellwork there is on a whim without any supervision from either Malleus or from a trained, experienced mentor. What's more, that unregistered coven of beginners is being lead by a boy who has absolutely no training in how to temper that group's ambition or teach them anything. Mr. Reid, are you familiar with the term criminal negligence?"

"I think maybe I should get a lawyer," he said.

Most people would have missed it, but because I've been paying very close attention to Burton, I see her give the tiniest of nods in my direction. Time for me to play good cop.

I leaned over to Burton and brought my face close to her ear, turning away from Reid. I whispered nonsense to her. She pulled away and looked at me as if angry, then sighed and got up. She walked out the door.

"Look, Vernon…is it okay if I call you Vernon?" I asked.

He nodded.

I smiled at Reid. "She's what we at the office call a real type A, you know? Do people out here in the real world still use that term?"

He laughed and I see his shoulders relax a bit.

"Look, man, I'm not interested in having to fill out a whole bunch of paperwork this afternoon for some penny ante little case of negligence. That's a whole lot of ink for something that's just going to get you a slap on the wrist. What I could use, though, is some information."

"Oh," Reid said, sitting up more straight, "Yeah?" It's always amazing to me, with the number of police procedurals on TV that show this technique how often people still fall for it. I've never tried to run it on a warlock or whatever before, but I guess that, magick or no, he still has to put his pants on one leg at a time.

"Yeah," I said. "We're trying to close in on a killer. Thing is, even though it's been a while, we're pretty sure you knew this person. We think maybe you have some information that could help us haul her in."

"Her?" he asked. Then he nodded and his features went dark, "Delores. You guys are trying to track down Delores, aren't you?"

I smiled, "See, we're already getting somewhere. Delores Vandecamp. Tell me what you remember about everything right there toward the end."

He cleared his throat. "After it became pretty clear that she wasn't going to get with anyone in the group, her behavior changed.

I mean, she was never the life of the party to begin with, but she really turned sour. We started to have more conversations about her than with her, if you know what I mean." He paused as if thinking about something, then went on. "I don't know why, but we could all feel it, too—that, after we'd made the sword, it was time to move on to other things. Like a team that gets together to win a championship, y'know? After they win that championship game, they tend to drift apart from one another. It was just like that. We'd been building up and building up and then we'd done this amazing thing but after that, we were aimless. Eric had the idea that we might start using the power to influence politics. Y'know, really start changing the world. Like those guys who tried to do a exorcism to remove the Pentagon back in the day." He smiled. I did, too, to keep him calm and talking.

"We all had different ideas about where to go next. Alex wanted to take on students, and I was kind of into that idea. Amy was thinking about visiting some of the cliché holy sites, maybe becoming a Buddhist for a bit. Journey inward kind of stuff. But Delores…" he drifted off.

"But she didn't want to move on, did she?" I asked.

"No," he shook his head. "She had another weapon in mind. She wanted to create something that she said we could use to defend ourselves if anyone ever tried to fuck with us. Thing is, no one had ever tried to fuck with us. None of us knew where this was coming from. Then came the disappearances."

"Disappearances?" I asked.

"She wouldn't answer her phone, wouldn't be home, no lights on at her place. That kind of thing. At first it was a week. We all thought maybe she just needed to go walkabout to get her head straight. That wasn't it, though. Not long after that it was almost a month. Then there was the whole summer she disappeared. That was right before the end."

"Did you ever find out where she went?" I asked.

He shook his head again. "We asked and she brushed it off. The one time Amy really pressed, Delores hit her."

"Slapped?" I asked.

"No, closed-fist punched her." He shifted in his seat. "Then she laid it on us that there was this organization called Malleus, and that they knew what we'd been doing, and that we were all in big trouble. She said that she'd been in touch with one of their agents and that she was the only thing keeping us all from going to jail."

"Did she give the name of the agent?" I asked.

"No. We gathered it was a he from the pronouns she used, but that was it. So she said we were going to give her this one last demand and make this one last weapon and then we were going to disband. Thing is, we were all at that point anyway. I think it maybe even surprised Delores how willing we all were to just get it over with. I swear to you, none of us were thinking she might do something horrible with the weapon."

"So you guys got the ceremony all ready and performed it to try to keep her protecting you from what you thought would be legal action?" I asked.

He nodded. "Look, I know in hindsight that seems like the stupidest thing you've ever heard, but it's true. We just wanted to be done with her. She had turned so dark, so mean…it was over, and we knew it, and we just wanted to take the easiest path to shutting it all down that we could."

"What happened during the ceremony that night?" Burton asked. Neither of us had heard her open the door.

He shifted in his seat again. "The early part went off like it normally did. Well, except that a little bit of the energy wasn't there because we weren't doing this for fun..or…well, you know what I mean."

"Go on," Burton said as she sat down.

"Eventually, though, the energy built and we were all… y'know…engaged with it. Then she began to speak these strange words in the direction of the blade. Like, we were all concentrating our energy on the center like she said to, but where I lead the last one, the ceremony that made the sword, she just took this one over. The words she was saying…I'd never heard anything like them before…they seemed to alter her voice as she spoke them, like a sound effect or something. I was afraid, but I kept on going. Like I said, I just wanted to get this over with. That's when things got even more strange and the...well, the blade kind of...it seemed to..."

"Seemed to pull energy from you?" Burton asked.

"Yeah," Reid said. His eyes said relief. "Just like that. It was pulling, like it sensed that we were where its energy was coming from, and that we weren't feeding it as fast as it wanted to be fed. It was...suckling...at us, but like...desperately, as if it was starving."

Burton nodded the whole time he was saying these things.

"She finished whatever spell or incantation she'd prepared and there was one last huge pull at all of our energy, then just like that," he said, snapping his fingers, "everything stopped. I've seen documentaries where people describe being in the worst part of a hurricane and then the eye passes over and the peace is surreal because it comes so suddenly. It was like that. Like we'd been in the middle of an enormous storm that stopped suddenly. Thing is, none of us had...y'know...gotten to the point that the great rite asks you to in order to have the maximum energy. We were all exhausted, but somehow she wasn't. While we were all still lying there, waiting to get the energy and focus back to move, she was already in her robe again, had picked up the blade, and was headed out the door. She wasn't even going to take the time to get dressed again. She hopped in her car and was gone and that was the last I saw of her to this day."

"Aftereffects?" Burton asked.

"Exhaustion. We were all so drained that just standing up to go get dressed made us all dizzy. I'm pretty sure we all just went home and slept for a few days. After a bit we did start to call one another again, but like I said, it was done. We all knew it. We drifted apart. Only Alex really stayed in touch with me after, and I'm pretty sure it was just to make sure I didn't let the house slip away. I gave it to him, in the end. I think he's teaching students there, now."

"He is," I said.

Reid nodded to himself. "Do you think that if you heard those words in that language again you could recognize it? Let us know which one it is?" Burton asked.

"Oh yeah," Reid said. "I won't ever forget those sounds."

Burton stood. I took that as a cue and stood up, too. "Don't go anywhere," she said. "We may need to get in touch with you soon. One last thing—if you had to guess where she might go, where do you think?"

Reid shrugged. "She wasn't exactly an orphan, but she was one of those people who walk away from their family. I don't judge, I mean, I get the impulse, trust me. I'm just saying that I don't think her family would be hiding her. Wherever she's gone, she's on her own. Unless that agent is maybe helping her."

Burton turned and walked out the door without saying anything. I followed.

"If you—," Reid started. When Burton turned around he stopped. He swallowed audibly, though, and then continued. "If you talk to Amy, tell her I said…that I said 'hi.'"

"You haven't spoken?" I asked.

"Not in a while."

I nodded. Burton didn't say anything. As soon as she started the car, I filled her in on what he'd said while she was outside.

"A male Malleus agent?" she asked.

"Yeah, that's what he said," I replied.

After a moment, I said, "He named Delores without us even pushing. I think we're on the right track. Should we maybe go ahead and call in a BOLO?"

She didn't say anything for a minute. "I want one more confirmation just to make sure we've *got* her. Agreed?"

"Agreed," I said. "So," I asked, "where to now?"

"It's time for us to talk to Amy Paulson."

The address we had for Amy was on the complete opposite end of town from the others. I wondered for a minute if that had always been the case. Traffic wasn't bad, so we arrived about twenty minutes later. It was another apartment complex, and not a very nice one. The kind of place people wind up because they don't have any other choice. We pulled up in front of one of the buildings toward the back of the complex.

As we walked from the car to the stairwell, I asked, "Do you think we need to talk to the professor? This Francis guy?"

"It's all going to depend on what happens here. I think that we might…" She drifted off as we entered the stairwell. She was looking up to the second floor. When I stepped behind her, I could see and hear it, too; lots of light, lots of people talking. She walked all the way to the front of the breezeway and before I followed her I saw it: red and blue lights reflected on her face.

"Shit," I said. She rushed back to where I was and took the steps two at a time. I followed.

Of the two apartments on either side, the one on the right and closest to the back of the complex was wide open. There were a couple of cops and a fireman talking outside the door that was wide open. I looked at Burton, but I already knew—that was Amy Paulson's apartment. I wondered why we hadn't seen the cop cars or the ambulance as we pulled into the complex, but then I thought about the layout—this far back from the entrance, and at this angle to the back of the complex, there was no way. I wondered for a minute what would make someone want to live so far back from the entrance, the pool, and the laundry room but then it hit me. This was sitting with your back to the wall so you could see all the entrances, only writ large.

Burton already had her credentials out. I fished for mine. She walked up to the firefighter. "Special Agent Miranda Burton, this is my partner, Special Agent Paul Lowe. Who's in charge here?"

"Guy's name is Peters. Detective. Just inside, guy with the glasses," the guy said obviously trying to keep his surprise under wraps.

Burton walked past him into the apartment. "Thanks," I said as I walked past.

Peters turned out to be a short guy with a military fade haircut and thick glasses. Burton flashed her credentials again and introduced us both. While Burton talked to the guy, I took the opportunity to look around. That stereotype you see in all the movies about how college kids live? Milk crate coffee table, cut-rate flat-pack furniture bookshelves stuffed with paperbacks, shabby carpet? That was Paulson's whole apartment.

"What've you got?" Burton asked.

"A mess. Kid's early twenties, lived alone. Not even a god damned cat. Sad," Peters said, running his hand over his hair and looking around. "I haven't even filed any paperwork on this, yet… what brings the Feds around? No offense."

"None taken. She's a potential witness in an ongoing. Was, at any rate."

I wandered back along the hallway. Only one bathroom and one bedroom. The crime scene guys were in the bathroom shooting pictures. Just past them I saw the body laid out in the tub. I didn't want to interrupt them, so I just craned my head in as far as I could to see past them.

No blood anywhere. Water in the tub was clean.

I wandered into the bedroom. No signs of struggle. Bed neatly made. Laptop sitting on it. I walked back to the bathroom and grabbed a couple of rubber gloves from the crime scene guys' pack. They go on fairly easy and I try to remember the last time I was at a crime scene like this. I opened the laptop and it came out of sleep mode. I'm not sure what I'm looking for, really, but sometimes something will jump out. Her email program was still up, so I tapped it open. Bill paid confirmations, emails from friends, though none of them being anyone from the group that I could see.

"Anything?" Burton asked from behind me.

"Not so far. I'm guessing there won't be, though. Whatever happened here happened fast, I'm guessing."

"Did you see the bath? No blood." Burton said.

"Yeah, I saw that. We'll need to wait to see the body, but I'm guessing…"

"That it'll look just like the others? I agree."

"Then you think she was here," I said.

Burton nodded, "and not that long ago."

"Should we warn the others kids?" I asked.

"Yes," Burton said, turning. I shut the laptop lid and followed her.

"Was her phone around here?" Burton asked Peters as we come back into the living room.

Peters nodded, "Yeah, but we got it bagged already. I can tell you, though, no calls today on it. A few yesterday, a few the day before. She wasn't exactly a chatty kid, I'm guessing."

"Texts?" I asked.

"None, but that's fishy, given her age. I'm guessing someone knew to delete them, and then to erase them permanently. Our guys will get on it, unless you want to step in and take over." I could tell from Peters' tone of voice that would start trouble. These kinds of jurisdiction things tend to get ugly.

"No," Burton said. "But if you would, keep me in the loop?" She handed Peters her card. He took it and put it in his shirt pocket. I thought that was a good sign that he might actually stay in touch. That doesn't always happen.

"Thanks," I said as we walked out. We got all the way to the car before Burton said, "Get on your phone and send a quick call to the others. Tell them that they need to pack a bag quickly and get out of town. Tell them that we'll be in touch, but not to tell anyone— friends, family, whoever. They just need to go."

We got in and she started up the car. "Where are we headed next?" I asked.

"To see an old friend who is very good at locating things."

"Why do you say 'friend' in that tone of voice?" I asked.

"What tone of voice?"

"Like you would really rather not see this person," I asked.

"Because," Burton replied. "They are an ex of mine."

We pulled up in front of a small house in a not so great part of town. As Burton shut off the engine I saw her take a long exhale.

"No badges, here," Burton said. "And you let me do all the talking."

As we walked up to the front door, I heard the sound of a motorcycle engine starting in the back yard. Burton waited a minute for it to stop, then knocked on the door.

"Come out back!" someone yelled.

We stepped around to the gate, which was already half open,

then through. The backyard was no more than ten foot across and maybe fifteen foot wide. On the back porch stood a beautiful Harley Davidson Softail Cruiser in black. The person who stood up from behind it was six foot three, slender but muscled. Something about the build said man, but the eyes had a softness to them, the face a roundness that could have gone either way. The hair, jet black, short and spikey. Feet firmly planted, like they knew how to handle themselves. The bulge of a gun under the left arm.

Burton didn't smile, but her voice softened some. "Sharkey."

"'Randa," the person said. They wiped a hand on a towel, then extended it toward a couple of plastic chairs sitting on the porch. Burton sat, and I follow her lead. The person grabbed a chair from the kitchen table and turn it around backwards as they sat, resting their arms on the top. Even when seated, they don't seem fully relaxed.

"Sharkey, this is my new partner at the Bureau, Paul Lowe."

Sharkey glanced at me and then back at Burton. It's funny, but in that second I know I've been scanned and assessed.

"What do you want?" Sharkey asked, but the tone of the voice undercuts the harshness of the words.

"Looking for this," Burton said, pulling out the picture she'd drawn earlier of the weapon.

Sharkey took the picture and stared at it for a moment. Sharkey laughed for a moment.

"What's funny?" I asked.

"Couple of people arrived here a little bit earlier. Looking for the same thing. Only they had more evidence than you do."

"Who? Someone from Malleus?" Burton asked.

"No. More like a PI or something. Paid in cash."

"Could you describe them?" Burton asked, taking out her notebook.

"Sure. He was tall, black, handsome, smart, she was…well…it was Stacey."

Miranda stopped writing at that name, then went on to write a few more things. "Okay."

"Sorry," Sharkey said.

"It's okay. Any idea why they were looking for this particular item?"

Sharkey's headshake is slow.

"What did you tell them," Burton said, pulling out her wallet. She pulled out two twenties and handed them over. Sharkey took them but doesn't put them away immediately. Burton cocked her head to the side and Sharkey shrugs. Burton whipped out another twenty.

"I told them where it was."

"Got an address?"

Sharkey gave us a number and a street. In my head, I ran through what I knew of the area just from the short time we'd been in town and it wasn't good. Burton closed her eyes and I could tell she'd just come to the same conclusion.

"It's good to see you," Sharkey said.

"Thank you for your help," Burton said. She stood up and I followed. "We'll be in touch if we have any more questions."

Sharkey nodded but didn't stand. Burton walked back toward the gate and I followed. Neither of us said anything until we were back in the car and moving. I expected that we'd head for the highway. Instead, though, Burton pulled back around and parked not too far from the house we'd just been to.

"What's going on?" I asked.

"There is one thing I know for a fact: When it comes to anything involving Stacey, Sharkey never tells the truth."

"Stacey, I take it, is also one of this Sharkey person's exes?" I asked.

Burton nodded.

"Can I ask if it was Stacey and then you, or was it you then Stacey?"

Burton doesn't answer.

"Ah," I said. "Okay. So you figure that Sharkey took your money and gave you a wrong address anyway?"

"I guarantee it," Burton said. "And, knowing how manipulative Stacey Durand is, very soon now, Sharkey is going to go to wherever they *actually* are out of some misguided sense of protection. So, all we have to do is wait and very soon Sharkey will lead us directly to wherever Delores Vandecamp actually is."

I nodded.

We didn't have to wait too long. About two hours later, once the sun had gone down, Sharkey came rolling out of that back gate on that pristine motorcycle. Burton turned our car on and followed after counting to ten. We stayed two cars back and one lane to the left as much as possible. Sure enough, the motorcycle was headed onto the freeway in the direction of downtown. We rolled through the outer district, which looked clean and vital, then slowly made our way downtown. Once it was clear Sharkey was slowing down to find a place to park, we pulled onto a side street and shut the car off.

"Take the safety off," Burton said. We got out and started in the direction where we'd last seen Sharkey. I reached over to my holster and clicked the safety off, then pulled out my flashlight. Burton already had hers out and on. I wondered as we walked, if it came down to it, would Burton arrest Sharkey?

We found the motorcycle fairly easily. It was near a large sedan. Both engines were still warm, but we couldn't immediately see anyone. Four buildings were possible. We walked around the one nearest the motorcycle, finding all the doors locked, and all the windows still intact.

"They didn't get here that much earlier than we did. So if they're not still out here searching, we have to assume they're almost on target," I said. Burton nodded. "That would mean they'd have to have someone…maybe…someone who could sniff out magick…is there something like that?" I asked.

"There is," Burton said. "Unfortunately, we don't have one of those."

We were just about to start to search the one next to it when we heard gunshots across the street. We rushed across and found that door open. We ran up the steps. We could hear sounds of fighting up above us as well as talking.

Just as we rounded onto what looked very much like it had once been a bar, we saw Sharkey, a woman, and a man, all injured. "Freeze! Federal Agent!" I yelled, my light landing on a young woman. The man stopped and straightened slowly, as if he expected what was happening. The young woman turned quickly and raised her hands, but her eyes bored into me. Burton yelled for them to freeze just a second after I did.

"She's getting away!" the young woman said.

"You got them?" Burton asked.

"Yeah."

"She's getting *away!*" the young woman said again.

Burton said walking up to the girl. "Are you Stacey Durand?"

"My name isn't important, I'm not the criminal, here," the young woman said. Burton helped her to her feet slowly. I looked around for Sharkey, but couldn't see her anywhere.

"And I know that because?" Burton asked. With one hand, Burton whipped out her wallet and showed her ID. "Miranda Burton, FBI. You two are coming with me."

"Wait, what?"

"Turn around and place your right hand at waist level behind you," Burton said, taking out her handcuffs.

"You're arresting me?" the girl asked, but complied.

"Let's say that I am naming you a person of interest and I'm asking you to come back to the office for a chat," Burton said, pulling the girl's other arm down and clicking the other handcuff closed. "Can you grab him?" she said to me.

I stepped up to the man. "Place your…" I started to say when he put his left arm in position to be cuffed.

"I'm a black man in America, do you honestly think I don't know how this works?" the man said. As I clicked one cuff closed, he moved his left arm down and I finished cuffing him. "Am I under arrest?"

"As I said, you two are persons of interest and I'm taking you into custody to get some answers," Burton said, already leading the young woman back to the car. I gave a small push to indicate to the man that we should follow. She already had the girl sat in the back seat by the time I got him around the other side. I put my hand on top of his head as I guided him into the seat, then I shut the door.

"Talk to you for a minute?" I asked, motioning away from the car with my head. She put her gun away and walked over to meet me. "What...what's the play, here?" I asked. "I mean," I said, "we got nothing on them, and Sharkey, the person who did seem to have some answers, is in the wind."

"We're going to take them back to the office and have a conversation or two and find out what they know," Burton said.

"Yeah, but the cuffs? I mean, are we officially detaining them?" I asked.

She stared at me for a second. "You know that if I ask them to come with us voluntarily, they say no. She was three seconds from going after Vandecamp even after what they just went through."

"I agree, but what's the procedure? Do we Mirandize them or...?"

"There won't be any need. They're not under arrest. We're just going to put them in a room long enough for them to get antsy and scared, then get them to spill what they know. We'll let them go at that point and they'll be so happy we didn't charge them with anything they'll forget that we started off in fairly murky water," she said.

"Look," I said, crossing my arms, "I'll back your play. But you don't think maybe they'd have been more cooperative had we just asked?"

"Him?" she said, gesturing toward the car, "sure thing. Her, though? She'd have fled. And something tells me she's the one with all the information we want."

"Federal Agent's intuition?" I asked.

She nodded and walked back to the car.

2. Derek Goldman

Being a larger, half-Jewish, bi-racial, gay, cisgender man on the wrong side of forty in a world obsessed to the point of distraction with 19 year old stick thin white boys with blonde highlights, my Friday nights are mostly spent in bookstores, anyway, so when my local indie bookstore was about to go under, I gave into impulse and decided to buy it. The loan went through in record time, the bank agent told me. Two weeks after the initial thought hit me over breakfast I was the owner of The Bitter End bookstore.

I mostly just wanted a quiet place to sit, shill a few Tom Clancy retreads, maybe turn some high school kid on to *The Master and Margarita*, and turn a profit every once in a while. Honestly? Had I known what was going to happen to literacy in America in the mid 2010s, I probably wouldn't have bothered. But, I'd liked the place since the moment I'd first walked in while scouting out the neighborhood before buying a house on that street. It was shabby but clean. There were no coffee machines anywhere to be found, which made me breathe a sigh of relief, but there were mismatched chairs scattered all over the store. Some overstuffed, some just thin seats held up by four mismatched and flimsy legs. That first night I found a pristine copy of Delany's *Trouble on Triton*, which I bought

71

to send back to an old friend in Illinois. My own tattered copy lay at home, never quite making it onto the bookshelf because every time I saw it, I had to pick it up and swim through a few pages. I took it as a sign, you see, because most bookstores won't even carry Delany, let alone one of his more—look, I'm going to use the term racy here, which makes me sound like a PTA mom, but you get what I mean, right?

The owner asked me what I planned to do differently to bring in business. He wondered if I was going to put in a coffee machine. Serve pastries. Hold combat card tournament games on Saturdays. I didn't have a plan, I told him. I just knew that, somehow, it was going to work out. Naïve, true, but I've learned to listen to these thoughts when they occur.

I tried to keep the staff he already had on, but they left. Some were going off to college anyway, some had been fighting for a while to keep the place open and were burned out, and a few just didn't care. So I wound up working open to close by myself. Eventually, I just moved my cat to the store.

Of course it gets lonely. For a long time I had friends who kept telling me that I "just needed to get myself back out there." To "stop moping around" and date. I tried to talk to some of them but it was no use. See, I'm like any other red-blooded human being—I'm looking at bodies, body parts, thinking of what I'd like to do to them given the chance. But after a certain age, the likelihood of that situation ending well kind of goes south. I got tired of being embarrassed by the fumbling and weirdness of it all. What still interests me is conversation, talking to people. The problem? Gay men aren't interested in that. If I were to say that out loud in public, people would scream bloody murder—"you're betraying your community!" "How dare you reduce us all to stereotypes!" "Of course people are still interested in conversation!" Explain Grindr to me, then, please. Explain Tindr. We exist in a culture that orders its sex like you'd order pizza. The idea of honestly talking to your partner before putting various body parts into various other body parts is completely moot.

And look, I get it. I was that age once, too.

But where does that leave an entire generation of us who were just a little too late to the techno-sex revolution?

Exactly where I'm sitting—in a used bookstore on a Friday night watching Ted Talks on YouTube while the entire rest of the world is off smearing God knows what all over each other. Once I figured out that I was just too old for this kind of thing (we'll call it a techno-sex era mistake made consensually but a mistake nonetheless and leave it at that), I took back up with reading. Like a lot of people in their twenties and thirties, I'd fallen away from reading so much. Not that I didn't love a book, and not that I wasn't reading, I just wasn't doing it in long sittings like I did in the years before my root chakra took over my life. As that flame dimmed to a dull, manageable warmth, I found myself back in the capable hands of Homer, of Anne Carson, of Samuel R. Delany (who insists that his friends call him "Chip"). Let the rest of mankind go on chasing each other around the maypole with visions of pistons in their brain—I will quietly wait out for the apocalypse in the halls of the great library.

So why don't I stop moping around and just date? It's not like I haven't. But the real reason it never works out?

Andrew.

I don't want to get into a whole long thing, but his name was Andrew.

The problem? Andrew was straight. Or, at least, straight enough to make anything I wanted out of the question. That old chestnut, as they say.

I've dated since then. Been in a few relationships. All of my attempts to find someone ending in cringe-inducing disaster. I wish I was exaggerating. Nothing lasting more than a few months. Well, one did, but he was just about to move to start a new job. Just enough time for us to really grow relaxed with each other, but not enough time for either of us to entertain the idea of moving with one another. Darrell his name was, and those few months were healing in so many ways, though I never told him that. Again…just long enough for me to have the thought, not long enough for me to say something like that without it seeming to be out of place. I hear from people every once in a while that he is a fixture at Burning Man every year, and that makes me very happy. He should be there among the free, the rainbow lights in the vast desert.

I think about Andrew every day, though. I know where he is. Our Facebook/Twitter/Instagram world makes sure that all the broken hearted can find out in an instant where all their "could have beens" are. What I've learned over time, though, which has been helpful, is *why* I was so powerfully drawn to him. It wasn't just because he was a magnificent half-Lakota Sioux, half-Brazilian androgene with long, perfect black hair. It was also because he had the spark, as I said. He carried within him a lot of raw, untapped power.

And it turns out, I'm drawn to that kind of thing. To magick. Nine times out of ten, I've found out, if you put me near a place where a ritual has taken place, I can tell you about it. I get feeling unsettled, jittery. I feel drawn to those spaces and can't stop thinking about them. A group of women I met along the way called me a "sensitive." The way they described that sounded a bit too close to the description of a drug-sniffing dog to be comfortable, but I got the basic gist.

I will never really be able to use the energy, the source, whatever you want to call it, but I can feel it. Sense how it moves. If I'm having a very good day, I can tell you what…I guess "flavor" would be the right word…it was. I can tell if someone is a witch or wizard or high priestess of some cult or another sitting across from them in a restaurant. Call it a kind of weirdness radar.

So I wind up staring at people a lot. Studying them.

Trust me, this does not win me a lot of fans.

Since puberty, my attention has always been drawn to weirdos. Not your run-of-the-mill show offs; those don't interest me. If the reason you have seven piercings on your head is to piss off mommy, somehow I can tell immediately. But if you have a single heavy silver ring on your left thumb, I'm immediately intrigued because I know what that means, even if you don't.

That's how I met Stacey. The first Friday night I was open, I was working alone (except for Jung, who I brought with me to the store on the first day, and who had very quickly made himself so at home there that I stopped taking him back and forth). In walked this person who looked like they might have been a boy or a girl. He or she came up to about my shoulder—jet black hair shaved on the sides. She had a thick silver ring on her left thumb but no other jewelry. Button down shirt with sleeves rolled up to his or her elbows and tucked in to jet black skinny jeans that tucked into enormous black steel-toed boots. Piercings all over.

And, yeah, okay, I'll admit it—I was attracted, and secretly hoping this was a dude, and that that dude was gay. Sue me, I'm human. And like most men of a certain age, the baby faces interest me (I was brought up in that culture that worships 19 year old stick thin white boys, too—hate it all I want, there's no escaping it).

At least, I'm pretty sure I'm human. It can get a little confusing sometimes.

Thing was, as this person browsed the shelves, I couldn't just go back to the podcast I was listening to (they're an addiction—again, sue me). I kept watching as she walked slowly around the racks. It took a while, too; she was looking at every single title. That's somewhat unusual—most people come in, go right to one or two sections (I'd worked very hard to get them all labeled) that they mostly read from, grab something or don't, and check out or leave. I'd learned over that week that the average person who walked in was out in under twenty minutes.

Several people came in and out, paid or left, during the time it took this person to finish and come to the counter.

"Excuse me," she said, her voice clearly female, "Occult?"

I found myself staring at the oversize ring on her left thumb more than her eyes.

"Everything I've got like that is in the 'New Age' section."

She sneered a bit and laughed, a habit I would come to know well. "They aren't the same thing." She thumped the ring on the counter, turned around and walked out before I could come up with any kind of response.

I wish I could say that I didn't think much about it. That I went back to listening to two musicians talk about how much of an influence Bowie had been on them and eventually locked up and went home. It bugged me, though. I kept thinking about her—and trust me, that's really unusual given the "her" part. Not to be stereotypical, but at the time I wasn't quite as reconstructed as I would eventually become. Plumbing still mattered back then.

I wanted her to come back so I could explain to her. Explain what, I'm not sure, to be honest. I felt like somehow I needed to show her that I did, in fact, know the difference between some guy who ripped off Cherokee herbal medicine with some of the shallow-end-of-the-pool beliefs of Kundalini thrown in for flavor and books by people who actually have walked the proverbial walk. I mean, I know what Ayahuasca is, y'know? I wanted to say all this to her and more, and for some reason it felt really important for me to. I think there was a copy of Castaneda filed next to Kahlil Gibran, in fact, and it hadn't made me cringe until just now.

I'll explain how I know all of this as we go, by the way. I'm not trying to be mysterious on purpose.

She didn't come back in that night, though. I closed up the store and went home. I couldn't get to sleep, though. I sat on my couch, the television off (unusual for me), absently running my thumb over the top of Jung, my cat's, head. As usual, I wound up half-dozing, half going through what I call the catalogue. The catalogue of exes and failures, one of my brain's favorite pastimes.

Another of my exes, if you could call it that, was a boy from high school. I guess we could say my first boyfriend, though we never had any kind of talk about what our relationship was...but that's how things are at that age. I think about how he took me to this place out near the bridge and showed me how, on a flat rock that sat pretty far back in the woods, he had put an old action figure, a yellow flower, and a small, chipped coffee mug. Every time he went out there, he would take a bit of whatever drink he'd been sipping all day and pour it into the cup. I went to reach for the action figure that first time, just wondering what it might be (looking back, I think it was a sunbleached and long neglected version of the blonde boy from a popular science fiction film). He stopped me and said I couldn't touch anything on the stone. When I asked why, he said that it all had to remain in place for them. When I asked who "they" were, he never answered. It was an early encounter with the world of Magick, though I didn't know it. On some level, he understood that you can't go touching someone else's altar. He let me blow him next to it, though. I don't know if he honestly knew what he was doing or if this was just what some people call naïve Magick. It made an impression, though.

I think about those instances a lot, about those boys a lot, because they touched me in a place higher than just sex. Don't get me wrong, the sex was magnificent, too, but they were involved with a deeper world. A world I wanted to have a part in, even back then.

When it finally truly started, it started with spiders for me. A woman I knew to be a Wiccan (mostly Gardnerian but with some personal flair thrown in, if you want to put a label to it) invited me to her home one day for tea. She was poet and I was a teenager, and whatever the equivalent of an enthusiastic toddler is to word crafting and we clicked. I think she mostly sensed that I was harmless. We got to know one another more and more and eventually she let me start coming to ritual. She vouched for me with her coven and I went to a Beltane gathering. The bonfire, the homemade wine, all of us howling at the moon at one point—it was powerful. None of them cared that I was half anything or whose thighs turned me on. All they cared about was sharing the energy and the night.

In late fall in that city by the bay, the large orb weaving spiders begin to stretch out and spin their webs. Over time, they start to connect and form colonies. It is at once terrifying and shatteringly beautiful. It just so happened that a colony sprang up between a tree near her bedroom window and the wall of the house. She invited me over to come see and though I was deeply arachnophobic at the time, when she pointed and said to step under, I did. As if they had left a doorway open, when I stepped under and then stood up I was in the center of this colony of spiders, some as big as my hand, all spinning their golden thread. Living together in harmony. The wind grew and the whole colony vibrated. I don't know to this day if there was a real sound or not, but in my memory, a faint whisper of a chime rose as those strings vibrated.

I knew that they were only there because of her power, the energies she danced with and wove in the moonlight.

No matter what I did, though, I couldn't connect with those energies myself. Too masculine for Wicca's feminine energy, too peaceful for chaos weavers, too skeptical for any of the various voodoo traditions—no matter who I found and no matter how hard I studied, I found myself further and further from my dream of finding a tradition and using it as a force for good in the world. At some point, you have to just admit that, no matter how pretty the reflection of the full moon is in the still water of the abalone-shell bowl that has been blessed and empowered in the circle, you're not seeing any visions of the future in it. No amount of wanting to will make it so.

More than one therapist said, "You're trying to find your people."

What I did learn over time, though, is that I can sense it. I have no power to wield, but I can see it working. Feel it. And from all my studies, I've learned the traditions. I know that world, even though I am useless within it. If you think that this is somehow okay, or that it is beautiful, you are mistaken. It is the single most frustrating thing that you can imagine. I've tried. Believe me, I've tried. There is simply no ability. I know the words to incantations, to prayers, I know how to call corners and the steps to summon so many deities and emanations. Show me the remnants of a ritual and I can tell you with a high degree of confidence the tradition the person believed in, and what they were trying to do.

I just can't do it.

I fall asleep thinking about that.

When Stacey (though I didn't know that was her name, yet) came walking in the second time, she had on a black denim bolero jacket, a white t-shirt that said Flying Lotus on it, skinny jeans faded to almost white, and silver Converse hi-tops. Her hair, freshly dyed so black it seemed almost blue, was done up in this short little faux hawk and her nose ring was in.

"Hey," I said. "You're back!"

"Hey," she said and walked right up to the counter. "Look," she said.

"Look," I said at the exact same time. She moved her head back a bit and squinted at me. I smiled.

"You go," I said.

She inhaled deeply then exhaled, "before he sold to you, Aldini and I kind of had a thing worked out where, when I needed money, he'd put me on the payroll for a bit."

"You want a job?" I asked.

"Not, like, permanently. I just need to get some cash together and I was wondering if, you know, you had anything that needed doing."

I hadn't thought of hiring anyone. The whole idea was for me to have something to do on the nights I wasn't sleeping, anyway.

"Also, I was wondering if me and some friends could use the backroom like we used to," she said.

"To do what?" I asked.

"Aldini didn't tell you anything?"

"Not much," I said.

"Yeah," she said, darkly. "Or something."

"What did happen?" I asked.

She leaned on the counter. "Did they not tell you anything?"

"Who is 'they'," I asked, drinking my coffee.

"Any more of that around?" she asked.

I turned to go to the back. She beat me to the door and walked in. For a second I was taken aback until I remembered she'd just said she had been in the store before. She was already at the coffee pot and had taken a large travel cup out of the purse I only just noticed because of the angle she had it slung across her back. She finished off the pot and then went looking through the cupboards until she found where I'd put the coffee and the filters. Some part of me thought I should be offended and angry about her presumption, but another part of me was tickled. Especially that she knew one of my basic rules in life: if you finish the coffee, start another pot (something none of my roommates or boyfriends had ever seemed to grasp as basic human decency).

As she set the filter and then scooped three spoons worth in, she said, "Aldini was a great guy. Old as dirt. That kind of old where they could be sixty or a hundred and twelve, you know? But still solid. Right up until the end I could have sworn he was every bit as limber as anyone else." She slid the filter tray closed and took the pot over to the sink to start filling it. "He owned this bookstore as far back as I can remember. Had a thing for all us kids who came through. Not like a pervert thing, though; just a spark. He liked talking to young people. It made him feel young, too, I think." She slid the filled pot back into the maker and flipped the switch. "Sugar?" she asked.

I pointed with my own mug, "Third from the left," then took a sip.

She found the container and started pouring spoons full into her own travel mug. I couldn't help but grin. "It's where we all kind of met each other."

"We?' I asked.

After she'd put six full spoons in, she stirred her coffee and then washed off the spoon and slid it into the little drainer by the sink. "All us neighborhood kids. He especially looked out for the ones who didn't have any place to go."

"Street kids?" I asked. "In this neighborhood?"

"Not as many as used to be," she said, closing the lid on her coffee and then taking a sip. My cat, awakened by all the sudden movement, walked directly up to her leg and started to nuzzle her. "Hello—?" she said.

"Jung," I said.

"Hello, Jung," she bent to rub his head. "Yeah, well, that's because of him." She stood and walked back to the front of the store. Instead of going back on the other side of the counter, though, she sat down on the stool near the register. "He networked with people and found them all homes or job opportunities so that they could find their own way out. He was good like that," she said, looking at the floor.

"I'm sorry. From the way you're talking, I assume he passed

on?"

She looked at me for a moment. I could tell that whatever test she was giving, passing was incredibly important.

"What's your name?" she asked.

"Derek Goldman," I said. As I'd been taught to do my whole life, I walked toward her and extended my hand to shake hers. This only made her scrutinize me more. When she didn't move to shake my hand, I thought to myself that I should be offended, but I could see that she wasn't done giving the test yet. Jung jumped up on the counter next to her, sat, and began grooming himself.

"Goldman? Jewish?" she asked, one eyebrow cocked.

"Half. My father was Jewish, but as you may know, that's the wrong half. Probably not a great thing to ask outright, though." I decided that, because I liked her, we could have the conversation about stereotypes and racism later.

"Ah," she said.

"Is that important?" I asked. "And you are?"

"Stacey," she said. She sipped her coffee. "Religious?"

"Not very, no. Why?" I asked.

She went quiet again. "Because I need to ask you something, and I'm trying to decide before I do if it's a good idea or not."

"What does your gut tell you?"

"That you probably already know what I'm going to ask," she said. "What do you know about magick?" she asked.

I leaned against the counter and cocked my head to the side. "That's not the question I thought you were going to ask me."

"You thought I was going to ask you if you were gay, yeah?" she said.

"Which, of course, I am, but how did you know that's what I thought you were going to ask?"

"Fifty-fifty shot. My gaydar, though, is impeccable. I didn't need to ask," she said. "Card-carrying lesbian since age four."

Something in the room suddenly felt more comfortable.

"But you didn't answer my question," she said.

"It all depends on what you mean by the word, 'know,'" I said. "It would be more than you think I do, but a lot less than you hope for whatever question it is you really want to ask me."

She set her cup down. Jung sniffed at it absently then went back to grooming his tail. She squinted a bit, "Wicca? Thelema? Stregone?"

"No," I said. She shrank a bit on hearing it. "To make a very long story short, I don't practice it. I know a lot about it, though. Which of those are you?"

"More of what they call 'other—idiosyncratic practioner.' At least, that's the box I check every year when it's time to re-up my registration." I could tell she was using the words to test my level of knowledge. "You know about The Conclave, right?" she asked.

"Yeah," I said.

"Well, if there is this Conclave, and that's the government for all people who use magick, then you know about the Malleus Maleficarum their sort-of FBI, yeah?"

"Yes," I said. I'd had more than one run-in with their agents over the years. Did I know the current whereabouts of this sorcerer? Had I seen this particular object in the last five years? Malleus agents tended to think that because I knew a lot of people in "the community," as they called it, that I myself was engaged in practice. No matter how many times I tried to tell them that I wasn't, they never seemed to listen.

"Well, if they have a kind of investigative branch, and that kind of resembles our own more 'regular' modes of government, don't you think there's also other related forms? Other ways that they are similar?"

"What, a kind of CIA for mages?" I asked.

She nodded gravely, "or an NSA."

I couldn't help myself and laughed. "Why would there be?"

"Why wouldn't there be?" she asked in return. "Who's to say that windchime over there isn't also charmed to record conversation? Whose to say that puddle outside the front door is actually a puddle and not a remote scrying work?"

"Come on," I said. When she continued to stare at me without saying anything, I said "Come on," again. She shrugged. She got down off the stool and turned for the door. "Thanks for the coffee," she said without looking back. She was out the door and gone before I realized I hadn't answered her question about a job. At the end, though, she hadn't reminded me, either.

It was two days later when she came back. I was in the back room making myself some lunch when I heard the bells on the door chime. The previous owner, Aldini (I now knew his name), hadn't installed artificial ones, but had an actual set of small bells that hung in the exact right spot. If the door opened or closed, they let out a beautiful melody that seemed very familiar but I could never quite place. I had assumed it was the customer who had been wandering around for the last hour, seemingly reading the back of ever book I had in the place regardless of genre, leaving.

I had just pulled the toast from the toaster and put it on top of the tuna fish sandwich when I heard her say, "Twelve fifty," and the rustle of a bag.

Another voice said, "You have such a lovely store, here."

"Thank you very much," I heard her say. The register drawer opened and closed and I heard her say, "come again!" in a bright cheery voice as I heard two coins clink. I came around the corner just as the man walked out the door, bag in hand.

She wore much the same outfit as before, only the T-shirt now said Deap Vally. "Is there coffee?" she asked walking past me into the back room.

I opened my laptop and after a quick search pulled up all the information on getting an employee's taxes set up. When she came back she sat down at the register.

"Last name?" I said, typing.

"I was hoping we could handle all this under the table," she said.

"Ah," I said.

"Like I said, it's not a permanent thing. I just need to put together some cash."

I shut the laptop. "I could get in trouble for that."

"I know," she said. "Durand," she said, "Stacey Durand," holding out her hand. I shook it.

"So, I'm assuming this is all to be a cash only operation?"

"Now you're catching on," she said. "First thing that needs to happen is to get the books in the 'new age' section split up. The fluffy bunny shit in one area the actual stuff in another."

"The 'actual stuff'?" I asked.

She sipped from the mug she had poured, closing her eyes and pausing. Then she started for that section of the store.

"I didn't change anything from how Mr. Aldini had it," I said.

"I can tell," she said. "Thing is, he and I fought about this constantly."

"Ah, I see," I said. "So this is all an old feud where you get the final word in?"

"Something like that," she said. She picked up a book. "See this?" I knew the book she was holding but I didn't say anything. I wanted to see what where she was going with this. "Carlos Castanada. That's real deal stuff. And yet here it sits next to a copy of a dream dictionary. Watered down second hand Freud sitting next to instructions for drug assisted astral projection. What if some kid came in here and didn't know any better and gave the two things the same weight? That kid is then out there trying to get through the doors with the idea that snake imagery is about fear."

"It isn't?" I asked with a grin.

"You could be responsible for leaving that kid misinterpreting his vision. His whole quest is for nothing. He makes the wrong decisions based on misinterpreting his vision and we get another world leader with delusions of grandeur," she said, shaking the book at me.

"But couldn't that happen anyway?" I asked.

"What?" she asked, pulling books off the shelf and sorting them into two piles.

"The idea that the universe unfolds as it should no matter what. If the kid goes for a dive in the deep water and comes back thinking he's the savior of mankind, isn't there an argument that says he would have done that no matter what?"

She exhaled dismissively. "Starhawk books sitting next to books shelved right next to…" she mumbled.

"What criteria are you using to determine what is 'real' and what isn't?" I asked.

"The truth," she said.

I couldn't help but laugh. "And if someone else came in here from a different tradition, wouldn't they just argue for a different sorting?"

She stopped, stood up straighter, and without turning to look at me said, "they might, but they'd be wrong." She flashed a lopsided grin.

"And how do you get that?"

"Because," she said and continued sorting.

"Because?" I asked.

"Because," she said and then sighed. She turned to face me. "Because some of the traditions are just nice ways to spend an evening and some of them are real deal no joke. You had to have sensed that, if you've been around all these other mages and warlocks and sorcerers and whatever they're called. That some of it is pretty and full of nice poetry while other stuff is real."

"Is that what this Conclave you talked about thinks?"

"No," she said, rolling her eyes. "Their official position is that all traditions have validity. All pieces of the puzzle. Blindfolded people touching different parts of the elephant."

"But that's not what you think?"

She shook her head. "Some of them are touching the ass."

"So why does the Conclave treat them all equally?" I asked.

"Because otherwise it would be all out war. I mean, they don't say that. They don't even acknowledge that delegitimizing any traditions is a possibility. But they know that if they do that, it's like putting a declawed kitten out at night. You'd have people who think they have juice trying to street fight with people who are actually carrying weapons. It would be a bloodbath."

"I see," I said.

"So they have to pretend that some nature poets who like to garden are the same thing as a serious Green Witch, and that some kid who reads a hex spell off the internet is the same thing as a high priest of Anubis. It's a waste of time." She takes the last book off the shelf and sets it atop one of the piles. "There."

"That's likely not a very popular opinion," I said. It was one I'd heard before, though.

"No," she said. "It isn't."

"Okay," I said. "So, now that you have what you've always wanted," I laughed and she cracked a bit of a smile. "What are you going to do with them?" I said, gesturing toward the books.

"Well, obviously," she said, "we can reuse the same shelf, just use an extra sign to separate them and make sure that when new books come in, they are sorted in the same fashion."

"I get that," I said. "However, you've run into another problem of politics."

She quirked her head to the side.

"What are you going to call the sections? You can't say one is 'the truth' and the other is 'bull.'"

She laughed. "We'll call one 'new age' and the other 'magickal studies.'"

"Doesn't that disrespect some of these other traditions?" I asked.

"No," she said. "I was careful. Even if it isn't a tradition I respect very much, if it is still magickal study, it goes in this pile." She put her hand on top of one of the piles. "This stack," she said, putting her hand on the other, "is purely for warmed-over pop culture rehashes of Jungian psychology and Erik Von Danyken. Sasquatch. Easter Island studies. That shit."

"Okay," I said. "We do sell other kinds of books here, too."

"Do we?" she asked without looking at me.

And it was in that way that Stacey came to work at the shop. True to her word, she didn't show up every day. In fact, I stopped trying to schedule her within the first week. I stopped trying to guess her schedule within the first three weeks. Eventually we settled into a rhythm. I started a list of things that needed doing around the place and left that list on the counter. When she did come in, whenever that would be, she fixed herself coffee, found the list, picked something off of it and set to that task. A shelf was made exclusively for Stephen King and placed close to the door because she looked over our sales one afternoon and discovered that we moved more of his novels than anything else in the shop. A set of holes was filled in and painted from where old shelves had been placed on the walls and when they were taken down no one had filled in the holes the anchors left. She decided what it was she did, and how long it took her to do it. As promised, I paid her in an envelope full of cash. She would stuff the envelope away and leave without saying anything. Her standard way of saying goodbye on any given day was to simply say, "okay," and walk out the door.

On any given day when she worked, our conversations could turn very deep. One day while sitting at the counter, she suddenly said, "Jabberwock."

"Excuse me?" I asked.

"The creature in the poem from Alice in Wonderland. The Jabberwock."

"I'm not following. Isn't the creature called the Jabberwocky?"

"No. And that's my entire point," she said. "It clearly says in the poem that the creature itself is called The Jabberwock. The poem's title is 'Jabberwocky.' Thing is, like you, you ask ten people what the name of the creature is and guess what nine of the idiots are going to say."

"Okay," I said.

"It says it right in the poem what the name of the creature is, but still nine out of every ten people are going to say what they *think* to be true, not the actual information. You see what I'm saying?"

"Walk me through it," I said.

"People get a thing in their head and that becomes a fact for them even if it isn't really a fact. It gets stuck in there and then they rely on it. Red wheelbarrow."

"Okay, what's that?" I asked.

"Another poem. 'So much depends on the yada yada.' The poem specifically says 'red wheelbarrow.' Let people read that poem and then give them a little time and ask them again, you know what they describe?"

"What?" I asked.

"A little red wagon. Most of the time so specific that they even give it the brand name, Radio Flyer. Nine out of ten times. They picture the wrong thing, that wrong thing gets lodged in their stupid little brains and then that becomes the fact they base their decisions in life off of."

"Red wheelbarrow, huh?" I asked.

"Yep."

"Jabberwock," I said.

"Fuckin A," she said.

Another day we were about an hour from closing up and I told her to go on, that I would lock up by myself. When she asked if I had anyone to go home to, I motioned to Jung, my cat. Since he seemed to prefer it to my apartment, I had migrated him to the store. I'd made him a cozy little cave back in the break room where I found him most mornings when I came in.

"Okay, but why?" she asked.

"Why what?"

"Why are you alone? I mean, you seem like a sweet guy and everything. You got a whole Richard T. Jones-ish kinda thing going on. Why didn't you ever settle down with someone?"

"I tried," I said.

She let that linger for a moment, but then asked, "what does that mean?"

"It means I tried. There were...complications...look, nevermind. Let's just forget it."

"Suit yourself," she said, turning her head away. "Did he die?" she asked after ten minutes or so.

"Did who die?"

"The One. The important one that left you so hurt."

"No. He's still...wait, how did you know?"

I looked over at her to find her looking back at me with a shocking intensity. She grinned, cocked her head to the side, and gestured as if to say, ta-da.

"Stop that." I said

"Stop what?" she asked.

"Stop doing whatever it is you're doing to pry into my life."

"Oh, dude, come on—I don't need any help from the spirit

world to see what happened. You were about to say there have been three loves of your life, which is kind of true, but also a little bullshit. There's been one and two others who came close. But at night, when you're thinking about the list of shit that's hurt you? It's his face you see. The One. The one that mattered, but didn't work out."

"Look, it's not important."

"It is, obviously. You've closed yourself off…"

"I said it really doesn't matter."

"…from the rest of the world and shut down because you think that if things didn't work out with that one, then they can't work out with anyone. It hurt you and you don't ever want to be hurt like that again, so instead you sit in your tower and…"

"I said let's drop it."

"…and what kills you is that his life didn't stop. I'm guessing, what…wife? Kids? Book deal? Speaking gig in the University of Wherever on Tuesday?"

I should have been angry. I should have been furious at being read so easily, but instead all I did was stare straight ahead.

"He must've been really something to mess you up like this."

"He was," I whispered. "He really was."

Minutes of silence passed, then she said, "You already know what I'm going to say."

I didn't answer.

"If things didn't work out, then he couldn't have been The One. If he was The One, then it would have worked out."

"I don't…"

"This is the part where you say that you don't believe in any of that 'The One' shit, but you obviously do, or else it wouldn't have hurt you so much."

"It was all a long time ago," I said so quietly even I almost didn't hear it.

She didn't say anything in return for a long time. Eventually, about ten minutes from closing, a customer came in, one of those who can only remember the color of the cover of the book that they want. We both got caught up in trying to help him that eventually any tension was forgotten. We closed out the register and said goodnight as I locked the door.

Somewhere toward the middle of the third week, she had brought in a small television and put it behind the cash register. I asked her how much she'd spent, intending to repay her for it, but she said she'd found it out behind a dumpster. Considering the age of the model, I believed it. She was sitting on the stool watching the television and minding the register when I came in from sweeping the front sidewalk. She was staring at the television with an intensity that I had never seen before. As soon as the door closed and she heard the bell chime, she jumped a bit.

"Fuckin A, Goldman," she said.

"What's going on?" I said with a laugh.

She said nothing but went back to watching the screen. On it, there was a picture of an alleyway and a body covered by a blanket. Then it shifted to a young woman in a turtleneck and a blazer behind a desk. "At this time, the woman has no identification. Police are asking anyone who might have been in the area to contact them."

"What's all that about?" I asked, leaning against the counter.

"Nothing," Stacey said, shutting off the television, grabbing her purse and walking out the door.

I didn't see her again for a week. When she came back in, she made no mention of what had happened. I didn't press. About a week after that, something very similar happened. I came in first thing in the morning to find the lights already on, the coffee already made, and her watching a similar news report. When I opened the door, she reached for something under her jacket as she jumped off the stool. I shut the door as gingerly as I could. "Lock it," she said.

"Customers?" I asked.

"Just...for now, okay? Fuck."

I locked it. The screen showed another picture of another body covered by a sheet in a different alleyway.

"Okay," I said, setting my thing down on the counter. "What's going on?"

"Nothing," she said.

"No, we're not going to do that. I know we haven't known

each other very long, but it is obvious that what is happening is not 'nothing.' So, what is happening? What is it about these killings that has you shook up?" I asked.

"Killings?" she asked.

"Don't try to tell me that the Jane Doe from a few weeks back with similar circumstances isn't somehow related to this one in your mind."

She held still for a second, then sat down on the stool once more. "I've...I've been homeless before. I mean, I have a place to stay for right now, but I mean, I've been on the streets before. I've had to live in those alleyways. I still know people down there."

"Were either of these two people you knew?" I asked.

She didn't answer.

"Do you have any information? If so, you really need to—,"

"Don't you think I know that? Fuckin A," she said. "Thing is, I'm not exactly what you'd call a model citizen. There's a reason I asked to be paid off the grid. You have to have figured that out already."

I nodded that I had.

"So I can't just go walking into some police station, even if what I have to tell them might be useful."

"Why don't you tell me, then?" I asked.

She looked into my eyes and started chewing her thumbnail. "Because it involves that stuff," she said, gesturing toward the section she'd set up for magick.

"Okay," I said.

"But is it?" she asked. "Is it 'okay?' You've been really cool, and that's great, but here's the thing. There's a difference between saying to someone, 'I think maybe what people say in some of these books is real' as a conversation topic over coffee on a Tuesday and asking them to believe that there might be a..." she said, but drifted off.

"A what? A killer on the loose? Someone who also believes?"

"A full fledged practitioner," she said, looking at the floor.

"Meaning what?" I asked.

She looked back up at me and held my eyes a moment. "I think

91

I know who is doing this, and I think I know why."

"How do you know those things?" I asked.

She thought about something, then nodded to herself. She got down off the stool and pulled up her shirt a bit until I could see a horrible scar across her stomach. "Because I'm pretty sure it was the same person who attacked me."

"Maybe you'd better start from the beginning."

Stacey said that she'd been born to parents who were one step above the stereotype we all carry with us of drug addicts. They were able to keep things together just enough to not have Stacey taken away, but she spent a lot of her childhood alone, locked in a house. She said she felt afraid of them when they were home from whatever jobs they'd been able to hold on to, so she actually preferred it when they were away during most of the day. She could pretend that the house was whatever she wanted it to be. Very often, she said, it was an endless kingdom of fairies and unicorns. The kind of things that our culture presses into little girls' heads pretty early. It wasn't until later that the parents lost their various jobs and couldn't scrape money together anymore that Stacey had to deal with reality. Later, she said, they would kick her out and wouldn't let her back in until almost night. She found herself wandering in larger and larger circles until eventually she found a kind of family in the homeless population in the alleyways. Whereas most people were afraid of their quirky ways, Stacey thought of it as a kind of play. They showed her their lives; where to get food, where to sleep that was safe, places to avoid. Several of them took her in and became a family. She eventually fell in love with another girl who was a bit older and they were very happy together. Stacey went back to her biological parents' house less and less until eventually she just stopped going altogether.

By then she was fifteen and she came in contact with an old woman everyone just called "The Bruhah" (after a minute, I figured out Stacey probably meant the Spanish word Bruja, which means Witch/sorceress). The Bruja took Stacey in immediately saying there were important things ahead for her. While this made some of the others who had taken on parental roles a little uneasy, they recognized that this was also an important thing—The Bruja was a kind of doctor and spiritual adviser to everyone in the alleys. Stacey was being groomed to replace her. Stacey didn't go into great detail about what she was taught, but she did mention the rudiments of herbal healing, how to be a good midwife, that kind of thing. It was The Bruja who knew the man who had owned the bookstore before me, and she had introduced Stacey to him, as she had so many other kids from the alleys. He took her in just as he had them, paying them for work and making sure they had a place to sleep that was warm and dry in the back room of the shop. He had discovered in her, though, something none of them had—potential. In this very shop she began to learn from him, as well.

As she spoke, I began to realize that the young woman sitting before me wasn't just another androgynous waif. I had allowed my lazy mind to put her in that box. I was looking at a young apprentice of great potential who had lost one of her master teachers—she had been learning two powerful traditions of magick simultaneously. It wasn't that I had kept her at arm's length on purpose before, but like all people when they first meet, I had done a fair bit of stereotyping. A part of me, some tiny door inside me, opened up to her in that moment.

It was one afternoon not long ago that she and The Bruja had been sent for. In the vast network of alleyways, a young man had been hurt very badly. They were called to heal him. When they arrived, she said, they found him sliced up badly. Much worse than what can sometimes happen to a young man asking for change in a big city. When the Bruja went to lay hands to begin the healing, she backed away quickly and began mumbling something in Spanish. Stacey said she'd never seen the woman act like this before. They healed the boy as best they could, but The Bruja said to Stacey privately that she didn't think the wounds would ever fully heal. When Stacey asked why, the old woman said that the blade had been worked with dark, dark magick.

Two nights later, Stacey said, while running an errand for supplies for The Bruja, Stacy found herself alone in a long stretch of alleyway. Out of the darkness, she said, came a woman who seemed blurry. Stacey said her eyes didn't seem to want to fix on her. When Stacey tried to run, she said, the woman was at her side instantly, as if she had teleported. Before Stacey could stop her, the woman spun and a blade, something like a very large version of the throwing stars Ninja use in all the movies only more curved, sliced deep into Stacey's midsection. She said she knew the wound was fatal as she collapsed. The woman, Stacey said, came in to cut her again, laughing the whole time, but just then a couple of off-duty cops happened to come out the back door of a bar nearby. For some reason, it was just enough to scare the woman off. The men being drunk and having just come from a place where there was light into the nearly complete darkness of the alleyway didn't see Stacey, so she was left alone and bleeding.

Again, the way I had seen her up to this point was gone. I was now looking at a survivor.

She said she came to in the bedroom of the abandoned house out near the paper mill that she and The Bruja shared. Her wound was dressed but The Bruja said, just as she had of the young man, that it would never completely heal. When she asked how the old woman had found her, all she'd gotten in return was a smile. She said she spent a week sleeping off and on and eventually came to. That first night she'd come into my bookstore was only the third night she'd been able to move. She'd come to talk to Aldini two nights before only to find him dead and the store in new hands. When she'd walked in, she had been testing me.

"So," she said, finishing, "I think that she's still out there. With that blade."

"What does your master, The Bruja, think?"

Stacey shook her head, "she left when she heard about Aldini. A promise she made to him about what she would do with his ashes. I don't expect her back for a long, long time."

I inhaled and exhaled loudly. "You're right," I said. "I don't think that's something you can tell the cops." She nodded. "There has to be someone from the Malleus, though, who is on the case, right?"

She gestured toward the TV, "does it look like it?"

"Well, I mean, they have to already know, right?"

"Maybe," she said. "Only, if they do, they aren't doing a very good job. I can't help but think…"

"Think what?"

"Nothing," she said, chewing her thumbnail again.

"Look," I said. "Haven't I proven that I'm not going to laugh you out of the store, yet? Haven't you seen that I know more about this stuff than your average book seller?"

Again, she waited, caught my eyes, then nodded to herself. "What if they do know, but they don't care? What if, because it's just street kids, they don't give a shit?"

"You figure that, magick or no, a cop is a cop is a cop?"

She shrugged.

"I don't suppose they'd have something like an anonymous tip line, right?"

"Do you honestly think they don't have ways of tracking things like that?" she asked. Had I been anyone else, I'm sure I could have talked that point away, but her level of paranoia was matching my own. I just nodded.

"I can't exactly say I don't agree that might be the case. But so then, if we're not going to call in the cops, and we're not going to call in these Malleus folks, then what exactly is it you want to do?" I asked.

"What do you mean?" she asked.

"Knowing what you know, feeling how you're feeling right now, we can't exactly just sit here. So, I'm asking, what exactly is it you want to do?"

She stared at me for what seemed like forever. "I want to try to track her down myself."

I let that sit for a moment. "And then do what?"

"Once we have some idea of where she is, of how to find her, *then* we can go to the Malleus. They won't be able to just shrug it off at that point."

"You feel like that is what will make the difference…having a location where they can just swoop in and pick her up?"

Stacey nodded. I let things go quiet again.

"And how exactly are you planning on doing this?"

She bit her lower lip, then nodded to herself. She reached into her jacket and pulled out a baggie that she laid gently on the counter. In it was a bit of metal and a scrap of cloth. "This was a bit of the blade taken from the wound."

I leaned forward and put my hand on the baggie. I expected that it might feel warm or vibrate, maybe, but it was cold. "And the cloth?"

"It was a scrap of the shirt she was wearing. It came loose from her somehow. I figure, I don't know…I figure maybe with my contacts, with the people I know, I can use these things to track her down," Stacey said.

"You don't think maybe she might use these same things to do the reverse?"

"To try to finish me off?" Stacey asked. "Why do you think I've been carrying this around?" she said. She opened her jacket and showed me the small black revolver she had stuffed in an inside pocket. This is what she had reached for when I had surprised her.

"That why you disappeared for a while?" I asked.

She let her jacket close. "Contrary to what every Republican asshole seems to think, it isn't exactly easy to get your hands on a gun off the books these days. Not to mention the ammunition."

"If she can move at the speed of a blink of an eye, though…"

"I didn't say any of this would be easy," she said. "So," she asked, looking at me, "you in?"

"Let's say that I am—is there a plan?" I asked.

"I have friends," she said. "The plan is we start by going to them and with their…skills…they give us information."

I nod. "Don't take this as a criticism, but you haven't already been gathering information?"

"Like I said," she sighed, "the gun thing took longer than I thought. So, I'm asking again. Are you in?"

I thought for a moment. Despite the fact that I'd been around people working magick my whole life, it seemed, I had never been involved with anything like this. This would be dangerous. I looked at her and knew, though, that she was going to pursue this on her own. I thought about how those other victims had died, and about how Stacey had almost died, already.

"Okay," I said. "I'm in." She smiled and put her arms out.

"Bring it in, Goldman." We hugged.

She told me to meet her the next night at the shop and to wear something "cool." When I asked what the idea was, she simply said, "We need to find Evan. If anyone can get us information on this thing," she said, putting her hand on the baggie, "it's him." So I went home and tried to sleep. I wound up pacing for hours thinking.

I slept eventually, once the sun came up, but not well. I woke to Stacey calling my phone. "I'm up," I said. "Meet me here," she said, giving an address that was far away from the store. I threw on my black suit, which I normally don't wear anywhere but funerals, and drove there, found a relatively safe place to park the car and walked to the corner she'd said to. She was standing in the alleyway nearby, dressed in full punk/goth mode. Leather jacket, hair swept to one side so that the shave underneath was more visible, knee-length combat boots.

"Nice," was all she said, turned, and walked into the alley. The further we got, the more I noticed that there were other people walking in the same direction as us. There were fat guys and emaciated guys and women who barely cracked five foot standing next to others who were five hundred pounds. And I know better than to let my eye linger on any one of them for too long because any one of these people could probably destroy me in less time than it takes to pronounce my name. I've been in places like this enough to know that an unarmed man would do well to stay humble when everyone else has a gun. More than one of them is marked with tattoos of symbols I know.

These are magick users.

There's no way of knowing, either, which are summoners, which are blood mages, which are enchanters, priests of some ancient death goddess, etc.

Stacey never deferred, though. She walked through the crowd, head up, shoulders back, almost daring any of them to come at her.

Eventually, we reached a door. She knocked and from behind it we heard a voice. "Pass?"

I had to stifle a laugh. This kind of shit only happens in cartoons in my world.

She stared hard through me for a moment until I calmed down, then said, "Shibboleth."

There were sounds of the door unlocking and chains being taken off. Once the door opened, the smell inside was both rank and welcoming all at the same time. Stacey pushed through without waiting to see if I followed. We passed by a short bald man with a goatee. He waved his hand and the door closed behind us, the locks clicking into place without his touch.

"Okay," Stacey said, stopping. "Here's the thing; where we're going—in there," she said, gesturing through the doors, "I need you to be cool. Not that I think you wouldn't be, but I mean I need you to *be cool*. You're going to see some stuff, and maybe you'll be okay with it, maybe you won't, but no matter what I need you to just..." she trailed off.

"To be cool," I said.

She nodded.

"Maybe it would help if you told me what all this is," I said.

"You've heard of underground boxing, right?" she asked. I nodded. "Same sort of thing, only with magick."

I must have given some sort of reaction with my eyes.

"Look, it can't come as any big surprise to you that there's any such thing. I mean, put two kids with ice cream in a room together and it's six seconds before they start having contests to see who can eat theirs faster, right? Same fucking principle here, only in this case, the ice cream is lethal. Or something like that. I'm not great on metaphors," she said. The door behind us opened and three men in leather jackets and sunglasses, even though it was night, walked by. The door closed behind them.

"But," she continued, "they come from all over. You got your folks who pledge their undying whatever to a deity or force or spirit that has walked this planet since before plants were the dominant lifeform. You got your kids who started out with the candles and what just about anybody calls 'fluffy bunny bullshit' white or green magick, making poultices from herbs they grew in their back yard and always smelling of patchouli, but then worked their way into darker stuff. You got your guys, and I don't know why, but it's almost always men, who picked up a staff or a necklace or gem or what have you and were instantly possessed by the remnant spirit of some nasty piece of work who decided they not only wanted to be a real fucker in the time period they lived, but cause plenty of fuckery for some other poor bastard later on. You got all kinds is what I'm saying," she said and then turned, and started walking again. The hallway seemed much longer than it should have been for the size of the building outside.

"Put any of these assholes in a room together and within seconds it's, 'well, at least I don't need to slice open babies' throats to cover myself in symbols and shit' or 'Oh, yeah? Well if your god, insert unpronounceable word here, is so powerful, can he/she/it/they do this?' and we're off to the goddamn races. The pecker contests aren't really necessarily about the size of the peckers involved, around here, but more about something else. Dicks are just what was on hand, if you will. And if kids are going to do that, then you bet adults are going to do it, and if it involves some kind of contest, you can bet there'll be deaths, both accidental and otherwise. And if there's going to be deaths, then that means there's going to betting. And in this town, if there's betting? It means you have to talk to Bennie the Fish," she said. We turned a corner and I could hear the sounds of a crowd nearby and growing louder. We passed another huge man with no hair in an expensive-looking suit. "I know what you're saying, 'Oh, that's super original—the whole insert name here then add 'the Fish' nickname.'" She continued. "Bennie, through various means and sundry combinations of powders, potions, spells, wards and whatever else strikes his fancy, is approaching his 800th year, despite looking a hard-bitten 41. Big eyes, large mouth, small nose. I think you get the picture. So, see, it's everyone else that got the idea from Bennie. This isn't just the guy, he's THE guy, if you catch my meaning." The crowd grew louder and I could now smell them, a jumble of expensive colognes and sweat. Blood and ozone.

"So," she continued as we turned another corner. Up ahead, I could see an opening and through it I could almost make out people moving around. "If this whole thing revolves around underground unlicensed spell boxing tournaments, at some point we're going to find ourselves standing in front of Bennie the Fish. And I know enough about that world to know, this is never a place you want to be. Bennie has been known to vaporize people for trying his patience. But…" she let that drift off as we entered the room.

Almost immediately a skinny guy in all black came up to us. "Place your bets?" He saw that it was Stacey he was talking to, though, and took a step back. "I haven't seen you in here in a while."

"Been busy," she said.

He looked over at me, then back at her. "Double card tonight. Wanna' bet?"

"Need to see Bennie," she said.

"Bennie got guests, tonight. Said no appointments."

"That's no appointments for the regular fuckers. You know he'll see me," she said. The kid rolled his eyes.

"You sure you don't just want to put a little money in circulation, then maybe go grab a bite to eat, maybe have a nice long talk?" he said, moving in closer and closer to her. I'm about to step in to push him back when she puts a hand on his chest.

"Go get Dane, tell him I'm here."

The kid stayed where he was, as in way too close, for a second, then rolled his eyes again and walked away into the crowd. While all this has been happening, people were milling all around us. Through another archway I could see the crowd gathered around a raised concrete slab. I don't have to be any closer to it to know that it's got bloodstains all over it. I'm just thinking about how often the world lives up to its clichés when a young black man, beautiful and huge, comes up to us. His hair is natural and his suit is very expensive and I'm instantly embarrassed for how I'm dressed.

"Stace," he said.

"Dane," she said back. "I need to see Bennie."

"Bennie isn't taking appointments tonight as I'm sure Frog told you." His voice was the exact voice you'd expect to come out of a man this powerfully built and handsome. I can't stop staring and, on some level, I know that he knows that because he doesn't even look at me.

"This will just take a second. Look, I can see him right there," she said, pointing through the archway. I can see a man leading a few other men through the crowd where she's pointing. They part for him without him having to make the slightest gesture. That's power, I thought.

Dane moved in front of her hand so that neither of us can see Bennie anymore. "Perhaps I can assist you with whatever information you're looking for."

She sighed. We can both tell that, while he has no intention of being rude, he is an impenetrable roadblock neither of us are getting through tonight. I could see her size up her options, shake her head, then give up. "Evan around tonight? Is he fighting?"

Dane smiled a bit. "The kid isn't here. It's a shame, too, because the action is particularly hot tonight.

"Any idea where he might be?" Stacey asked.

"He said something about taking the week off for a legit tournament, last I heard. Upstate, maybe? Why are you interested?" Dane asked.

She looked at me, then back at him. "This killer going around. I think...I think maybe they might be...you know...one of us."

Dane's smile faded a bit. "We deal with all kinds around here," he said, "but I'm sure the kind of person who would be out there carving people up wouldn't be the kind of person who would wind up in the ring. Seems to me, that's a different kind of itch."

"You don't think Bennie would maybe know something, do you?" she asked.

Dane flicked a glance at me then back at her. "I'm sure that if Mister Bennie has any information he thought would be relevant to an ongoing case, he would communicate that information to the proper authorities." At that moment, a young woman in a very short dress came up to Dane. He bent down some and she whispered something in his ear, then walked away quickly. "You are of course welcome to stay for tonight's event. I'm afraid I'm needed, though. If you'll excuse me." With that, he faded into the crowd. I watched him go until I couldn't see him anymore. When I looked back for Stacey, she was already halfway to the exit.

I caught up with her in the alleyway headed back to where we'd met.

"Did you drive?" she asked.

"Of course," I said. "This guy Evan, is there some other way we can catch up with him?"

"Yeah, I think so. We just have to do a quick search for martial arts tournaments upstate. I'm sure there can't be more than a handful. Still, though," she said, stopping. "I bet Bennie knows something. I bet he knows a lot more than Dane thinks."

"It was pretty clear we weren't getting anywhere near the guy tonight, though," I said.

"Yeah," she said. "You're right. Still. Fuckin' A."

We walked to my car. I unlocked it and we both got in. "Where do you live? I can take you home."

"Drop me by the shop," she said.

"I can take you home," I said. "It's really no trouble."

She sighed. "So, okay. I need you to not freak out."

"Okay…"

"I've been kind of living there for a bit. In the shop, I mean. Jung and I share the office," she said.

I start the car and head for the shop. "Surprisingly, I'm not mad. It would explain why he got so comfortable with you so quickly. You don't have an apartment or a roommate or something?"

She shook her head, "I lived with The Bruja for a long time. Then I lived at the shop and then I was on the streets for a bit until I finally came to meet you."

I nodded. We didn't say much else until we pulled up to the shop. I shut off the car and we both went in. "Start some coffee," I said. Jung, surprised at the sudden activity, opened one of the cabinet doors and launched himself inside, the cabinet closing with a loud thunk behind him.

After clicking around for a while, Stacey tells me we're in luck—

there is only one tournament upstate this weekend and it starts the next day. We can get there fairly easily.

"And," she said, "the good news is that's on the way to another one of my friends that I want to have take a look at the piece. We can stop off and see him first."

"If we leave now, we could be there by midmorning," I said.

"You don't need sleep?"

"I don't sleep much these days," I said.

We finished our coffee, I poured a bit more food for Jung, and we got in the car. I told her to print off the directions and she laughed. "What is this, 2005?" she asked. She asked for my phone and transferred the information over. "Just an analog guy in a digital world, Goldman," she said.

"Oh, I see. Well, if you're so advanced, why don't you have this guy Evan's phone number so you can just call him?" I teased.

"I don't know. I just never thought to get it from him, I guess. Whenever our paths crossed, there was always something more important going on."

We drove straight through, stopping just after sunup for breakfast. She didn't say anything and I didn't press, though I had so many questions. Once we pulled into the town she'd indicated, I asked, "So, where to now?"

"Take a left up here and then follow it out to 54th avenue," she said. After a while I could tell she wasn't going to talk, so I flipped on the radio. Her chin was resting on her hand and she was staring out the window. On the speakers, Sammy Hagar was wondering why this couldn't be love.

She stayed quiet except for directing me to turn right or left. Eventually we arrived in a shabby neighborhood. No one out walking around or sitting in their driveway looked particularly worrisome, but I could tell we were along the edges of the suburbs. "Over here," she said, gesturing toward a house on the left. I pulled up to the curb and shut off the radio. As soon as I did, I could hear someone was playing very loud guitar. The thing is that it wasn't the sort of riff that someone would normally play loudly. It was delicate and complex, but still very loud.

As soon as Stacey and I both stepped out, someone from down the street a bit yelled, "Hey, get him to turn that down, willya?" I didn't turn to see who said it, and Stacey was already halfway to the garage door. When she pulled it up, inside was a wall of speakers of odd shapes and sizes, a wall of thrift-shop amplifiers. In front of them stood a guy who was maybe five eight with wavy black hair left long on top but short along the neck. Even though it was hot, he was wearing a thin black leather jacket over a plain white t-shirt, and grubby jeans with a hole in the right knee. The guitar slung over his shoulder looked cobbled together. It had a hole in it, like an acoustic, but it was plugged into the wall of amplifiers by a long black curly cord. His eyes were closed and he didn't even seem to notice that the garage door had been opened. He moved from one chord to the other on the neck and it was in that quiet that his eyes opened and he saw Stacey. He stopped playing.

"Stace?" he said, cocking his head to the side.

"Eddie," she said.

He used the heel of the palm of his hand to roll the volume knob and the sound died except for a slight hum still coming from the wall of amplifiers.

"What are you doing here?' he asked.

"Need a favor," she said.

He pulled the guitar over his head and set it down on a stand, then walked over and flicked a switch on a surge protector on the floor nearby and the hum died. He gestured to me to lower the garage door so I stepped in and did. The garage turned gloomy and almost cold. "A favor like what?" he asked, turning to meet her eyes and crossing his arms.

She reached into her pocket and pulled out the baggie. "Need you to read something for me."

He smirked and shook his head, "Of course. Him?" he asked, looking over at me.

"He's cool, but we are in a bit of a hurry."

He didn't move for a minute, but then walked over to the wall where I noticed there were lots of smaller objects and instruments. Small bells, triangles, wind chimes, etc. He turned his back on us like we weren't even there any more and started to pull off one chime or bell after another. This went on for what felt like half an hour.

"I'm sorry to…" I started to say but Stacey, talking over me, said, "Bit of a hurry, Eddie."

"Look," he said, setting the chime he had in his hand at that moment down. "This kind of thing you're asking for? It isn't like figuring out some charming little throwaway yacht rock number, you know what I mean? We're not talking about Vampire Weekend, here. This is like trying to figure out art pop…like working out how to play Lindsey Buckingham. The easier it looks to do the more unbelievably complex. I need a minute."

Stacey walked over to me. "Are we sure this guy can…?" I asked.

She nodded and sighed. "Could take a while, though," she said.

"So he said," I replied. "Explain it to me again."

"Every surface can take on impressions of things going on around it. You already know that because you know what a toucher does. Well, they also take on sounds. Normal regular old every day sound producing equipment can't pull that stuff out unless it's physically marked on the surface, but guys like Eddie, here," she said, gesturing. "That's their whole gig is to pull sounds off of objects."

"I admit it, you got me there. I've heard of a lot of different kinds of abilities, but I've never heard of this one," I said.

"We call 'em strummers. Y'know; 'strumming my pain with his fingers,'" she halfheartedly sang. "Thing is, most of them don't know what it is that they are. To anyone who doesn't know any better, they look like cream of the crop musicians. Name me anyone who has ever made you cry or given you goosebumps on a record and it was probably one of these guys. The reason you've never heard of them is that they tend to die. Usually right around the age of 27 or so, oddly enough. The ones that live beyond that usually have to take a lot of drugs to stay alive too much longer, but eventually they all go early."

"Why?" I asked.

"Their channeling the one place where emotion can't be hidden or lied about—sound. Next best thing to an empath."

"Which reminds me, why didn't we just go find one of those?" I asked. I'd at least heard of empaths, before, and I'd seen them deliver usable information.

She rubbed her thumb and index finger together, "have you seen what they charge these days? Especially the good ones. I don't know any of them. Eddie, here, though? He's a friend of a friend. Fairly good, at least for the level he plays at."

As if on cue, there was a ringing sound that went on for over a minute. Eddie was moving a long thin piece of metal over a ceramic bowl in his palm. He shook his head and set that one down. He picked up another and rang it, then shook his head and sat that one down. He picked up a third bowl, rang it, and then nodded to himself. "I bet that's got it," he said, and gestured us over. We walked over to him, and Stacey handed him the baggie.

"Do I even want to know what…?" he said, letting the question trail off.

"No," Stacey said. He nodded.

He set the bag down and put the bowl he'd selected next to it. One of his amplifiers in the corner began to feed back a bit even though it was off. Eddie nodded to himself. He took the piece of blade out and set it into the bowl. A few more of the amplifiers began to feed back. It wasn't loud, but it was undeniable—with nothing plugged into them, they were feeling a vibration and amplifying it.

"You might want to stand back a bit—I have a feeling this one is going to be wild," Eddie said.

Stacey and I both took one huge step backward.

He picked up the rod he'd been using before and tapped it to the side of the bowl that had the piece of the blade in it. The sound that came out started sweet but as it grew, it turned more and more sour. Eddie stood before it, his eyes closed, his hands spread wide like radar dishes. For a moment, he seemed to glow. As if someone was manipulating it somehow, though, the sound began to wobble, stretching back to the sweet note it had begun with, then thickening as if plunged into mud. I felt sick to my stomach. Stacey put her hand to her mouth and clutched at her stomach. As the note began to fade, I saw Eddie staring at the bowl, his eyes wide with shock. The thick, muddy end of the note got more and more quiet but it was as if I could hear someone speaking through it. It sounded like a huge voice whispering through a crack in a wall, and I wondered, even as I felt that, how I knew what that might sound like. Still, though, I was certain that was what I was hearing. Eddie reached out and put his finger on the bowl and the sound stopped completely. I was left with that same feeling I had as a kid after a roller coaster—emotionally drained and physically sore.

"Fuckin A," Stacey whispered after a few minutes of silence.

Eddie stepped back from the bowl still staring at it.

"What, um—," he began but then fell quiet. "Um…okay. So." Eddie turned and walked to a chair nearby. "Shut the fuck up for a second," Eddie said. I could tell from Stacey's body language she was not at all used to him talking this way. "Just everybody shut the fuck up." He fell into the chair and fished in his pocket for a cigarette. He lit it and took three puffs before he finally looked at Stacey, then at me. "What the fuck is that?" he asked, gesturing toward the bowl.

"It's a piece of a blade that—," Stacey began.

"What did you hear?" I asked.

His eyes had shifted back to the bowl. They slid back to me for a second then returned. "That," he said, gesturing with the cigarette. "That is…that thing is…hmmm," he stammered. He closed his eyes and took a deep breath, then opened them and said, "there's something in there."

"I don't understand," I said.

"There's, like, something *in* the piece," Eddie said. "The metal itself had something going on, which is what I expected to hear, but then, at the end, you…I mean, you heard it, too, right?"

"I think I did," I said.

"Me, too," Stacey said.

"I think maybe you guys should like, y'know, go."

"But we need more infor—,"

"I mean it, man. I think, yeah, I need you guys to take whatever the fuck that is and get out," Eddie said. He'd already finished half his cigarette.

"Do you think that there's any danger, though, of it—," Stacey began.

"Just *go*, man!" Eddie said, closing his eyes. It was only then, with his hand held outward, that I noticed how badly he was shaking.

I walked over to the bowl. I could feel it still vibrating some. I picked up the shard and put it back in the baggie. Stacey followed me out of the garage.

Neither of us spoke until after we were pulling onto the freeway. Since I couldn't think of what else to do, I continued on our route to go to this tournament and find her friend Evan.

"So," Stacey said and exhaled.

"Yeah," I said. "What do you think we take away from that?"

"I've never seen anything scare Eddie. I mean, granted, I haven't been around him doing his thing more than a few times, but still. Never. Whatever…that…is," she said, gesturing toward the back seat where she'd tossed the baggie, "it's more than he's encountered before."

"Okay," I said. "But then what should *we* do in response to that. I mean, we're just walking around with that thing. You just had it sitting in your pocket."

Her eyes got wide as she nodded. "In all this time, it hasn't… y'know…it hasn't spoken to me, or whatever."

"You're sure?" I asked.

"Trust me, Goldman, I'm not secretly doing the blade's bidding, or whatever," she said.

"And you're sure of that? I mean, in Tolkien, the ring whispered for a long time before…," I trailed off, not completely sure what my point was.

"Yeah, I get it. Still, though, I think I'd know. And I think maybe what Eddie was saying is that it isn't the blade itself that's doing the whispering. Remember, he said that there was something *in* there. Whatever it is, it isn't the object itself, but something…something maybe somehow *inside* the blade."

"Okay, I can buy that. That did seem to be what he was saying.

And I heard…I don't know…I think I heard something whispering there at the end," I said.

"Fucking A. I'm glad you said that, because I was thinking I had somehow lost my mind. Yeah, that's what I heard, too."

"Something…something very large trying to whisper through a very small opening. That was the image that came to my mind," I said.

Stacey nodded.

"Okay, so we're in agreement—that wasn't exactly a waste of time, yeah?" I asked.

"No, it wasn't. Whatever is going on with this woman, it may not be her fault. There may be something in the blade she's carrying around that's…manipulating her, like you said. Like something out of Tolkien. So maybe along those lines, this thing, this blade, is something she found by accident and its warping her the longer she has it?"

"That's a thought, but we don't have anything to back that up. Let's not go too far," I said. "The funny thing is this—as many of these type of people who grow up reading Tolkien, you'd think they'd have paid attention to his big message: magick items cause big trouble," I said.

The display said we had another 4 hours until we reached our destination.

The gym during a martial arts demo, whether it be local, regional, or national, smells exactly like you'd think it would. There's a difference in how young people's sweat smells. I think about that sentence for a second and decide that I will never say it out loud for fear of sounding like a pedophile. That doesn't mean it's not true, though. It also sounds exactly like you'd think it would. All the stereotypical sounds that kids who don't know a martial art make when they play like they do? Those are pretty much the real sounds people make. Add occasional bursts of music and applause and you've got it.

She stopped us for a second, staring around the gym.

"He's here," she said, then moved forward.

"I think the older kids are over this way," I said, motioning toward the back end of the gym.

"I know," she said and moved us to the left instead.

We wade through adults standing near mats with arms crossed, staring at their child as if the child was a circus animal. Kids rushing from one area to the other, barely having time to register how they did in one event before having to start another. Mostly there is just a sense of hurry and energy.

Eventually, she stopped. She slowly shoulders up to the mat past a few adults and I follow her trail. When we got to the front, we can see a young girl just finishing up her routine with a beautiful long sword. She and the sword flashed around in circles and lines like a deadly steel butterfly, the blade so thin it seems to wobble a bit. She hit a final pose and held it, then stood. I felt the blast of positive energy flow off of her and the crowd applauded and the girl bowed. Only then does she smile and walk off the mat. The judges smiled to themselves and wrote on their pads.

"Here he is," she said, and crossed her arms.

As the crowd cleared a bit, a thin sliver of a boy with spiky black hair walked on to the mat. He has two katana strapped to his back. He is only a bit taller than they are long. I'm tempted to laugh at the juxtaposition, but something about him carried a level of gravity, and almost pulls the room toward him. When he stood in the center of the mat, the rest of the room seemed to quiet, as if everyone, everywhere, was watching. He bowed to the judges. He announced that he was Evan Parker and that he has graduated from working with his master, Master Yamaguchi of the Black Rock dojo, and that today he will be demonstrating the exquisite art of something (I don't speak Japanese, remember). He delivered these lines at almost a yell, but even then the kid has more poise than I would have on my best day ever.

Stacey nodded as if she knew exactly what he was going to say the entire time and had just been waiting for him to say it.

Without warning, he moved. For the next three minutes, there is nothing but movement. I've watched as many martial arts in movies as the next guy, but seeing it in real life, done by a body that sharing the same air as you, is different. It is also less easy to describe. Remember that the people doing it in the movie are posing and stopping, they want it to look impressive. The kids performing all around me want their form and performance to be impressive, too, but there is no pausing, here. One move flowed into the next into the next into the next, like a word flowing into a sentence then into a paragraph. The swords moved together then independently then together, the kid's body slid through a dance.

Then I felt it. As I did, I saw Stacey grin. The swords glowed a bit. Just a tiny bit of a spark at the tip of both as they sail through the air, leaving a blue arc behind them. I saw the judges register it, but before anyone can get an idea of what just happened, the energy disappeared. Around me, the adults and few other kids gathered gasped just a bit, probably without realizing they just did it, and leaned in.

The boy never stopped. He continued, a whirling top of death, a minute more, then abruptly made one final slicing motion, came to rest in a pose with one final sound, and slid both swords home across his back. He paused for a moment, then bowed to the judges.

The crowd clapped. The judges, who I'm gathering aren't really supposed to clap, do. One even stood up while clapping, which, from the looks of the other judges, is *definitely* something they're not supposed to do. The kid walked off the mat.

"Come on," she said, already moving to catch up to him. I followed.

Even after all that, though, there is another kid coming onto the mat already. As we moved to catch up with Evan, I marveled at the efficiency. I wondered what the kids must feel having given a performance so powerful and unique only to have it vanish and another happen almost immediately. Something of the mandala in that, I think, building something through effort and concentration, only to have it disappear as soon as it's completed.

We walked up to Evan just as he sat down.

"Aren't you going to stick close by to hear your scores," she asked.

He looked up and almost immediately smiled, laughed, and

wiped his face with a towel. "Nope. Not interested."

"You sound like the old man," she said. "How is his cough?"

"Worse. He keeps saying allergies allergies allergies, but we all know what it is." I noticed that he makes no move to unstrap the swords. Up close, the kid is even younger than I thought he might be before. He wiped his forehead, then his neck, and looked at me.

"This is Derek Goldman," she said.

He nodded, then looked back at her. "I can't imagine that you came all this way just to see me compete, and you bringing a stranger here means whatever it is, it isn't good. The fact that no one is shooting at you right this second means that it's important but not blood urgent, so," he said with all the battle weariness of a general, and looking toward the corners of the gym then toward the rafters, then toward the front door. "There's a coffee shop just across the street. Let me go get cleaned up and I'll meet you there in about ten minutes."

The latte isn't half bad. I feel like a shitheel for ordering it, though, because I've been around long enough to know that no self-respecting person in Europe would order one. It's a kid's drink that has caught on in a powerful way in America. What does that say about us to the rest of the coffee drinking world? The problem is that, as I get older, and my blood pressure goes up, both from the fat and from my unerring capacity to get myself into life threatening danger, I can't handle caffeine anymore. That's how pathetic I am—the thing that most people need to have to get through their day, one of the mildest stimulants on the planet? I can't tolerate it.

What might Darwin have to say about that?

She, of course, has water. She ordered it completely unconcerned with the look that the barista, who can't be more than fifteen, maybe sixteen, gave her, too, which impresses me. I don't know why I care what teenagers think of me, but I do.

"So, how—," I started.

"He'll turn fourteen in a few months."

I whistled and shook my head.

After that, we waited in silence until he walked in. I glanced at my watch and it's exactly ten minutes from before. Cleaned up, the kid looks like any other kid you'd see. None of his clothes have any labels or logos, I notice. If you were to see him in a crowd, your glance would drift right over him, which is completely at odds with how things were back on the mat. He slid over a chair, put down the large black gym bag he has, then sat.

"You slipped a bit in there," she said, sipping her water.

He grinned, "For a split second, I got lost in a memory. A particularly interesting chase from about a month ago."

The girl who had served us earlier brings over what looks like a green tea with ice in it and a straw. She set it down in front of him and he looked up. A moment passed between them, then she walked away. He removed the straw from the plastic and put it into the cup in one motion.

"I'm glad you caught yourself. The last thing you need is to be outed like that at a regional."

He nodded, glanced at me, then back at her. "So," he said.

"So," she said, and it feels like a tiny part of a ritual has just happened. "Here is what has happened," and she tells him the story so far.

When she finished, he exhaled and sat back.

"Okay," I said. "So, what's next?"

"She wants me to read the blades, see what we can pick up off of them, obviously," he said. "It's going to take a minute and I need to get changed and set up the space for the ritual. Meet me at my house in like an hour or so?" He picked up her phone and typed in an address. Stacey nodded and Evan got up and left, walking directly to an older man who looked almost exactly like him but with salt and pepper hair. I watched them walk out and get into an expensive SUV together.

Stacey slumped in her chair.

We pulled in to a fairly nondescript suburban neighborhood and turn onto a perfectly forgettable cul-de-sac. Stacey stopped the car in front of a house that I honestly couldn't tell from any of the others around it if I had to. I almost asked her how she knows this is the right one. "Here we are," she said, shutting off the car. The front door opened and Evan gestured us inside.

He shut the door behind us without saying anything. The house smelled of lilacs and new dry wall. In one of the rooms, someone was watching the news, but I couldn't see them. A large dog raised its head as we passed by but made no noise.

Evan lead us through the main hallway and out the sliding glass door into the back yard. The grass stood perfectly green and off to the side there was a pool. A beach ball floated in it, lazily moved by the breeze. I kept thinking that none of this could be real. My mind fought the bland pleasantness of it all.

Evan stopped in front of the padlocked door to a small brown and white shed. He made a gesture over the lock and something in the back of my head tingled for a second. The lock opened and he shoved it into a pocket. The door to the shed creaked as it swung open a bit and it is dark inside. Once we step in, Evan closed the door behind us and my eyes adjust.

"Here we are," he said.

The floor of the shed is dirt and there is a large circle made out of white chalk. The circle is cut into four segments. The segments are all empty, but at the center point of the "x," Evan has put a large black candle. The flame sputtered a bit but settled as we did.

"Shoes and socks," he said, stepping to the wall and pulling down a bundle of sage. He grabbed a white candle from a shelf along the wall, lit it, and set it on a small plate on a knee-high table nearby. From the flame of the white candle he lit the sage.

I rarely have my shoes off anywhere other than my bedroom, so this feels more than a little odd. Stacey already has hers off and neatly piled near the door. To me, as I tug at the laces and try not to fall over, this feels invasive, embarrassing, and also a little erotic.

"Come on," Stacey said, gesturing with her hands.

"Gimme a second," I said.

Evan stood near a spot on the circle that I would bet money was exactly due East. This isn't my first time being around circles. I got my socks off and stuffed them into my shoes. The ground carried a chill, but felt clean and solid to my toes. Evan was already running the sage under Stacey's limbs and over her hair. It's an interesting mixture of what I would have thought were very separate ritual cultures. When Evan finished, he gestured to the side and Stacey moved to where he pointed. Again, the juxtaposition of power strikes me as odd, but I remind myself that in the world of the supernatural things like age and height don't have anything to do with power. This is one of the most important differences between it and "normal" fiscal year, bank holiday world.

Evan gestured for me to come over. I raised my arms and he moved the sage under them. He continued smudging the rest of me, gesturing for me to bend so he could send the smoke around my head. Once he was done, he gestured for me to stand over near Stacey. He smudged himself purposefully and then sat the sage down in its dish, which looked like it might be an abalone shell. Once he turned back to the circle, the level of concentration in his eyes had grown by a thousand percent. He is focused to a razor's edge. He clapped once, waited, then again, waited, and then a third time, all the while his lips moving slightly. He stepped into the circle, then moved to the next division to his left in one large step. He repeated this twice more, moving from where he started, in the East, through South, then West, ending up North. Stacey repeated all of the same actions, ending up in the West.

Once we were all in our segments, Evan clapped three times again and then sat cross-legged. Stacey repeated the same action. I guess that I'm supposed to do the same, so I do. It's hell on my knees, though.

"Okay," Evan said. "So, what is it we're looking for?"

Stacey took out the small sandwich bag with the shard in it.

"Will this be enough?"

"You know me," he said with the exact kind of cocky grin you'd expect. He set the drawing down next to the candle in the center, and then examined the sandwich bag.

"It was used to make this cut?"

"Yes," Stacey said.

Evan nodded. He took the scrap of cloth from the sandwich bag and set it next to the candle. He handed the empty bag back to her. She stuffed it in her pocket.

"Alright, so you know the drill," Evan said, looking mostly at me. "No matter what don't touch me, no matter what don't leave the circle, no matter what don't interact with anything you might see, yada yada yada. Kay? Kay."

He shifted his body to put left leg over right, then left hand over right and settles them into his lap. With a speed I've never seen before, he leaned his head back a bit and his eyes rolled back in his head. The circle is suddenly charged and with way more power than I've felt before. The hairs on the back of my neck stood up. Stacey looked at me, but then the small flame from the candle in the center makes a roar and spits out a huge flame. Evan has closed his eyes and is mumbling something. I want to know more, but I also know that these are the second most slippery moments of any ceremony. Only the ending is more important than these opening moments.

Evan started to move his upper body in circles from the waist. That's when I felt the energy begin to circulate around the room. Think back to a time when you felt a warm, pleasant wind come up out of nowhere on a winter's day, or a cool breeze hit you on a hot Summer day and you'll know something of what it feels like. The candles flickered a bit, but the flames grew brighter.

Just for a second, in the middle of the circle, I thought I saw the outline of a heavily armored and armed warrior. He bristled with sheathed knives, swords, a quiver of arrows. I blinked, though, and the outline was gone. Evan goes a few shades more pale than he was when I met him and his hair is damp. His mumbling grew louder, and his eyes, though closed, wrinkled at the edges with concentration.

His eyes opened and glowed with a faint greenish light. He began talking in a language that I felt like I understood but so fast that I couldn't keep up with it. Stacey responded in the same language at the same speed. They talked back and forth, Evan's speech growing more and more concerned as they did. Out of the corner of my eye, I could tell someone was there, near us, but I knew if I looked, there would be no one. Eventually, Stacey grew silent and Evan quieted. His hands moved in circles and ovals in the air and his eyes closed once more.

He said one more word, then collapsed without moving from where he sat. The winds around us calmed down. The faint outline of the warrior I saw before is visible once more but then goes as Evan sits upright. His eyes no longer glowed and he began mumbling again. The energy around us calmed gradually until it stopped. Evan stood, wobbled a little, and then walked counter-clockwise back to where we all entered the circle. He stood outside and gestured for Stacey to do the same. Once she left, he gestured toward me. After I'm out, he walked counter-clockwise along the outside of the circle and clapped in the direction of each candle, causing the flame to go out. Once he was back to the place we all entered the circle, he clapped three times and it felt like the shed grew three times smaller instantly. Looking around, I'm amazed at how we all fit in it, now. He's already moved out the door as I grab my shoes. I tried to slide back into them as he and Stacey sit down at the table on the porch. Evan put on a pair of sunglasses that were waiting on the table and leaned back in the chair. As if on cue, a woman who looks a lot like Evan brought out a tray with a pitcher of lemonade and three glasses. She set it down, turned, and walked back inside.

"So," I said as I sat down.

"Give him a second," Stacey said.

I noticed that neither Evan nor Stacey brought any of the items Stacey gave him back from the circle. In fact, I don't remember seeing them as we left. Evan picked up the glass, his hand shaky. After a long gulp he set it back down deliberately.

"Spill," he said, looking at Stacey.

"I don't know what you're—,"

He shook his head, the sunglasses giving him a decided older than he is look to the gesture. "You know what I know, now, so tell me."

"I didn't know what you'd be told and what—,"

"You know who he might very well be. Just because we haven't confirmed it doesn't mean it isn't possible. And if he is who you and

I think he is, what made you think you could keep anything from him? Why would you want to try?"

She didn't say anything.

"Who do you believe it is that you summon?" I asked.

Evan looked at me and, even though the sunglasses masked his face, I could tell that the subject was dead.

"Did he find it?" Stacey asked.

Evan turned his attention back to her and nodded. "It's worse than you thought, though."

"How worse?"

"The spirit that's stuck inside that thing? It's not just some vengeful wife who was murdered by her husband or something. It's a monster."

"What does that mean?" I asked.

"It means that this thing, this blade you're looking for? When they were making it they hit the jackpot, only I'm guessing it wasn't in a way they wanted. They hauled in something from the deep, deep parts of the other side. Like catching a whale on a fishing pole meant for trout. He," Evan said, gesturing back toward the shack with his chin, "doesn't have any idea how they managed to land the thing. It shouldn't have been possible."

"Fuckin A," Stacey said.

Evan took a sip of lemonade.

"And now it's seeping into her," Stacey said.

Evan nodded. "She may have been powerful for a witch or whatever she wants to call herself, but she has no defenses against this thing. It's too big. Clint Eastwood versus Godzilla."

"Did...did he," I said, moving my head toward the shack, "did he have any idea where she's at?"

Evan nodded. "Told me basically where she's at. Too much energy to disguise fully, though she's trying. But she's already made some kills, and with every one it gets her to make—,"

"She gets just that much further down the hole, yeah. What if," she said and stopped. I waited. "What if that's what we're dealing with, here. A kind of Tolkien meets Lovecraft kind of thing? Something using the object as a way to try to come through from somewhere else into our dimension?" she asked.

"As far as I know, this kind of thing isn't possible," I say, even though some dark part of my brain was already running with the idea.

"Yeah, no shit," she said. "Thing is, every time someone says something is impossible, look what fucking happens."

"Okay. Let me rephrase. This kind of thing isn't supposed to be possible. The exchange has to be balanced for anything to enter, right? Isn't that the rule?"

"Fuckin A," Stacey whispered.

"Okay, so if these people pulled over something big, something really big, then…"

"Then the books are unbalanced and something's got to give? Yeah. Pre-fucking-cisely."

"Okay, then…?" I asked.

"Why do you think the thing is compelling her to kill? It's trying in some way to balance the books, in the only way it knows how. It says to itself, like fucking minute one, 'hey, what am I? Oh, yeah, I'm a god damn instrument of destruction and death.' It's doing what it knows how. And, I bet you dimes to fucking doughnuts that this thing that's gotten stuffed in there isn't exactly a gods-damned Boy Scout, either. Like draws like, even across the veil."

"But the killing isn't balancing the energy deficit," I said.

"Ding ding ding, give the man a prize."

"Then…?"

"Well, I didn't want to speculate, but yeah…chances are there's a tear in the veil somewhere where this thing came through and that tear is only getting bigger all the time," she said.

"Great," I said.

"Fucking A," she said.

Evan, who had been completely silent as we talked, finally said, "so what is it that you want?"

Stacey turned to him and I could see it on her face; like me, she'd honestly just gotten so caught up in the exchange of ideas she had forgotten where we were. "Sorry," she said. Evan nodded, and I can't decide if it's the most kind or most obnoxiously smug gesture

I've ever seen someone make.

"He says she's in an abandoned building somewhere downtown. I mean, I know that's like the single most cliché thing anyone has ever said ever, but it's the truth…something is…hiding her. Making her hard to see, so I can't pinpoint which, but that was the general impression I got."

"Listen, Evan, thank—," Stacey started.

"Because I know that eventually I'm going to be asked by at least one Malleus agent," Evan said, "is there some reason I'm not giving one of them this information? I mean, it's great to see you and all, but…" Evan lets his thoughts drift off. Stacey is having to stare directly into her reflection in his glasses.

"Trust issues," Stacey said and stood up.

"At some point, you're going to have to get them involved, Stacey. Like it or not."

Stacey shoved the baggie into her pocket. She finished her drink in one gulp and then said, "Thanks."

Evan put two fingers to his forehead and extended them to her like a half-assed salute. I honestly cannot decide if this is the coolest kid I've ever met or the most obnoxious human on the planet. "Yeah," I said, "thanks." I got up and followed Stacey back through the house to the door. I kept expecting someone to come meet us and escort us out, but no one did.

"Okay. So, we kind of know where the blade is now. What do we do next?" I asked once we were headed back toward the freeway.

Stacey sighed hard and pulled around a man going under the speed limit.

"Stacey?" I asked.

"Yeah."

"What do we do next?"

"Well, Goldman, this is the part I've kind-of been dreading."

"Why's that?"

"Because in order to tell you what we have to do, I have to tell you what's already been done, and that means a story. A story where I don't come off looking so hot."

"What do you mean?"

"I'm hungry, are you hungry?"

"Fair enough." I said.

We stopped at a fast food place. She wanted to sit outside for some privacy. The wind was up, so we spent a lot of our time trying to keep the food from blowing away. After she'd finished about half of her burger, she said, "So, the top page on this one is this—I fucked up."

"Okay." I said after a while.

"I was going to join Malleus. I wanted to."

My eyes got bigger.

"Yeah. Well, don't act like that. Once upon a time, I was a good girl. I mean, I could summon spirits and scrye and shit, but still basically a fucking good girl, y'know? When I read cards for people, I genuinely wanted things to turn out well for them and shit."

"Okay." I said after a long silence.

"So I found out about Malleus fairly early. I hadn't done anything that broke any of their laws, so they hadn't come knocking on my door. See, that's what tends to happen with a lot of young folks. Their eyes get bigger than their stomach, if you catch my drift." She laughed once. "My mom used to say that all the time. I haven't thought about her in a while."

"She still alive?"

"I don't think so. The cancer, y'know." She sighed. "Still, so, I trolled the internet and the dark web, or at least what passed for it back then, for weeks and find out all I could. Back then they weren't what you'd call all that tech savvy, so there were websites where people talked openly about their encounters. Usually rants. Usually including threats of hexes and whatever." She shook her head. "Like admitting to other crimes in writing was a good idea. Still, it was a different time." She crumpled up the garbage left over and gestured toward mine. I nodded and she took what I had left, crumpled it up, then tossed all the garbage into the can nearby. We walked back to the car in silence. She started it up and pulled back out onto the road. We had pulled off in one of those small towns where it only takes one stoplight to get back on to the freeway, so in no time we were back up to speed. She pulled around a small hatchback that was doing exactly the speed limit.

"So I figure out where they are headquartered by triangulating encounters. Not that hard to do, but most people who use magick? Turns out, not that good at geometry. Which is kind of funny when you think about how fifty percent of the shit we do involves drawing fucking circles. But I digress. So I show up on their door step all bright eyed and whatnot and I'm like, 'one job, please.' They laugh me away after just a few minutes of conversation and one scan. I'm too young, not 'potent' enough yet or some shit. I forget exactly what they said, but the effect was the same: scram."

"I'm sorry," I said, not knowing what else to say.

She tiled her head to the side then back. "So, in their minds, that was that. But you've known me for a bit—how likely am I to take the word 'no' as final?"

"Not very."

"Fuckin' A. So, I hung around outside and watched. I started to follow the agents when they left. You can probably already see where this is going."

"You followed one who had a run in with the blade we're looking for and it didn't go well?"

"Worse—the bitch saw me before he did, and she took me hostage."

"Oh no."

"Yeah, so not only did I get seen, which was a fuck up, but... well...I'm the reason they didn't apprehend her and the object early on, when they still really had a chance."

"How did...?" I asked.

"When she grabbed me, all of her attention was on him. She must have thought I wasn't a user or something. She left my hands and my mouth mostly free, so I did all that I could think to do with no powders or circle or anything."

"What was that?"

"The devastating one-two combo of a flash glamour to her eyeballs and an elbow to her left tit."

I barked a laugh.

She was smiling, too. "I know, right? Super sophisticated magickal combat maneuver number 1. Still, you'd be surprised how highly effective it was. She dropped me and when he went to make a move, she phased through the nearest wall and bounced. He looked for a good long time to find her but couldn't. Then he came back and dealt with me."

"You didn't try to leave?"

"I told you—I was a good girl back then. I did what I was told."

"I can't imagine that conversation went well."

"No. No, it did not. The upshot was that he was personally going to file a report about me and that if anyone from Malleus ever saw me again, even if it was happenstance, they were going to haul me and snip snip."

"'Snip snip'?"

She watched the road for a time. "They have a ritual left over from a culture that lived long before white people were around. Mad bad juju and shit. It…it cuts a person off from the source of magick. All sources."

"That sounds awful." I said.

"Indeed it does. It's the highest punishment they can inflict next to a death order. And so…"

"There went your hope of being in the Malleus."

She nodded.

"No wonder this case is so personal for you."

"Been wondering, yeah?"

"Well," I said, "I mean, I expected the sort of standard deal. The 'if we don't stop her, the world will come to an end' speech. The standard call to action. But it isn't that. I mean, from what you've said, she's already growing into a serial killer and something even worse will come out of it if we don't get the blade away from her, I get that. But you're pouring a lot into this for someone who doesn't have an official job title. But you're hoping if we catch her then…"

"Yeah. Maybe. I dunno. It's fucking stupid, maybe, but…"

"I get it," I said. "You haven't told me who we're going to see, by the way."

"Their name is Sharkey."

The pronoun immediately hit me. "And Sharkey is…?" I asked. Stacey didn't respond.

"Our next stop," Stacey said.

The last few minutes we rode in silence as she pulled off the freeway and then onto a street near the offramp. I watched the neighborhood get worse and worse as we pulled through the blocks. Eventually, in a block that could only be described as scruffy, she pulled the car to the curb and shut the engine off.

"We're here."

"So, Sharkey is…" I asked again as we got out of the car.

"An ex," Stacey said. "And I need you to be cool when you're around them."

"Them?" I asked.

Stacey sighed again, and I could see her tensing up for a fight.

"No. I meant…look, you've used 'their/them' the few times you've mentioned this person, and I have a radar for that kind of thing. I admit that though I'm a gay man, I find I fall back on all the standard cisgendered stuff when it comes to first meetings with people. I'm not super proud of it, but it happens. Sharkey is…?"

"Fuck," Stacey stopped and turned while sighing heavily. "Not that it's any of your business, or anyone's really, but Sharkey is nonbinary. Is that going to be a problem or something?"

"No," I said. "I just wanted to know so I could use the right pronouns. I'm trying to be respectful of the people you introduce me to."

She closed her eyes for a second. "Have you never met a nonbinary person before?"

I shook my head, "I've met all kinds of people, but no, I've never met anyone who identified as nonbinary before. I've read about it, but…"

"Okay. Well then I guess we'll be lucky if we get through all that without you fucking it all up."

"Nice," I said. "Look, I can't help it if I need you to maybe give me a bit more information than you like. Remember, my role in these kinds of things is usually to sit back and listen. I'm not normally a 'go out in the field' kind of person."

"Look, just say 'Shark' or 'Sharkey.' They respond just fine to their name. When you're talking to me about Shark, just say that. If you need the pronouns, Sharkey prefers "they" and "them," but you don't need the pronouns because I know who Shark is, and you know who Shark is, and anyone else will probably have a good idea. We were...we were fairly well known."

"Why's that?" I asked.

She turned on her heel and walked to the front door, "That's a story for another time, Goldman. Sharkey is a good friend and will help us." She knocked and waited.

"We couldn't have just called?" I asked.

"This," she said, "this is not the kind of hello you manage with a phone call."

"It's open," someone yelled from inside.

"Be cool," Stacey said just before she opened the door and walked inside.

I try to not be offended. I know what it's like to introduce new acquaintances or friends to old ones. Still, though. The house is dark and smells a bit like lavender but also motor oil. We walked through a short hallway into a room with two large couches and what I'm sure is a motorcycle when it's assembled. The parts were all laid out in neat little piles.

"I'm in the back. Go to the den," the voice yelled again from somewhere deep in the house.

Stacey turned left and I followed her down another short hall. We stepped down twice into a sunken area. Two sectional couches faced each other; the hook ends on opposite sides so that they made a kind of rectangle. No matter where anyone sat in this room, they would be facing someone else.

The young person who walked in was about six foot two, wearing what people sometimes call a Canadian Tuxedo: jeans, Iron Maiden t-shirt under a denim jacket. Doc Martins polished to high gloss. There was a bulge in the jacket just underneath the right arm that said gun, though I wondered why they might need it in their own home, especially after simply inviting us in without seeing who we were. The jacket revealed bulging arms. Their hair was jet black and cropped tight and spikey in places, and the ears were gauged large.

"Shark," Stacey said.

"Stace," Sharkey replied, then looked at me.

"He's cool," Stacey said.

Sharkey tipped their chin up at me then looked back at Stacey as if I wasn't there.

"What's up?" Sharkey asked sitting on the arm of the couch and gesturing for us to sit, as well. Stacey moved to the center of the opposite couch and I moved to sit with her.

"Need a favor," Stacey said. Something in the way she said the word, though, told me that she meant something more.

Sharkey's eyebrows went up. They stood and walked to the middle of the other couch and sat. They spread their arms out to the side, leaning back. "Okay," was all they said, though.

"Are we cool?" Stacey asked.

Sharkey made a gesture with their palms upward and a shrug that I took to mean things were okay. Stacey reached into her pocket and pulled out the baggie. She put it on the small coffee table between the two couches. Sharkey looked at it for a moment, then back at Stacey. "Ah," Sharkey said. "I see," they said, but made no move toward it.

"I was hoping you could take a look at it for us," Stacey said, gesturing toward the baggie.

Sharkey inhaled and exhaled. They tilted their head to the side, looked at the floor, then back at Stacey, then shook their head. "Him?" they asked, pointing toward me with their chin.

"He's cool, like I said," Stacey said.

Sharkey exhaled one more time, then leaned forward and looked at the baggie. They made no move to touch it, though. "Wait…," they said. "Is this…?"

"Yeah," Stacey said.

"But you said…"

"I know what I said," Stacey said.

Sharkey leaned back. "So you lied."

Stacey nodded, "Yeah. I lied. I'm sorry."

Sharkey frowned. They shook their head. "Even after all this time, I still keep tripping over your lies. Even now. You show up to my house and want me to read something for you and in the process I'm still slapped in the face with another lie."

"Stop performing the hurt ex for him," Stacey said, nodding her head in my direction.

"None of this if for him," Sharkey said.

"Isn't it, though? Are you going to take time parading through the streets, the grief stricken widow, or are you going to get up off your ass and help me?"

"See what I mean? None of this is about me, or you, or how you walked out. I'm just here to help you with your quest. A fucking plot point," Sharkey said.

"Fuck this," Stacey said, grabbed the baggie and stood up.

"Sure," Sharkey said, "run like you always do. Even if it means not getting what you want or need."

"Stop," I said before I realized I was going to say anything. They both looked at me like I'd just killed someone for daring to interrupt. "Look, I don't know what went down between you two, but I can tell it hurt. I can see it's unresolved and that it would tell a helluva lot more time than one afternoon to fix. I get that," I said. "And before you even say it, no, 1 don't think you two are being irrational. But maybe, maybe, we can remember that finding the person who has this item means people won't die tonight. That there's a greater good to remember. So, Sharkey, even though we just met, I'm asking. Please. Can we move past the anger, the hurt, with the understanding that this won't be the last time you two talk? That there will be future opportunities, after this is all done, to work things out?"

"She's always known where I live," Sharkey said.

"Do you...do you even want to talk?" Stacey said.

"Why would I not want to talk about what happened? For fuck's sake. Why wouldn't you want to talk about it?" Sharkey asked.

Stacey shrugged, "What was there to say? I...I fucked up. Was there any way that wasn't going to mean the end of things?"

"Yeah, of course it meant the end of us, there was no way around that," Sharkey said. "But didn't it ever occur to you that if you were that important to me that I might still want you in my life after we had time to cool off?" Sharkey reached for the baggie. "Here," they said, "give me the goddamn thing." As Stacey handed over the bag, as soon as Sharkey saw it was metallic, they sat back in their chair.

"First, though, Stace, Please tell me this isn't some left-over Third Reich, Spear of Destiny bullshit. Swear to me we're done with all that," Sharkey said.

"No," Stacey said. Then she thought about it for a second. "Well, mostly not." Then she thought about it for another second. "Well, at least half not." Then another second. "Okay, kind of not, but then, they were pretty thorough—a lot of shit is connected to them at one point or another."

Sharkey's eyes rolled.

"I'm kidding," Stacey said. "Kidding. Please..." she said, gesturing toward the baggie.

Sharkey shrugged out of the jacket and sat it on the table, then picked up the baggie. Out came the metallic bit and then scrap of cloth. Sharkey sat the scrap aside and clasped the metallic bit in one hand, then leaned back in the chair. Sharkey's eyes slid closed.

We all sat like that for several minutes. Nothing moved. At first it was the usual kind of boredom, the same thing you might experience while waiting for an elevator. Then the air became thick. Sharkey took on a kind of glow. By that I don't mean that a light emanated from their skin, but that suddenly they seemed vital and powerful to my eyes in ways that they hadn't just a second before. There was a smell in the air like fresh cut basil. I looked over at Stacey to see if she was registering anything happening, but her eyes were locked onto Sharkey.

It faded, though, and time started moving once more. Sharkey's eyes opened. Without moving, Sharkey said, "What have you gotten yourself into?" I knew she meant Stacey.

"What did you see?"

Sharkey sat the metallic piece on the table and rested their elbows on their knees. Sharkey glanced from Stacey to me and then back. Stacey's eyes were desperately trying to say something to Sharkey. With a heavy sigh, Sharkey said, "So, it looks like the same old bullshit. There was a group. They came together organically it looks like. Eventually they moved to working objects. The internal politics got complicated because of sex," Sharkey said.

"Doesn't it always," Stacey said.

They both smirked.

"From what I can tell, it looks like the toxic emotional environment started to taint the workings until one night it got to the point where the group was going to break. Rather than just break clean, though, it looks like they did one more working," Sharkey said.

"And that's this thing?" I said, pointing toward the bag.

Sharkey nodded. "Shit," Stacey said.

"Yeah," Sharkey said, leaning back in the chair. "Looks like while they were trying to pull in some spirit or power to put into this thing, they managed to pull a whopper. I've heard of this kind of stuff they were doing before, I mean it's all over the place in theory, but somehow these people pulled it off."

"Stuff like what?" I asked.

"It looks like they figured out how to pull entities from other regions and somehow bond them to a working with a solid object."

Stacey leaned her head into her hand, "Fuck me."

Sharkey laughed bitterly, "Yeah."

"So..." I started.

"So," Sharkey broke in, "it means that what you're dealing with here isn't something that was controlled and tempered to do what it does. It accidentally happened."

"Shark?" Stacey asked.

"See, accidental workings, even if they don't involve something that supposedly doesn't actually exist, like bonding an entity from another dimension to an object, are bad news, and for all the same reasons you can think of. There is literally no telling what they might do, what characteristics they might take on, what price the magick will extract for its use. That guy who wrote about the black rune sword wielded by the albino elf? He got pretty fucking close to what we're talking about—incredibly powerful weapon, true, but the price for using it was utter chaos and destruction."

"How do you know about this kind of stuff?" Stacey asked.

"Blades," Sharkey said. "It's always about blades."

"Did you see any of its use, maybe what it looked like?" I asked.

"Yeah. It's like…kind of like this," Sharkey said, leaning forward. A small spiral notebook and a pen were nearby. Sharkey sketched for a couple of minutes, producing something that looked a bit like a triskelion, only with blades instead of the curlicues that most people put on it. "Kind of like that," Sharkey said, sitting back.

Stacey tore the paper out of the notebook, folded it, and shoved it in her pocket.

"Not super practical as a stabbing weapon," I said, noting that Stacey had grown pale.

"Any chance you can find a location?" I asked.

With a shake of the head, Sharkey said, "No. And that's unusual. I don't mean to brag or whatever, but I'm good. Normally, you come to me, I can get you to within a couple of blocks. This, though?" Sharkey said, with a gesture toward the drawing. "It's putting off some kind of screen. Either I'd have to be a helluva lot closer to it to feel anything, or…"

"Or?" Stacey asked.

"Or there isn't anything really to feel," Sharkey said.

"I don't get…," I started to say.

"Thanks," Stacey said, standing. "Let's go," she said.

"But…" I started to say.

"Let's go," Stacey said, already moving for the door. I stood and followed them.

"Thanks," I said to Sharkey who only smiled.

Once we were outside, I said, "Your friend might have had more information for us."

"We'll call later and ask," Stacey said, opening her car door.

I slid into the driver's seat and closed the door. I turned to her, about to ask more questions when I saw that her eyes were closed and she was running through a breathing exercise. I started the car and turned on the AC. I pulled away from the curb and moved us through the maze of streets in the subdivision until we were back out on the main road. About that time, Stacey took a large breath and her eyes opened.

"Okay?" I asked.

"Okay," she said.

"Do you want to tell me what happened?" I asked.

She took another breath, "I don't know. All of a sudden, just seeing it, the object, brought back so many memories. I don't know if I'd been hiding them from myself or if…"

"If maybe something in the object's power made the memories harder to get at after it cut you," I said.

Her eyes got wide.

"I keep telling you, this isn't my first rodeo. I haven't exactly seen this before, but so far nothing we've encountered has surprised me all that much," I said.

After a moment, she said, "yeah…like maybe after it cut me, the memories of what happened got…fuzzy? I don't know. Seeing a drawing of it, though, made all that stuff come rushing forward, and I can see the woman's face clearly. I can hear her voice."

"So if you saw her again, or a picture of her, you could identify her?"

"Yeah," she said. "That doesn't really help us, though; we don't have a name."

"Yeah, but we're closer than we were, and that's not nothing," I said. "What now?"

"Gloria," Stacey said.

"Who is?" I asked.

"She's a specialist with memory stuff. She can help. There's only one issue," she said.

"What's that?" I asked.

"Head downtown," Stacey said. After I turn the car down the on-ramp to the freeway, she said, "the problem is how to get to her without her brother knowing and sticking his nose into it. There's one more person I want to talk to before we talk to Gloria."

"Whose that?" I asked.

Stacey's voice took on a blank quality, as if far away, "'Madame Sosostris, famous clairvoyante…with a wicked pack of cards.'"

Stacey asked me to turn right onto one of those downtown streets that seem to exist in every city all over the world; a side street that is in plain view, but once you are on it, it seems like another world—for a moment, despite knowing it's a ridiculous thing to think, you're certain no one has ever been on it in their lives.

She told me to pull over to the curb next to a storefront that simply said, "Madame Annalise" in blinking red neon in front of a black curtain. The shops on either side had signs in the front window that say "for sale." As we get out, I say, "Well, I will give you this; I'm certainly getting an education in my own city today."

"You think you know a place…" she said without looking away from the sign. She closed the car door and walked directly to the front door of the shop. She opened it and walked in, head down, full of purpose. I followed.

Inside, as I closed the door behind us, I saw there was a long black couch and a coffee table against one wall and an open doorway with a black and red bead curtain against the far wall. The beads were still swaying a bit because an enormous black cat had just come through them. He sat down on his haunches and stared at us without blinking.

"That's more than a little unnerving," I said.

Stacey stopped in the center of the room. The ceiling fan above us spun lazily, hardly moving the air at all.

"One moment," someone called from the other room. The large black cat stood up, turned around, and walked back through the curtain just as a woman came through it. She stood about five five in her flats and wore all black except for a gray cardigan that was at least three sizes too big for her. Her black hair was clipped loosely at her neck.

"Stacey," the woman said as if she'd already known who it

would be.

"Annalise," Stacey said without moving.

They stared at each other for a moment, then Annalise looked at me. "And this is?" she asked

"Derek Goldman," I said, stepping forward to shake hands. Annalise reached out to do the same but Stacey said, "Don't" so abruptly that I stopped, midstride. Somehow, I knew that it wasn't meant for me.

Annalise smiled, then put her hand down.

"Not that it isn't pleasant to catch up every once in a while, but..." she drifted off.

"We should talk in the other room," Stacey said.

Annalise considered that for a moment, then stood aside and gestured for us to go through the bead curtain. Stacey went through and I followed. The room was quite a bit smaller. There was a knee-height table with one chair on one side and two chairs on the other. Stacey sat in one, and I followed suit. Annalise took the solitary chair across from us.

"Need a favor," Stacey said.

"And what's that?" Annalise asked, settling back in the chair and crossing her legs.

"Umm...We...we need a reading. A second hand reading," Stacey said. I tried not to laugh. I hadn't know her a long time, but I'd never seen her this affected by someone.

"I see," Annalise said. "Someone you know or someone you know of?"

"Does it make a difference?" I asked.

Her eyes slid over to me and for a second even I was caught up in her beauty. I marveled at that for a second—one hell of a glamor to be able to work no matter the sexuality of the target.

"A very large one, monetarily and otherwise," Annalise said.

"Ah," I said.

"I was hoping we could work this on a sort of pro-bono footing. Or maybe quid pro quo?" Stacey said.

"I don't do charity work. It disrespects the Gods," Annalise said.

"Aren't you supposed to do the work regardless of payment?"

I asked.

"That's an old way of thinking about things, my friend," Annalise said. "My practices are squared with my Gods. Can you say the same of yours?"

I had to admit that I'd never thought about it.

A large blue-gray cat came in and jumped into Annalise's lap. It gently tapped its forehead to her chin, then swiveled its blue eyes to look directly at me, then Stacey. Annalise whispered something to it and it blinked once, then jumped off her lap and disappeared into the back of the store.

"Your sign outside says a 3 card pull is only thirty-five dollars," I said.

"If the reading is for you, and only 3 major arcana, then yes. What you're asking," she said, nodding to Stacey, "is something quite different. Much more difficult. And a bit more dangerous."

"We don't have any money," Stacey said. "But we're...we're looking for someone. Someone dangerous. A killer. Isn't that...isn't that maybe worth..."

"How much?" I asked.

The corner of Annalise's mouth quirked and without looking at me she said, "Someone you know, or someone you know of?"

"Know of," I said.

"Physical object?"

I nudged Stacey's shoulder. She brought out the baggie with the cloth and the shard and set it on the table. As soon as she did so, both of the cats reappeared and began to sniff around the table. Annalise's composure was broken. She leaned forward immediately and almost touched the bag.

"Is that some kind of...what is that?"

"Be kind of careful," Stacey said.

Annalise disappeared into the back of the shop and returned with a black wooden box. On the cover a single rune was carved: Uruz. Her cards were like none I'd ever seen before. They seemed almost home made, but still of the same level of artistic quality of a Rider-Waite deck. Though clean and well-maintained, I could still tell that they were very old.

"You'll need to hold the object in your hands and think as hard as you can about this person you are seeking. Remember that we have to convince the cards that you are her, or at least acting in her behalf." I could hear the doubt in her voice.

"How many times have you ever done this?" I asked.

"Do you really want to know?" Annalise responded. It did not fill me with confidence.

"You or me?" Stacey asked.

Before I could answer, Annalise said, "It would be better for things to be closer to the original. You identify as female, yes?" She was looking at Stacey.

"I do."

"And you identify as male, yes?"

"I do," I said.

"Best if we use you," she said, gesturing at Stacey as she fanned the cards out in a half-moon in front of her. "Sit," she said without looking at me. I pulled a chair from the wall to just behind Stacey's right shoulder. "Pick it up," Annalise said and Stacey picked up the bag. "No. Skin to skin. Has to be." Stacey looked at me, worry in her eyes. I nodded some kind of encouragement, though I think we both knew we were back in the deep end, again. Stacey opened the bag and picked up the blade shard.

"Feel it. Feel the weight of it in your hand. Feel the coldness of it," Annalise said. Stacey's eyes drifted closed and immediately the room felt smaller. Both cats had drifted into the room and were now sitting on either side of Annalise's chair. "Think about her. Feel her name on your tongue." Stacey's brow furrowed. The large gray blue cat slipped silently onto Stacey's lap. I moved to put the cat back down but Annalise gestured for me to stop. "Cats. Half in and half out of this world. He's helping her." Its blue eyes caught mine and for a second I could have sworn I saw it smirk. "Think about her," Annalise said again. "Feel her in your mind."

It was at that moment that Stacey started to glow. Not a huge, bright light as you see in the movies, but I could tell that she was giving off light. She moaned a bit, but the sound was distorted, sounding as if it came from a deep canyon.

"Good," Annalise said. "Good. Now, feel her in your heart."

Stacey's face became a grimace as if in pain. The glow increased. A steady yellow light drifted off of her like smoke. Annalise's eyes had gotten large and she seemed to be vibrating. "Now, pick three cards. Quickly! Don't think about it, just do it!" Stacey picked three quickly and turned them face up.

The Hanged Man but reversed.

The Wheel.

The Devil.

I couldn't help but notice that Annalise was taken aback, physically. "Alright," she said. "Okay. I need you to let go. Let go of the shard. Let go," Annalise said.

Stacey shook her head and the light that had been coming off of her, a kind of golden haze, started to change, shifting toward green.

"Let go now. It's time to let go of the shard," Annalise said. The cat meowed and slid off of Stacey's lap. The light continued to move toward a sickly green.

"I need you to let go…"

"Stacey," I said.

"…Stacey. I need you to let go, now, Stacey."

Again, Stacey shook her head no. The light had moved to a kind of green I remembered seeing on a Stephen King book cover, sickly and foreboding. I reached for her but Annalise shook her head no.

"Let go! I command you to let go of the shard now!" Annalise said.

Stacey's eyes shot open and in a voice three octaves too low, she said "No! The weapon is mine! I will have it!" Blood was coming off of her palm from where her grip, gone far too tight, had made the remains of the blade cut her skin.

Annalise stood up and, opening her shirt, revealed a necklace of silver with large oval glass beads worked into it. She laid her hand on it and it lit up as though the beads were light bulbs. Annalise's eyes began to glow with the same violet-ish light that the necklace gave forth. "In the name of Anubis and Set, of Bast who sees all in darkness, I command you to release the weapon!"

I was pinned to the chair as if some force was emanating from her. It seemed as though a tendril of the sickly green light was reading out and colliding with the whitish-violet light coming from Annalise. The two seemed to be pushing against one another. Stacey's eyes had begun to glow with the pale green light, as well.

"No! It is mine!" Stacey said in a low growl.

Annalise spoke in a language I dimly recognized as Egyptian, though an older, more guttural form than I had ever heard before, and the greenish light was slowly being pushed back. The necklace's light increased and I felt as though I were under water. Stacey began to talk back to it in a language I have never heard before, though just as guttural. I couldn't understand the words, but I could tell they were a curse. Twisted, profane cursing words that should never be uttered on any material plane.

Finally, with one flourishing gesture of her free hand, the other desperately clutching the necklace, Annalise's white-ish-violet light flared out in a shockwave from her and Stacey was knocked back in her chair. The light that had been surrounding Stacey disappeared and her eyes closed. Annalise slowly drifted to the ground and only then did I even notice she'd been levitating about an inch off the floor. Her eyes came back to normal and the necklace slowly lost its glow. She slid into the chair, laying her head back and closing her eyes.

For a moment, the room was silent.

When I had my wits about me again, I stood up and went to Stacey, kneeling by her chair.

"Hey," I said, pushing against her shoulder. "Hey!"

Stacey's eyes drifted open.

"You with us again?" I asked. She nodded. I went to Annalise, but before I could touch her, the black tomcat planted himself in my way. I understood that I was to come no closer.

"Annalise?" Stacey asked.

Her eyes came open and she sat up. "Well," she said after a moment, but didn't continue the thought.

"Fuckin A," Stacey said. "I could use a drink."

"What happened?" I asked.

Without opening her eyes, Annalise said, "An unclean spirit entered. To say the least."

"I don't understand."

"You do. Let yourself process it. Whatever…" Annalise said, paused, then continued, "whatever is in that weapon, it is powerful. And old. And in a great deal of pain. You could have probably guessed all that already, and I'm not a specialist in these kinds of things, but consider that even a small fragment of it was powerful enough to posses your friend."

I looked at Stacey. Stacey was staring at the floor.

"But your necklace," I started. "It was powerful enough to…"

"Only barely. Had the…fragment…of whatever it is been any stronger, we would not now be having this conversation." Annalise opened her eyes and sat up. "What have you gotten yourself into?" she asked staring at Stacey.

"But that must mean it worked. I wasn't just faking that I was her, I became her."

"No," Annalise said, sitting forward and examining the three cards that were pulled. "You became it. Or at least a piece of it that was separated from the…bulk of itself. I told you, I'm not a specialist in these kinds of things. What I do know, though, is that these cards pertain to it, not her. I don't know if you'll find that at all helpful."

"What do they say?" I asked.

She looked at them for a moment. I noticed that the cats had again taken up positions next to her legs, the blue-gray one staring me down, and the black one directly between Stacey and Annalise, staring daggers through her.

"If we hadn't just had a very direct demonstration of possession, I'd have guessed it from these cards. They're about being taken over by very base impulses and a lack of forward movement…a kind of frustrating time without much control or advancement." She exhaled and rubbed her temples. "It's stuck."

"Stuck?" Stacey asked.

"That's what it pulled. It's stuck. I don't know what that might mean to you, but that's what these cards are about. A desire to break free but a complete lack of movement and the need to abide because this time, this time of very brutish impulses, of Freudian ID working, this time will come to an end but not quickly, and that whoever…*what*ever pulled these cards, will have no power over this time period. It will end when it ends, but not through any actions it takes."

"That would seem to suggest, though, that…that maybe whatever is in that weapon…that it doesn't really want to kill?"

"Maybe," Annalise said, "or at least that its murderous abilities are being used in a way that are foreign to it…somehow below its sense of what it is for."

"Fuckin A," Stacey whispered.

Annalise picked up her phone from the table beside the chair. With a few flicks of her finger she saw whatever it was she wanted to see because she nodded. "Your time is up. I would like for you to go now."

"Thanks," I said, and put my hand on Stacey's arm to steady her as she stood up. She shrugged it off as soon as she was up and I followed her out the door. I noticed the black cat followed about two steps behind us. When I turned to shut the door after we'd gone through it, I saw the cat sitting there at the doorway to the back room. It was calm, but I couldn't help but get a feeling of warning. We were not to return here ever again.

Back in the car, we drove for almost twenty minutes before either of us said anything. In the end, it was Stacey who broke the silence. "Gloria," she said.

"Is that where we need to go next?" I asked.

"Yes," Stacey said. "But I won't lie, I'm dreading it."

"Well, considering what we've already been through today, how much worse can it possibly be?"

Stacey laughed.

"Do you want to tell me why you've been dreading it so much?" I asked.

"Head west. We're going toward that edge of town."

I turned the car that direction at the next intersection.

"It's not so much that I dread talking to Gloria. I mean, she's batshit crazy. Certifiable. But still mostly harmless. It's her brother, Simon. If he's around, that could make things...complicated," Stacey said.

"And why's that?"

She sighed. "They're both Malleus agents."

My eyes grew three times larger. "I see."

"Yeah."

I let that sit for a while. "So, if you dread seeing her, and seeing her might cause all kinds of complications, then why are we going?"

"She has a knack for...finding things. Now that we have a lot of information, information they might not have, we can bargain. That's...that's what I hope, anyway."

"So you're hoping that we can give them enough information about this killer that they'll just give us the location and then we can...what?"

"Go stop her," Stacey said.

"And what's to stop these agents from simply saying, 'thanks for the info, we'll handle it from here?'" I asked.

"That's why I want to talk to her and I hope he isn't around. She is often...confused...befuddled...enough that maybe we can sneak this around her."

"And why is that a good idea?" I asked. "I mean, why haven't we just gone to Malleus with all of this to begin with?"

She said nothing for a long time.

"Are you seriously thinking that we're going to confront this killer by ourselves?" I asked.

"If we can find her. Take a left up here," Stacey said.

"You think this Gloria person will be able to do what your friend Sharkey wasn't able to?"

"I'm almost certain of it. Let's just hope the price is right," Stacey said.

"Why don't you want to know about or go see any of my contacts?" I asked.

She shifted in her seat to look at me but said nothing.

"I mean, you know that I know people, too, right?"

"Goldman, please don't take this the wrong way, but I don't know the people you know. I wouldn't trust them," she said.

"You know, paranoia isn't a good thing for a young person," I said, only half joking.

"Just because someone calls how you feel paranoia doesn't mean that it isn't still a good idea," she said.

Stacey guided me through more one-way streets and along a service road until we reached a tiny building next to a small, obviously man-made pond.

"Is this where she'll be?" I asked as I pulled the car to a stop.

"Maybe. Maybe not. It's just the first place to look on any given day. Come on," Stacey said, getting out.

The sign out front said Museum of Witchcraft. Like so many things I was learning on this day, I had no idea this was even here. "Normally you'd find something like this much closer to Boston or Salem, but there's this one. She likes to hang out here."

We opened the door and the little bell above it chimed. Very small aisles led off from the center of the building where a desk sat. Behind the desk was a very tall and skinny young man with long black hair. Not my type, I thought, but sexy in his own way. He set the book he'd been reading down. "Stacey?"

"Yeah. Hi."

"Wow," he said, suddenly growing awkward. "Hi. It's been... wow." Stacey didn't say anything for a minute. "You cut your hair," the young man said. His eyes shifted to me and then back to her.

"Yeah. Listen, I'm sorry to be in a rush, but...have you seen her lately?"

He looked confused for a second, then nodded. "Yeah, she's out back."

Stacey walked past the desk toward a door behind it. I followed. Through it was a porch that overlooked the pond. On a bench beside that porch was a woman with black hair that hung down to her knees. She had on the darkest eye shadow I'd ever seen, all but hiding her blue eyes. They were the same color as pictures I'd seen of an iceberg that had flipped over. When they hit me, I had to force myself to continue walking.

"Gloria," Stacey said coming to a stop next to the bench.

"Do I know of thee?" Gloria asked, turning her head to the side a bit as if she were a dog hearing a new noise. Her voice sounded exactly like the singer Stevie Nicks.

"We've met a few times, but never really spoken. My friend and I are in a bit of a hurry, so I'm going to skip ahead to the important stuff…"

"Hurry often just produces more worry," Gloria said in that tone that comes when someone is quoting something. She closed her eyes and looked away.

"I know you work for Malleus Maleficarum, you and your brother, and I know you have extensive knowledge about the things that go on here in the city when it comes to magick," Stacey said all in one breath.

Gloria's face never shifted. She didn't move. We stood there for a while waiting for her to respond in some way, but she didn't.

"Gloria, I need to ask you some questions about something that is happening here in town. I know I'm not a part of the agency, but if I ask, will you answer?"

"This is the way the boy and the sword come to us," Gloria said, her eyes still closed.

I looked around for some indication of what she might be talking about. My eyes met Stacey's. For a second there, I could have sworn she had just said those words to the tune of "All Around the Mulberry Bush."

"May I ask you some questions?" Stacey asked.

Gloria's eyes opened slowly, and I was hit with them again. They made it hard to concentrate. She was definitely humming the tune to "All Around the Mulberry Bush," but too slow and almost off key, and she was grinning as she did.

"The problem is not in the asking, it is in the way thou shall phrase them. The words will betray thee. But, if thou must, thou must. Begin thy questions." Gloria said and then went back to humming.

Stacey pulled the baggie out of her pocket. Gloria immediately slid back away from it. "Where oh where did that come from?" she asked. For the first time since I'd seen her, I felt like we had her full concentration.

"A woman who attacked me had it. This is a piece that was left after she sliced me open pretty good. I need to know more about it because it might help us," she said, gesturing to me, "find her and stop her from killing others of us."

"'Us'?" Gloria asked.

"People who use magick."

"I see; so thou believst there is a woman in the city who useth a very special blade to harm others who are using magick. Art thou making a formal report, then?" Gloria asked. I couldn't place it, but I knew there was more behind her words than what I was hearing.

"No," Stacey said. "I can handle this on my own."

"Come now, little mouse. Versus something frightening enough to bring thou to *my* feet?" Again, Gloria cocked her head to the side and I had the distinct impression she stifled a laugh.

Gloria gestured toward herself, "None ever come looking for me unless deeply overhead with something nasty. This time, though, thou hast brought a lovely hound to play." There was no denying that she was looking right at me when she said that.

"A hound?" I asked.

Stacey shook the baggie. "I'm looking for this woman. I think maybe I can stop her."

Gloria stood up and I won't lie; I took an involuntary step backward. Her eyes never left mine. She walked straight to me. "Such a lovely beast," she said. With a speed I couldn't believe her index finger was on the tip of my nose. "Does it know what it is, she wonders."

"Gloria," Stacey said. "I need you to try to focus."

Without looking, Gloria reached out and snatched the baggie away from Stacey. Our eyes were still locked, but out of the corner of mine, I saw a faint glow around the shard blade. "Dost thou feel that?" Gloria asked me.

"I don't know what you're talking about," I said.

"Oh, the happy things we could do if you were with us," Gloria said. The glow changed from an almost pleasant golden to a harsh blood red, though, and her attention was drawn from me to it. "This is nastiness," she said, and dropped the baggie. She spit at it and kicked it away. "This is abomination. A thing that should not be."

"Can you sense it? Where is it?" Stacey asked, stepping closer.

"I should call my brother. He would know what to do with twisted ugliness such as this."

"No!" Stacey said. "No. Please," Stacey reached out toward her. "Let us handle this. Why bother your brother, eh? He's got other things on his mind, right now. Things he has to do. Just tell us where it is, yeah? Tell us where it is and we'll go handle this."

Gloria watched her as you'd watch an angry animal in a corner. She looked away off to the distance for quite some time. I began to wonder if she'd forgotten we were there, then she turned her attention to Stacey again and said, "Thou art of twisted mind. I see thee," then she whispered, "I see thee," vehemently. "What you seek is in a building that no one uses anymore. One of those that still has power. She hides among the living but will not be able to do so for very much longer, as I think you've surmised already. Give," Gloria said, gesturing to me, and standing to her full height.

"What is it that you want...?" I began to ask.

"Thy phone! Swiftly!" Gloria said, punctuating each word with a snap of her fingers. I handed it to her. She tapped a few things then typed something in. She handed it back to me with an address displayed. "Whatever wickedness shields thy prey, beware it. It grows more powerful by the second. Are you *sure* you would not rather simply give this over to my brother and I to deal with?" That last was said in the same tone you might use to taunt a child.

"Got it?" Stacey asked. I nodded. "Thank you, Agent Gloria. We thank thee." Stacey bowed to her, then turned and walked quickly toward the parking lot. I turned to follow but Gloria got in my way.

"And thee, houndish courser? Dost thou thank me when the wind is high and the prey's scent is in thy nose?" She asked. The gleam in her eye was pure cruelty.

"I thank you, Agent Gloria," I said, and made no move. When she saw that she wasn't getting any reaction, she turned and walked back to the bench. I took off as fast as I could without running. I slid into the car, started it, and backed out.

"Now you see why I saved this for last," Stacey said as we pulled back onto the freeway.

"What's a hound?" I asked.

"Let me have your phone. We're going to need to call Sharkey in on this one," Stacey said.

"What," I emphasized heavily, "is a hound?" I already had a feeling I knew the answer to the entire question, but some part of me wanted, no...needed her to confirm it.

"Hand me your phone, please. If I call Sharkey now before she goes out for the night, maybe I can—,"

"WHAT," I said again, louder, "is a hound?" I handed her my phone and she started tapping in texts.

"Okay, look, I didn't know. Not for sure. I had to find this thing, though, and I had a feeling...a million to one shot, really, because I've never had to do something like this before, you know? But I had to find this thing—," Stacey rambled as she typed. Replies started to come back, pinging each time. Stacey didn't stop, she was already typing the next response. "—and to do that, I had to find myself a hound—."

"What's a hound?" I asked.

She stopped typing and set the phone down on her leg. "Derrek—"

I didn't say anything.

She sighed. "Haven't you ever wondered why you constantly find people who are witches? Who can scrye? Haven't you wondered why none of this," she gestured to the world around us, "makes you even the slightest bit nervous?"

I said nothing.

"You're a hound. A sensitive, I guess would be the proper word for it, though no one I know uses that term. You can—"

"I get it."

Neither of us said anything for a moment. She finally looked up and into my eyes.

"Haven't you ever wondered, though? Wondered why you constantly find yourself around magick even though you yourself don't use it?" she asked.

"I said I get it."

"At any rate, I wasn't sure. Not until now. It's just...when you talked about how often you ran into people who were users, I started to get a hunch." A few more replies came in. She picked up the phone and typed a bit more, then handed the phone back to me. I put it in my jacket pocket.

"You're using me," I said. "You've been using me from the start. This isn't about friendship or—,"

"Bullshit!" she said. "Fuckin A, Goldman, you *are* my friend. At least I consider you to be. Who else would have come even half this far? Who? Who else would still be with me now? I mean, you can put out the call all day long, but someone who is going to answer it? That's a *friend*."

I took the off ramp that was going to lead us to downtown and pulled into the slow lane. The streetlights passed by, lighting the car, then plunging us into darkness again and again.

"Come on, Goldman. I mean, yeah, I had suspicions that you were a sensitive. The fact that you didn't have those suspicions is kind of crazy to me, to be honest. But what if I'd told you what I thought and I was wrong? I mean, I didn't have any proof. Still wouldn't if we hadn't just gotten finished talking to Queen Psychobitch back there. And have I asked you to do anything today that you wouldn't have done without being a sensitive? No, because you didn't know you were one. Everything you did today, you did because we *are* friends. At least I hope we still are." She waited but I didn't say anything. "Come on, Goldman—are we still friends?"

I pulled the car to a stop against the curb. The building address that Gloria had given us was just up ahead and around a corner. I figured it would be better for us to approach on foot, quietly. "Open up the glove compartment," I said. When she did, an old .38 pistol nearly fell out.

"Fuckin A," she whispered.

I took it and slid it into my other jacket pocket.

"You've had that the whole time?"

"It was my grandfather's. I don't even know if it works. Still, though, I have a feeling this isn't going to be good." I got out and shut the door quietly. Stacey did the same. I locked the doors and put the key away, then started walking. Stacey fell in behind me.

"So, I mean, like…are we cool?" Stacey said.

I didn't say anything.

"Goldman," she said.

When I didn't respond after a long couple of minutes, again she said, "Goldman."

I stopped and turned around. "Yeah. We're cool. You explained yourself and when I think about it, you're right—I didn't do anything that I wouldn't have done otherwise, so we're cool. Next time you feel like you have information that's about me? I want you to tell me immediately. Got it?"

"Cool," she said. "100% cool." She slapped my upper arm. Just then there was a roar that startled us both. Sharkey pulled up on the massive Harley, put the bike's kickstand down, and slipped the helmet over one of the handlebars, then walked toward us.

"Shark," Stacey said.

"Stace," Sharkey said, then nodded to me. I nodded back.

"We saw her. She gave us the building number. Three of us? I figure we can get her pinned and into custody, get the blade away from her, and after that, I bet dimes to doughnuts she calms right down."

"So that's the plan?" I asked.

"Yeah," Stacey said. "That's the plan."

I noticed Sharkey had a gun as well. Stacey started walking and quickly turned the corner. Both Sharkey and I followed. The building we were looking for was directly across from us. It was one of those that had been abandoned a long time ago. Either no one had ever attempted to reclaim it or the attempts had stopped after they had taken too long. It had become one of those structures that are just background noise after a while, framing for other more important buildings. As anyone who has ever had to live on the streets will tell you, after a while, even the derelicts of the city won't stay in buildings like that for fear of disappearing as the structure slowly slides into obscurity.

"This is it," Sharkey said, and stopped us in front of what had once been a beautiful revolving door but was now just a gaping open hole, like a missing tooth. Sharkey had brought along a pistol that sat in a shoulder holster so comfortably it seemed to have always been there, simply another part of the body. Everything about Sharkey was angles and lean lines like a poster of a movie star playing a secret agent. Just having Sharkey with us made me feel more confident. Sharkey gestured toward the open entrance. The last rays of the sunset made the skin on Sharkey's hand seem like cooling bronze, fresh from the forge.

Stacey exhaled. "Okay."

"And you're sure we shouldn't maybe, I dunno, call someone?" I asked.

Stacey looked at me over the top of her sunglasses. "Who, Goldman?"

"I don't know, someone. Maybe we *should* call in Malleus."

Sharkey laughed. Stacey did the same a second later. A look passed between them.

"Ready?" Stacey asked Sharkey. Sharkey gave a single nod.

"Here," Sharkey said, passing me a skinny pocket flashlight. Stacey took one out of her own jacket. Stacey walked through the gaping entrance into what had once been a lobby. Sharkey followed, and I came in last.

The second we were inside, I got a feeling across the back of my neck. As I always did, I reached up to brush it away, thinking it was a web I had accidentally broken. When my hand came away with nothing, I said, "I can feel it. Sharkey was right."

"Where?" Stacey said.

Sharkey pointed to the stairs at the far end of what had been the lobby. "Up."

I hadn't thought about it, but the elevator wouldn't be working.

We'd have to climb stairs to get to whatever floor the killer was living of hiding on. So, we began to climb. Every creak and groan of a stair or support beam convinced me I was seconds from falling to my death. The itching sensation at the back of my neck got worse the more steps we went up.

Not being in nearly as good a shape as the other two, I had to call for a rest around the fourth landing. I sat down on a stack of boards that had been left there and tried to catch my breath. Stacey waited near me patiently while Sharkey took the opportunity to explore, shining the light around what had obviously at one time been some kind of piano bar or lounge. There was a raised platform in the far corner too small and at too odd an angle to the rest of the room to be a stage. A circular bar dominated the center of the room.

"I wonder if there's any booze left," Sharkey said, making a beeline for it.

"There isn't," someone in the darkness said. Immediately my whole body tensed and my hands started to shake. Stacey spun in the direction of the bar and began to wave her light around. Sharkey had frozen in place, body in a loose but threatening stance. "Trust me, I looked." The person with the voice emerged from the far end of the room past the bar. It was like the blackness had been a curtain that parted for her.

"Hello," Stacey said.

The woman had long brown hair parted on the side in a fashion I hadn't seen since high school. She wasn't tall, and her weight wasn't too little or too much. Her eyes were a shade of brown I'd seen a million times before. In other words, nothing about her would stand out in a crowd.

"I don't know you, do I? I feel like I might know you, somehow," the woman said without coming any further. "I'm Delores."

"You know me. You tried to kill me," Stacey said.

"Ah. I think I do remember that vaguely," Delores said. There was a thunk as she set the blade down on the bar. Even in the dark, it gleamed and glistened. I knew if I touched it, it would feel hot, and that just being near it felt wrong. "How did you find me?" With that, her attention shifted to Sharkey.

"You're not hard to find with that sitting at your hip," Sharkey said, gesturing toward the blade.

Delores laughed and seemed to relax. For a split second I was stupid enough to feel like this might work out without bloodshed.

"I see," Delores said. "I've been doing my best to stay hidden, but it…it keeps drawing me to places like this. The empties."

"It's taking you over, Delores," I said before I could stop myself.

"Who are you?" she asked.

"It doesn't matter. You know that it's taking you over, Delores. There isn't much of you left and what there is won't be here for much longer. You can't fight it alone. Let us—," I of course was about to say "help you" when she picked up the blade and then slammed it down on the bar again. If you recorded the sound of a huge bell and then ran that recording through a massively distorted guitar amplifier the size rock bands use to play an arena, that might get at about half of how loud this was. While our vision was blurry and I was doubled over, Delores whipped into action.

She was over the bar and at Sharkey before the ringing had stopped. In one motion she pushed Sharkey's hand aside before it could connect with the pistol and brought the blade upwards across Sharkey's body. Blood flew from the force of the cut. Sharkey flew backward, landing fully prone, laid out.

I had just enough time to register that this had happened before Delores was in front of Stacey. Stacey somehow managed to bring up an arm and put it in the way of Delores' wrist, but I heard the heavy snap as she did. Stacey was also knocked backward and wound up on her back on the floor. Sharkey was already up, had taken a knee, and was aiming the huge hand cannon carefully. I thought that if I could just keep Delores distracted for a second, Sharkey would get off a shot.

I have never been more wrong about anything in my entire life.

I stood and moved in the direction of Delores and she whirled. Less than one second later, Delores had her back nearly against my chest and her elbow was deep in my ribcage while the blade itself had sliced through the air and cut Sharkey's pistol in half. As I collapsed to my knees in pain, Delores reached out her hand and the blade whirled back to her. She caught it and pivoted smoothly, landing an expert kick to my chin. It was my turn to land on my back flat out on the floor.

"Let us help you," Stacey said through a groan as she fought back to her feet.

Delores stopped moving for a second and cocked her head to the side. "Help me do what?"

"Help you get away from its grasp, its power," Stacey said.

Delores laughed the single most cruel, demeaning laugh I've ever heard in my life. "Oh, pumpkin," she said, taking a step toward Stacey. "What on Earth makes you think I want this to stop?" She spun the blade in her hand, then brought it across Stacey's chest. The blood flew from the cut.

Sharkey was up and moving toward Delores when we all heard something downstairs. From where I was laid out, by moving my head just a little I could see high powered flashlights below through the holes and gaps in the flooring. Someone cried out something that sounded like "Federal agent" but I couldn't be sure. I looked back at Delores just in time to see her face change for the first time since we'd encountered her. She was genuinely worried. She took a stop toward Stacey then stopped, as if thinking better of it. She then growled. Not in the way a human might growl when angry, but an even lower, more guttural growl. The growl of an animal denied its prey. In two bounds she was off up the stairs.

The high-powered flashlights were coming up the stairs to this landing.

"Sharkey," Stacey managed to say. I saw movement, but by the time I got my head up high enough to see where Sharkey had been, they were gone.

"Freeze, Federal Agents!" a man said, the flashlight moving across Stacey, who was now on her feet clutching her chest, and me, still lying on the floor. "Freeze, Federal Agents!" the woman's voice said, just a second behind the man. I didn't have the breath to tell her she was wasting her time—at that moment, I couldn't have moved if I had wanted to.

BOOK 2

"In the universe, there are things that are known, and things that are unknown,
and in between, there are doors."

—William Blake

3. Derek Goldman

There really are only three ways to describe time—it either crawls, it flies by, or it stands still. If you had to guess which one it does while in custody, police or otherwise, you'd be right to guess that's the kind that stands still. All you can do is keep looking at the clock wondering when someone is going to come in and clear up whatever the mistake is. For Stacey and I, this was no different. Made worse, if I'm being honest, by the fact that she was furious and unable to sit still.

"Fuckin'..." she muttered to herself nonstop and that was the only word that became clear every few moments, as if punctuating the sentence.

After a while, a man came by and moved me to a tiny room with a metal table and a chair on either side of it. I've seen enough TV to know what comes next.

I don't know how long it was, but after another long while, the door to the interrogation room opened and the agent who identified herself as Burton came in. She had a thick stack of file folders and a Styrofoam cup in one hand, a second identical cup on the other. She closed the door behind her with her foot.

"We're out of creamer," she said, setting the cup down in front of me. She flopped the folders down on the desk and sipped from her own cup. "That stuff will give you cancer, anyway."

I blew on the coffee and then sipped. It was weak, but warm. She sat down across from me and flipped open the top folder.

"So, I'll dispense with all the Gestapo tactics they tell us to use to soften you up at first and get to the point. Tell me how you got involved with Ms. Durand."

"The bookstore," I said.

Burton flipped a page, then another, then said the exact address of the bookstore. I don't know why it surprised me that she would know it, but it did.

"She, what, she came in, got to know you then, maybe, I don't know, she comes in one night after she figures she can trust you and she says, 'you've got to help me with this thing'?"

I nodded. There's not much more to say. Burton nodded back, then leaned back in her chair.

"I pride myself on knowing who is going to lawyer up and who won't, you know," Burton said. "Miss Durand is going to lawyer up. Why haven't you?"

"Because I didn't do anything wrong."

"You're way too smart of a man to think that's actually a defense. Out with it—why haven't you even asked about seeing a lawyer, yet?"

I leaned forward, "I know that you spend most of your time dealing with people who are crooked and that they try every trick in the book to get out of whatever situation they are in other than telling the truth, but it's been my experience that telling the truth first is usually the best way to proceed."

Her right eyebrow cocked. She nodded with a grin. "Refreshing."

"As you figured—we really haven't known each other long at all."

Burton nodded. She flipped the folder closed. "Tell me the story," she said.

So I do. I tell her everything, no matter how crazy it all sounds. I figure it's just easier this way. Tell the truth and no matter how badly the system treats you, at least you know you tried. I'm about halfway through the whole spiel, just now getting to the part with the tarot card reader when I notice something: she hasn't even blinked the whole time. Nothing I'm saying to her is surprising. She hasn't even looked at the mirror where, undoubtedly, her partner is standing. She just stays focused on me. I finished by telling her everything about the attempt to take on Delores. "…and that's when you and your partner showed up."

When I said the name, something happened behind her eyes. She tried to hide it, but it was there. She tapped her index finger on the desk twice. Then she opened up the file folder and slid two pictures of Delores at me. "This is the woman you were chasing?"

"Delores Vandecamp, yeah," I said.

"Under what authority?"

"Someone had to—,"

"I asked," she said, "under what authority?" She's staring at me like there's a specific answer she expects. Like there's a code word I'm supposed to use.

"Someone has to try to stop this woman," I said.

"And you thought it would be you and Ms. Durand? Why?"

"Let me ask you this," I said, leaning forward, "were you there to stop her? I mean, were you there specifically about her?"

She waited a moment, then tapped the folder with the pictures again, "What do you think?" She flipped that folder closed and pulled another one. She opened it and I see that it has a large stack of paper and clipped to the top of the first page is a picture of Stacey. "You claim that you had only met Ms. Durand recently, is that correct?"

"Yes."

"And that you employed her at your bookstore based on, quote, 'a good feeling about her.'"

"That's right," I said.

"When did you find out that she was a practitioner of magick?" Burton asked without looking up from the page.

It was as if thunder had peeled forth in the room.

"So…wait, so, you believe?" I asked.

"When, Mr. Goldman?" she asked again, this time looking up

at me.

"Not…um…not for a few weeks. Like I said, she came in with a pretty extensive knowledge about new age stuff, but I didn't know that she was actually someone who practiced," I explained.

"Are you aware of the existence of the investigative body that calls itself the Malleus Maleficarium?" Burton asked.

"The witch FBI? Yeah, I know about them."

"At any point, did you consider that this might be a case better handled by them than by two non-affiliated amateur detectives?" Burton asked.

"Hey, there's no need to get mean," I said.

"Answer the question, please."

"No, I guess I just got so caught up in all of it that I didn't really consider that we should tell them. I'll be honest, I've never really had any run-ins with them, and I wasn't terribly sure that they even really existed."

She tilted her head to the side a bit. "Well, they do. Not only do they, but your friend, Ms. Durand, has applied to the agency on more than one occasion," Burton said.

I didn't say anything.

"She was denied both times, as you can well guess. Do you have any guesses as to why that might be?" Burton asked.

I shook my head no.

"Both times, that agency deemed her…" Burton said, flipping through a few pages until she found the one she wanted. She traced the sentences with her finger as she read aloud "…'too violent.' They say she is 'too prone to non-diplomatic thinking,' that she is 'incapable of de-escalating situations,' and that she is 'prone to vigilante thinking.' These are their exact words."

I wanted to argue with her because she was attacking someone I'd come to care for, but I had to admit that these things did line up with the list I'd started to keep in my own head. Burton leaned back in her chair and crossed her arms over her chest. "I'm guessing right about now you're thinking that these things line up pretty well with what you've noticed of her behavior, am I right?"

I didn't want to agree, but I had to. I nodded. She nodded back.

"I'll level with you, Mr. Goldman, there are two basic questions I have—one is this: if you knew about the existence of the Malleus organization, why didn't you just report what you were learning due to Ms. Durand's unauthorized investigations to them to handle once it became clear that you were out of your depth? And two is this: Once it became clear that Ms. Durand's endgame was a physical confrontation with Delores Vandecamp, an actual hand-to-hand combat with the woman, why didn't you report what you were seeing to the Malleus organization, or even maybe just to your local law enforcement agency?"

I wasn't trying to be flippant, but all I could do was shrug. "I don't know," I said. "I got...caught up in the momentum and suddenly, we were there, standing in front of Delores."

Burton nodded. "Had anyone died in that confrontation, Mr. Goldman, you would be headed to trial for, at the very least, manslaughter. Do you know that? Simply because these things involve supernatural forces does not negate the law. You're a very lucky man that no death occurred." She flipped all the folders closed. "Very lucky on two accounts, now, because I believe that you went into this without actually thinking through what could have happened. I buy that you got caught up in all of this before you really thought it through. Ms. Durand, however..." she said, letting it trail off.

"What's going to happen to her?" I asked.

"That all depends on what she says to my partner. They're having a very similar conversation right now, but I expect that her answers are quite a bit different from yours." Burton stood up. "Someone will be by in a moment to release you."

"That's...that's it, then?" I asked.

"You're free to go. Something tells me, though, that this is not the last conversation we're going to have, so don't leave town."

I nodded. She nodded back and walked out of the room. Time crawled again for who knows how long before a man came in, unlocked my handcuffs and lead me out through a maze of hallways to the lobby. "May I sit here and wait for my friend?" I asked. The man shrugged and walked off.

Again, time went strange. I had forgotten to put on a watch before we left on this adventure of ours, and they had my phone until I went to the window near the front door to retrieve it. Eventually, though, Burton came walking down the hallways.

"You're still here?" she asked, stopping in front of the bench. She checked her watch, "I told you to go home hours ago."

"Yeah," I said. "How much longer, do you think?"

"Well," Burton said sitting down. "As it turns out, Ms. Durand had quite a bit of information. Not only does her story check out with yours, but it happens to move us a bit further along in our own investigation. In a way, it's fortuitous that you're still here because we're going to do," Burton said. "We are going to sit down and share information. You saved us the trouble of having to wait for you to come back. So," she stood and gestured for me to do the same, "if you wouldn't mind." I stood and followed her down the hall. "Would you like anything? More coffee? Something?"

"I'm good for now," I said.

We entered a room almost exactly like the one I'd been in earlier. Stacey was sitting in a chair on one side, Burton's partner was on the other. Stacey's face lit up to see me, but before she could say anything, I shook my head. Burton gestured for me to sit next to Stacey while Burton took a chair next to her partner.

"Derek Goldman, this is my partner, Special Agent Lowe. Paul, you remember Mr. Goldman," Burton said as she sat.

"I'll ask again, shouldn't we have some sort of legal representation present?" Stacey asked.

"If we were charging you with anything, yes, but we're not. It's not exactly a reset button, but I'm hoping that we can let the past few hours go and start from scratch," Burton said. I looked at Stacey. Her jaw was set, but I could tell she understood we were being offered something, here. Neither of us said anything.

"Okay," Burton said, "good."

She flipped open a few folders and explained what they had gathered about the group that had made the weapon that Delores was carrying. They'd gotten just far enough to understand that it was a physical object, but that it was also acting in some way like a

160

portal. Burton also let us know that Delores had begun to kill the other members of the group along with giving us an idea of how many people she'd murdered beside. Burton let us know that one of the effects of the blade was that it was drinking the blood of the victims. I felt sick to my stomach as she talked and showed us the pictures of the victims.

"So, what have you come up with so far?" Burton asked.

Stacey looked at me and made a gesture. Lowe stepped out. So, I went back over it again—let them know that we'd visited other people who had examined the fragment of the blade. I let her know what the different examinations had come up with and that it all added up to the fact that the thing that they had tried to put in the blade was, instead, still in some other dimension and was using the blade to try to come through. Whatever parts of it had come through were seeping their way into Delores and making her superhuman.

Lowe came back with a strange look on his face and an envelope in his hands. On the back, where he'd already opened it, I could see a glop of wax and some kind of symbol pressed in. Stacey's eyes went huge.

"What's that?" I asked.

Lowe handed it to Burton along with another, thinner slip of paper. "Lab report is back on the metal she had, and then this." She pulled out the letter, written on what I was sure was hand-made paper, then her eyes cut to Stacey. She folded the letter back up and handed it to Lowe. "Where did this come from?" she asked.

"Courier," Lowe said. "Arrived just as I walked past the front door."

Burton set the envelope down and I saw that the symbol in the wax was a hammer crossed with a branch that came to a point. Then it hit me: a wand. The symbol was a hammer crossed with a wand. In fact, it almost looked like one of those circles with a slash through it that people use to mean "no" or "against." As in the hammer was slashing through the wand saying "no wands" or maybe "no magick." The message, it came on me all at once, was from the Malleus people.

"We've had the lab run tests on the shard you had in your custody. Tell me, how did you come by it, again?" Burton asked. Something in her tone had changed from earlier.

"What did that message say?" Stacey asked.

"Why don't you just tell me how you got that shard of the blade?" Burton asked.

"What did the message say?" Stacey asked again, slower this time.

Neither of them said anything, they just stared at one another. I began to feel like all the momentum we'd built up was seeping away. We'd lose it if one of us didn't do something.

"Stacey," I said. That broke Stacey's concentration just enough. "Let's share."

"I don't know, Goldman; I don't think they're sharing all that they have with us, so why should we share everything we have with them?" she asked. We were all sitting less than two feet from each other.

"I assure you," Burton said, "we are sharing everything that is relevant to this case at the moment."

"And so are we," Stacey said.

"You don't think how you came to be in possession of a shard of this magickal blade is important to trying to track down the killer that is using this same blade?" Burton asked.

"Maybe, maybe not," Stacey said.

"Stacey," I said.

Then no one said anything for a few minutes. "Can we have a minute?" I asked.

Burton looked at Lowe, then they both got up and walked out of the room. I heard the door lock as they closed it.

"Look, you can feel it, right?" I asked.

"Feel what?"

"That we've gone about as far on this thing as we can by ourselves. We found the woman, and we tried to confront her, and she made short work of us, even with your friend Sharkey there. If we try it like that again, someone is going to get hurt very badly. Maybe even die. So we have to change up how we play this next

step." Stacey didn't say anything, but I could see the wheels were
starting to turn. "Now, here come these Federal agents who not
only believe that all of this is true, but they want the same things
we do. So, how about a little cooperation, yeah? I mean, what's it
going to hurt?"

"I want to know what that letter said. I mean, it was obviously
about me," Stacey said.

"And I get that, I do. However, is it a hill you're willing to die
on? I mean, is it such a deal breaker that you feel it's worth turning
down the level of resources and help these agents can bring to the
whole thing?" I asked.

She thought about it, then sighed. "Fine. Fine, I'll let it go. But
I have a feeling about this, Goldman—whatever they just learned
about me? It's going to come back and bite us in the ass."

I tapped on the door, knowing they probably hadn't gone far. I
was right. They stepped back in and sat down.

Stacey explained it to them as she'd explained it to me. Burton
gave the tiniest of nods at the end. "Okay. So, then, here's what I'm
proposing. You were able to locate Delores Vandecamp quickly. Do
you think that you could do that again?"

"I think that we can," Stacey said.

"Okay. So then I'm going to ask for your help in doing just that.
Once we have her in custody, we will then take possession of the
blade and dispose of it. At that point, you will have the thanks of
the Bureau."

"The fateful 'we'll take it from here,'" I said.

Burton nodded, "something like that, yeah. We acknowledge
that it seems we've been drawn together on this and I want to cap
this case as quickly as possible. It seems like the best way to do that
would be to ask you two to come on as consultants. Will you agree
to that?"

I looked at Stacey. She nodded at me, then reached out to shake
Burton's hand. Burton shook it and the tension in the room fell just
a bit.

"One thing needs to be very clear, though, before we go even
a step further—you are not to attempt to engage with Delores

Vandecamp physically. Is that clear? You leave all of that to my partner and I," Burton said.

"Okay," Stacey said. I don't know that I believed her, though.

"So look, what do we do with these things once we get hold of them? I mean, is there some place to just drop off this kind of stuff?" I asked.

"We're going to need to find neutrals."

"The what now?" I asked.

"Neutrals. People who actually put out a kind of anti-magick field," Burton said.

"There are people who do that?"

"Yeah. Haven't you ever been around someone that just seemed to…well, someone who just kind of lacked any sparkle? Seemed lifeless? They are often the person talking about a dead relative in the corner of a party. Kind of person who launches into the story about a dead pet three seconds after meeting you?" Stacey said.

"Oh," I said.

"They're not always like that, but it's a pretty good sign. Anyway, you take an object like one of these and give it to someone like that and it becomes just another piece of rusty junk sitting in an attic. At least until the neutral dies, then there's trouble. So, we need to find a fairly young one. Therein lies the problem," Burton said.

"What do you mean?"

"Well, they're going to have to be a fairly powerful neutral for objects like this. Finding a young person who is this much of a buzzkill is going to be difficult work. We're going to have to look in some fairly bad places."

"Goths?"

"Worse. Young Republicans, or the kinds of people who organize college campus ministries," Stacey said.

I looked at Burton, who nodded. "So, the problem we have has multiple layers. Find a woman who is now very likely under the control, or at least the influence, of some sort of large power from another dimension, subdue her non-lethally if at all possible, take the weapon and get it to a very powerful neutral and then contact someone from Malleus to come and either destroy the weapon or at least find some place to put it where it won't fall into anyone else's hands."

"None of this is shocking to you?" I asked.

"We didn't have time to get properly introduced—my partner and I work for the division of the Bureau that is specifically tasked with examining crimes that involve the supernatural," Burton said. I looked over at Lowe. He smiled back at me.

"Like that TV show?"

Burton exhaled. "We're where the idea for the show came from. Or, at least, someone who used to work for the Bureau was."

"Still, even with that being the case, these circumstances aren't...I don't know...this level of direct other dimensional involvement isn't shocking to you in any way?" I asked.

"No, this isn't my first rodeo, Mr. Goldman," she said, and flipped the folder closed. She looked at me for a moment, then settled back into the chair. "My first week as with the bureau was the week we started what the guys were calling the 'the voodoo case' at the time. Very imaginative, eh? You see, on a tip about a mass murder case they'd been working, the two senior detectives in the department, well, they'd found a warehouse downtown full of human bodies hanging upside down. Massive air conditioners working overtime to keep the place nearly meat locker cold. That's why no flies."

"I'm sorry?" I asked.

"When we first got the case, I asked, 'how come there weren't any flies?' I figured a warehouse full of bodies, there'd be flies all over it. You see, I was still stuck in that mode of thinking that the world worked the way I expected it to. I figured, the kind of people that would store a large number of bodies in a warehouse, they'd have to be hotheaded people. They wouldn't think through a problem like how to keep the place hidden. But you know what the world has taught me since that day? That there are really only two types of bad guys—the dumb ones and the smart ones. That's why our whole system is set up to recognize different levels of murder. Some are so thorough about murder, though, they think to buy enough giant air conditioners to keep every square foot of a huge warehouse cold enough that human flesh stays frozen." She took another sip. "Turns out, there was an…agreement…between several of the local gangs and a few of our more colorful groups of magick practitioners, and you better believe that since that case, I know the difference between magick with a 'c' and magick with a 'ck,' Mr. Goldman. Turns out, even some of the more stupid local groups could envision a world where human sacrifice was important. That's where so many of these groups, these covens or solar lodges or what have you, have the jump on us in the police. We still expect that the world functions the way we think it does—scrambled eggs are for breakfast, when it rains you open an umbrella, etc. In that world, a man walks into a nice restaurant with a young boy, you think 'must be custody weekend.' You don't think that maybe he bought that kid at an auction and this is the one night a week he lets the poor little bastard out of his chains, cleans him up, and lets him pretend to be a human. In that world, we don't think that the reason we can't find any evidence in an important case is because some priestess cut the entrails out of a 23 year old former employee of Enterprise rent-a-car while he screamed and then she fed those guts into the fire while chanting the name of a powerful spirit from the other world, asking it to block the way to our victory. I certainly didn't think any of those things that first day on the job when I walked into that warehouse and saw those bodies. You know what was worse?" she asked.

"What?" I said, only just then realizing I'd been leaning further and further across the table to hear what she had to say.

"They were labeled. The bodies were labeled. Little toe tags just like we use, only these not only checked height, weight, and sex, but they had prices. See they weren't just killing these folks and then hanging the bodies up, they were selling them. Had a whole system for how much they would charge for that person. Even better, there were sometimes three or four different numbers on those tags."

"Like MSRP on a car?" Stacey asked.

Burton nodded and leaned forward in her chair, elbows on the desk, "I asked my partner at the time, he's since retired, who was the more experienced detective, why multiple numbers. He didn't hear me. I think maybe he was just as much in shock as I was. After about ten minutes of wandering around, though, I saw it."

"What was it?" I asked.

"It was race, gender, and age. Now, most of the gangs that were doing the catching and storing of these bodies we would eventually find out were black or Hispanic. But the tags on white kids' toes had higher prices than the black or Hispanic ones. They were participating in something this fucked up, this far outside, and there was still racism and sexism at work. White, teenage girls were the highest prices, black adult males lowest."

"But that still doesn't..." Stacey started but trailed off.

"Explain the multiple numbers? Well, see I eventually got an answer on that, too. We hauled in a man on an unrelated charge and as he was talking about what he did for a living, the two guys questioning him started to put two and two together and figured out that his whole job in the gang was that he was one of the transporters. He and a buddy would get a call with a street corner and a car and a color. They'd go to that corner and there they'd find the car that was the color named. They'd find the keys in one of the wheel wells then take the car to the warehouse and the body or bodies would be in the trunk, but they didn't have to handle them. The people who worked at the warehouse did. Once the bodies were out, they just took the car to the chop shop. Eventually, though, the guys got to know the other guys and they would have a cigarette or three and talk. When we got far enough to give him immunity to spill on the whole operation and asked him about the numbers, we found out. See, the numbers were based on how likely it was that this body could be pawned off as a virgin."

"Jesus," I said.

She nodded. "It was an entire industry, up to and including ways of trying to rip off the customer. That warehouse was organized like a showroom. Need a black male teenager who was probably a virgin? We have that right over this way. Middle aged white woman with blonde hair? I think we have one of those over here. That day, in that warehouse, though? That was the day I stopped believing in the world the way I'd seen it for almost twenty-five years, and started to understand that there were borders far beyond what I could see."

Burton paused for a moment, then said, "As a hound, you were using your ability to home in on Ms. Vandecamp, right?"

I looked over at Stacey. She shrugged, "I didn't say anything."

Burton's eyes never left mine. "No, but you *have* been using his abilities to help you find Ms. Vandecamp, haven't you?"

"I was only just informed about it," I said.

"You didn't know that you had this ability?" Burton asked.

I shook my head. "In my whole life, I have always been around people who use energy in lots of different ways…mind you, none of them as direct as some of the people that I've met today…I've always found myself attracted to them, but it never occurred to me that there was a specific ability involved."

Burton nodded. "I see. And Ms. Durand, here, only just let you in on the fact she was using your ability to her advantage?"

I nodded back. "Look, it's not like he was hurt or anything. I mean, fuckin' A, we managed to get pretty far even without all the fancy tech you guys have. Just plain old detective work got us here."

"Sharkey is good, but not that good. Did you have other help?" Burton asked.

Stacey's eyes got huge. "How do you know about Sharkey?"

A tiny smile played across Burton's lips, but was gone almost instantly. "My first name is Miranda," Burton said.

I watched as Stacey put it together. "Oh."

"Yes. Oh," Burton said. "But, again, they're not good enough to do something like that all on her own, not unless *a lot* has changed in the last few years. Did you have other, outside help?"

Stacey nodded but didn't say anything more.

"From whom?" Burton asked.

"It's not really all that important. Thing is, we won't be able to use her information again."

"Her?" Burton asked. "So this was a female someone?"

Realizing her mistake, Stacey folded her arms and looked away.

"Was it someone from Malleus?" Burton asked.

The air was thick with tension.

"Ms. Durand...Stacey...the only way we're going to move forward is if we share information with one another. Who did you talk to?" Burton asked, leaning forward onto the desk.

I nudged her with my elbow, but Stacey still wouldn't say anything.

"Ms. Durand," Burton said.

Stacey still wouldn't say anything. I looked at Burton. It was clear that, though we had agreed to hit some kind of reset button, that newfound sense of cooperation was disappearing fast. I didn't know what, but I knew that Burton was going to make a power move if Stacey didn't say something.

"We talked to—," I started to say, but Stacey elbowed me in the ribs. I looked over at her and she continued to stare forward. Burton looked at me pointedly. I stared at the floor.

Burton closed her eyes and shook her head, "Enough." She turned to Stacey and stared her down for a second, then turned to Goldman. "You're A positive, right Ms. Durand?" Burton asked in a tone that told me she already knew.

"Yeah, so?" Stacey said.

Burton nodded again. "One of the prelim results we've gotten back from the blade shard so far is that there is blood on it. One tiny little spot, about the size of the head of a pin is A positive, but the other splatters on it?" Burton said, then stopped. Stacey sat back. "AB negative. Now, anyone will tell you that this whole blood typing thing has some margin for error, especially when it's coming off of a weapon, and especially with some age, but to have that big a difference in blood types, that's...that's really something." Lowe whistled. I thought to myself that was a fairly cheap bit of theater, but I could see that for Stacey, it worked. "Mr. Goldman, do you know the percentage difference in people in the US who have A positive blood? It's one of the most common types. Do you know the percentage that has AB negative?"

"I'm guessing not many," I ventured.

Burton nodded again, and waited. When Stacey still hadn't said anything, Burton shrugged. "Did she tell you about Michael Velmoor?"

Stacey flinched and whispered, "Shit," involuntarily.

"Or did she give you the 'I used to be homeless and I lived in the back alleys' backstory, instead? The story of her time as the apprentice to the great Bruja of the alleys?"

"Who is—," I started to say.

"Now wait a—," Stacey started at the same time.

"When were you going to tell him?" Burton asked, turning on Stacey once more.

Everyone fell silent. Goldman was looking from Stacey to Burton and back like he was watching tennis.

"Michael Velmoor was a sensitive, like you. A hound, or a sniffer, the kids say. That's a pretty vulgar expression, but it gets to the point. When we dug up Stacey's folder, I knew I'd heard her name before. Turns out there *was* another case right around the time she had her first run in with Delores Vandecamp, the one that lead to her being denied entry into Malleus."

"Look, I think maybe we ought to—," Stacey began.

"Hold on," I said. "Let her finish."

"The blade sample she's been using? It did wound her, that's true, but it wasn't lodged in her wound," Burton said. Stacey shook her head and walked away. I knew this had to play out, so I kept an eye on where she was going while Burton finished talking to Goldman. "It was lodged in Michael Velmoor. She removed it before police got on the scene. Or, at least, that's what the medical examiner thought. That there had been massive trauma due to some kind of bladed weapon, but that the weapon had been removed. I had thought that the Velmoor case was unrelated until I saw the bit of blade she's carrying around. It matches the wound from that case, and the drawing I had one of the forensics guys do. He guessed that it would look exactly like that. Then, all of a sudden, this case comes along and it all clicks together."

"I'm guessing the day that she walked into your shop would have been about, say, middle of March?"

"What makes you..." I drifted off.

"That would be within a few days of the day that Michael Velmoor was killed," Burton said. "Technically, he was one of the first victims of Delores Vandecamp after she fell under the influence of the shadow blade that was made by the group of extremely gifted amateurs that called itself The Order."

I didn't say anything.

"You, Mr. Goldman, were her second choice as a sensitive. She knew she needed one to find Delores. I'm betting she had a list of, maybe, four names? Five, maybe?"

"Why that number?" Goldman asked.

"Because that's the number of sensitives that we know of who live in the area," Burton said. "I don't know how, yet, but somehow, Stacey Durand had or has access to some part of our files, or maybe someone else's who would have that kind of information." She looked at me. "The message we just got? That was what it was tipping us off to. She isn't who she's been telling you she is."

"I don't understand," I said looking at Stacey. It wasn't the truth, though. There was a part of me that was starting to put some things together, as well, and I didn't like the picture they were adding up to.

Burton's phone rang. She pulled it out of her pocket and said, "Burton." She listened for a few minutes then said, "We'll be there." She pressed the red circle and then put the phone away. "We need to get to the medical examiner's office."

"Another one?" Lowe asked. She nodded.

"I put in a call to the local medical examiner. I wanted to know when Amy Paulson was brought in. Not only did she just hit the slab, but there's been another one."

"What about them?" Lowe asked.

"I think maybe they have a conversation they need to have," she said. Turning back to us, she said, "We have to go take care of this, but we'll be back. You aren't under arrest, of course, and technically you're free to go. However, I would ask that you stay put. We shouldn't be too long, but if you need food or anything, tell the officer out here at the desk." She opened the door but then stopped. "When we do come back, I hope that our partnership is a little less...strained." With that, she walked out and Lowe followed.

The silence that fell was deafening. I shifted in my seat a bit, cleared my throat.

"She's wrong, you know," Stacey said.

"Wrong about what?" I asked. I tried very hard to keep the heat out of my voice, but I didn't do such a great job of it.

"About a lot of it."

"Michael Velmoor?" I asked.

"I just knew him as Big Mike. He worked security for The Fish. As you can imagine, The Fish isn't big on having people walk in knowing something he doesn't. So, he's got all these kind of people working for him who sniff out all kinds of things. It's so no one can get the drop on him. So, I asked Big Mike to help me out. He…kind of had a thing for me. So he agreed to help," Stacey said.

"Why didn't you ask one of your other people—the ones who can see and feel remotely?" I asked.

"I don't know," she said. "I didn't think of it. I…I wanted to find Delores, only I didn't know that was her name, fast."

"Why?" I asked.

Stacey shifted in her chair. She shook her head and muttered, "Fuckin' A."

"Look," I said. "As of right now, you and me? We're on thin ice. So if there's more to say, you need to say it, because I'm not going to have another thing drop on me out of nowhere like this. If someone tells me something about you and me that I don't already know, I'm going to walk. Honestly, I'm about three seconds from walking out of here anyway. So…" I let that hang in the air.

"I was trying to get in to Malleus, like I said," she said.

"Ok…and?" I asked.

"The stuff I told you about the Bruja? That's true. Well, I mean, most of it. At any rate, I wanted to get into Malleus. It's why so many of the people I know are…iffy…around me. They knew I'm trying to go Fed, as Sharkey puts it. But, I mean, I want to try to help. Especially with things like this. The problem is that they didn't like something in my application, like I told you."

"What do you mean?" I asked.

"I don't know. They were never super specific. See, they don't have any laws or regulations breathing down their neck about what they have to disclose to an applicant or whatever. So all they said was 'we're still thinking on it.' But I'm not stupid, you know? I know what that means. So, I thought to myself, okay, I'll go out and solve a case on my own. I'll bring someone in and then they'll rethink their position."

"And somehow Delores Vandecamp wound up being the case you were trying to bring in?"

"At the time, all anyone in the alleys knew was that there was this woman who was teasing guys into thinking they were going to get into her pants and then cutting them. She hadn't killed anyone, yet. It was all just getting guys alone and all worked up and then slicing into a leg or an arm. So, I asked Big Mike if he would help me track her down."

"He was there when you were attacked?" I asked.

Stacey nodded. "Whatever she was, then, she didn't look it. She looked like some stereotype of a librarian. Thing is, though, when Big Mike moved in to grab her, she went nuts. Fuckin A, Goldman, I've never seen anything like it except in kung fu movies. I didn't know what to do. She cut me once, but she…she sliced Big Mike to bits. He must've had something on him, though…some kind of charmed weapon or armor or something. There was a loud 'clank' like a machine might make if a huge gear got caught. She stopped for a second, long enough for me to get a fairly good look at her, then she leapt up the fire escapes."

"And that's when you found the shard?" I asked.

Stacey nodded, "Yeah. It was sticking out of one of his ribs. By that point, someone had managed to get a hold of the cops and I could hear the sirens. But I know from dealing with cops, you know? They don't buy any of this shit, though they see it every day. So I snatched the shard and ran. I was lucky that she had only really sliced me shallow, like a warning or something. I managed to get away."

"And…?" I asked, because I could tell there was more.

"I hid out a few places for a while, a week or so maybe, until I had healed enough to move again, then I went looking for Aldini."

"And instead you found me."

Stacey nodded. "That's why I don't want to tell them I talked to Gloria. Because then they'll want to talk to Gloria, and if they do, what's to stop her from telling them I applied?"

"They seem to know a lot already," I said. "But let me ask this—why do you not want Burton and Lowe to know you applied and were rejected and that was what started this whole chase?"

"It'll just sound stupid, now," Stacey said.

"Try me."

"It's embarrassing," Stacey said.

"We're trying to catch a killer who, every minute we don't, is becoming more and more possessed by something that several different people who know these kinds of things have described as extremely powerful, and you're worried that these people will look down on you?"

Stacey exhaled loudly, "I mean, I get it, when you put it like that, but…"

"We have to tell them that it was this Gloria person who tipped us off, Stacey."

"Fuckin' A" Stacey said, folding her arms and laying her forehead on them.

4. Special Agent Paul Lowe

On the way to the car I kept thinking that even for Burton, this was strong-arming. I hadn't known her very long, though. What I had gathered up to that point was that she was someone who always had a plan. So if she came down like a ton a bricks, it must be leading up to something.

"Something is on your mind?" Burton asked as we got into the car.

"Yeah," I said. "Look, we haven't known each other all that long, and all of this is way more your territory than mine right now, but…"

"You're wondering why I would come down so hard on Durand if I'm trying to build some kind of coalition with her, even if it's just for information sharing?"

"She seems like a good enough kid. But I mean, even just basic psychology would say to be nice if you want someone to be nice back," I said.

"That's true, but you have to have run into people like her before. She's a classic manipulator. If someone is nice to her, she starts thinking about how to get what she wants from them. You saw Goldman's face when I gave him the Velmoor information, right?" I nodded. "Imagine if that were us. Imagine if we were in confrontation with Vandecamp and she got the drop on us because Durand only gave us half-truth about something? We can't take that risk. So, right up front, I let her know that I'm not someone she can play."

I shook my head. "Risky."

"Everything about what we're doing is risky," she said.

We were downtown in a few minutes. The medical examiner's office seemed more like a long hallway behind a door. His desk was to one side. He was a tall man, bald, with thick glasses, in a white coat.

"Special Agent Burton?" he asked, standing. "John Gonzales"

She walked to him and extended her hand. They shook and then he said, "I just finished doing the workup on the body you asked me to contact you about, and, as I said, there's been another one that I'm almost certain is related."

We arrived at the last door on the left. Gonzales opened it and we went into a large bay with green tiles and a drain in the center. Along the wall were six small steel doors. Gonzales walked to the top door on the left and opened it, sliding the long shelf out. On it was a man who had been quite tall when he was alive. He looked to have been in his early twenties and in extremely good shape, physically. Though he had olive toned skin, he was obviously very pale in death. The man took a second to look at Burton, then flipped open his folder. "Agent Burton, meet James Abadi, twenty-three. Up until recently he was a grad student in science at the university."

"Cause?"

The man moved the sheet back and we could see that his torso was shredded.

"Multiple stab wounds, as you can see. All of them fairly deep. Not particularly well aimed if the idea was a quick death, either, so I'm guessing that wasn't a goal. Of course, like the other young woman you asked me to contact you about, cause of death ultimately was exsanguination. Just like that body, too, the crime scene guys say the place was clean. So, where did all the blood go?"

Burton didn't say anything.

"You figure, though, with this number of cuts, she...what...she tortured him before draining it?" I asked.

"Looks like," Gonzales said. "Compound fracture on the left tibia, clean break on the left elbow—snapped right through it. Also, interestingly enough, some evidence of sexual contact relatively recently, possibly right around the time of death but not postmortem."

"So," Burton said, leaning in toward the torso, "she lures him to bed, she gets off, then she...what...she takes the opportunity to subdue him and torture him?"

"Why go to all the trouble?" I asked. "Why not just kill him outright?"

"Or, more to the point," Burton said, "if she wants information, why not just go right to the torture?"

Silence settled in as Burton moved around the body looking closer at all the cuts.

"Any fragments left?" Burton asked.

"Negative," Gonzales said. "Whatever she did it with, it was beyond razor sharp. Not even any micro-serration. These are single cuts that go that deep. You say you think this is a woman?"

Burton didn't say anything.

"I have to tell you, I'm a feminist and all, but look...she'd have to be immensely strong to make cuts this deep in one motion, no matter how sharp the weapon, and with no serration of any kind. The edges of these cuts are perfectly smooth. I have serious doubts that this could be a woman."

Burton didn't say anything for a while, then straightened. "Can I get a copy?"

He handed her a small stack of papers from the back of the folder, "I figured you'd ask, so..." She smiled at him and took the papers. "And now, can we see Amy Paulson?"

Gonzales nodded and walked us to the last door on the right. He opened it and pulled the shelf out. She was completely intact; the only obvious cuts were on her wrists. She was just as pale as the Abadi boy had been.

"No torture, here, just straight for the blood," I said. Burton nodded. "Same basic idea—she bled out, but again, the crime scene guys say there was no blood in the bath, so where did it go? Some signs of sexual contact, though nothing as definite as with Abadi. Mostly because of the bath."

Burton tapped the folder on the shelf and asked, "If any more come in like this...this kind of clean exsanguination, you'll call me?"

Gonzales nodded, "You bet. Should I let local PD in on the fact that you think this may be serial?"

Burton looked at me then back at the doctor. "You do what you think you have to, but I'm going to bet that if you do, they aren't going to believe this. That could cause trouble for you down the road. Besides, we're hoping to wrap this case up by tomorrow at the latest."

"Okay," Gonzales said.

"Thank you, Doctor," Burton said then walked briskly for the door without waiting for him or for me. I hurriedly followed.

"Agent Burton?" Gonzales called just as she hit the door. She turned. "Is this going to keep happening?"

Burton said, "I'm hoping we can stop her soon." Then she went through the door with me in tow.

Back in the car I asked, "She's getting stronger, isn't she?"

Burton nodded. "The blood isn't just being pulled into the blade. We've seen that before. No, somehow, it's fueling all of this. She gains more strength from the blade drinking blood. But is it direct transmission, blade to her? Or is it because the more blood it drinks, the wider the portal becomes, and the more of whatever it is that is on the other side comes through and into her?"

"The sex somehow charges the thing, doesn't it?"

"I think so, yeah," Burton said. "There's this old idea that sex is the point where all of a person's energy is stirred up and available. Some practitioners use that moment to work their magick."

"Sex magick. Yeah, I've heard about that stuff," I said.

"It's a big part of what these kids were doing in their circle. The 'great rite,' so to speak, it's sex. The idea is that both people involved work to get their energy in balance while having intercourse, then get to the point where they're both about to climax and then, as they do, they cast their thoughts toward whatever it is they are wanting to happen," Burton said. "And there's also the idea that at the moment of death, someone's full energy is released whether they want it to be or not, so…"

"So she gets them to the point of orgasm, then she kills them and the energy comes through the blood into the blade?" I asked.

"I don't know, but it's starting to look like that might be the case," Burton said.

"So there'll probably be another one tomorrow?"

"I think so, yeah," Burton said.

"Is there some way we can use that to catch her?"

"I was wondering the same thing. Problem is that, so far at least, from the other files and this one, I can't see a…if you'll pardon me…a 'type.' It seems like she just grabs whatever is handy, not that she's looking for something specific. Still, though, I'd be willing to bet that if we can somehow predict who she's going to want next, we could catch her before she goes after them and she'd be at her weakest."

I waited for a moment or two, then asked, "Do you think it's her preference we have to worry about or—?"

"—Or is it the preferences of whatever is trying to come though the object? More importantly, why Amy Paulson? That's not random, and certainly not male." she finished my thought. "What if…what if Vandecamp wasn't upset that none of the men in the group liked her? What if…" Burton said and then let it trail off.

"What if she was actually into Paulson the whole time, you mean? That it was that relationship, not any of the others, that made her upset?" I asked.

"We need to be careful, here," Burton said. "This can't turn into some kind of 'she was bisexual so she went crazy' kind of scavenger hunt. The signs might point that way, but then again, they might not. At least not at this point. We have to be better than any of that 'blame the crime on the stereotype' nonsense."

"Just throwing ideas out there," I said. "Besides, could be like I said…the preference of whatever is coming through might be changing her M.O."

"We're going to need to talk to Reid again," Burton said.

When we pulled back up to the station, I half expected to find Goldman and Durand gone. They were still sitting in the room where we'd left them, though. "I think we're ready to give you the last piece of information you wanted," Goldman said. "But, you need to understand, the information is sensitive."

"How so?" Burton asked.

"As in, if you want my help, and I'm thinking you do, then that means you need to take into account the fact that Stacey is my friend. And that she may have done things in the past that she isn't super proud of, but that doesn't mean you can browbeat her with those facts," Goldman said.

I looked at Burton pointedly. Burton nodded. "Agreed. As long as Ms. Durand comes clean, then we'll call this," Burton gestured toward the room, "an amnesty zone. Will that do?"

Goldman looked at Durand. Durand nodded. Immediately I felt the room relax.

"The connection we used was Gloria. She's a…" Stacey started but Burton's reaction was so visceral that she stopped.

"Gloria?" Burton asked. "Did I hear you correctly? Black hair, about five eight, says 'thee/thy/thou? That Gloria?"

Durand sat up straighter in her seat. "Yes."

Burton pulled out her phone, flipped through a few pictures and came to one where a woman who looked remarkably like the actress Cate Blanchett but with black hair was shown standing next to a man who was taller, with short, sandy-blonde hair and thick glasses. I was about to say something about the resemblance the woman had to the actress, only the next thing I knew, I was on the floor and Burton, Goldman, and Durand were all standing over me.

"Paul? Paul, can you hear me?" Burton was saying. She slapped my face lightly.

"Yeah," I said. "Yes. I can hear you."

Burton settled back on her heels. Goldman and Durand stood up.

"Everything okay in here?" a uniformed officer asked, sticking his head in the door.

"I think so," Durand said. "Do you think we should call the paramedics or something?"

"They're right next door," the officer volunteered.

"Paul?" Burton said.

I sat up on my elbows. I was light headed and embarrassed, but there was no real damage. "No, I think we're okay."

"I think we have it from here," Goldman said sort of shooing the officer out the door and closing it behind him.

I tried to get up, but Burton put her hand on my chest. "Paul, do you have any idea what may have just happened?"

"No," I said.

"Can I test a theory?" Burton asked.

"Will it hurt?" I asked only half joking.

"Not if you stay down here on the floor." Burton reached back to the table and got her phone again. She pushed slightly on my chest and I lay back down. "Okay, I'm going to show you a picture, and you just..." I didn't hear her finish her sentence because I passed out again.

When I came to, they were all crowded around me again. "What'd I miss?" I asked with a groan.

"How many fingers am I holding up?" Burton asked. She was holding up three so I said three. She nodded to herself.

"Here, let's get him into a chair," Burton said and Goldman extended his large hand. I took it and he pulled me to my feet. I was still fairly unsteady and they helped me to sit down.

"So, what's going on? What is it about that picture that makes me pass out?" I asked.

"I have a theory, only it complicates matters quite a bit," Burton said. She sat down across from me. Taking that as a signal that things were relaxing, Goldman and Durand sat down around the table as well. All eyes were on Burton.

"In an interesting bit of irony, it is now time for me to give you all some information. I promise, though, the only reason I hadn't included any of it in our earlier conversations was that I thought it was a separate case. It seems, though, that the two cases are going to end up connecting somehow," Burton said. Just then the door opened again and that same officer from earlier came in with four Styrofoam cups.

"One of the other officers says you guys could probably use some coffee, so I poured some up," the young man said. He was about six foot, had freckles and red hair, and large, blue eyes. As he passed out the coffee and set down some packets of sugar and creamer I saw a look pass between him and Goldman. Ah, I thought to myself, so that's how it is.

"Thank you," Goldman said. We all chimed in our thanks right after. The officer left.

"They're spying on us," Durand said. Burton nodded. "Probably think we're here as some kind of review of their efficiency or some such shit," Durand finished.

"It's not half bad, actually," Goldman said after he took a sip.

"Paranormal Investigation division has almost always been a two person job. At the very beginning, there was an idea of making it a three or four person squad, but that just didn't work out, trust-wise. So when I was brought in it was as a partner to the man who had been there for quite some time. He passed quite recently and so, when there came an opportunity to choose a new partner, I chose someone who had actually been a target in a recent case," Burton said. She gestured with her cup toward me, then took a sip. "Special Agent Lowe had recently been abducted right out of our own building."

"What?" Durand asked. I nodded but didn't say anything.

"By agents of Malleus Maleficarum," Burton finished. "Two of them. A male and smaller male or, more likely, a male and a female. They waltzed in and, using spells they had pre-prepared, they took Lowe for a total of maybe thirty minutes or so, then returned him. They wiped his memory of it, only, for some reason, they forgot to wipe the footage of them doing it. Now, here we are, on a completely separate case and simply showing you," she said, gesturing to me, "a picture of two Malleus agents makes you pass out. Twice. And it just so happens that this picture is of a male and female set of agents who tend to work together because they are brother and sister."

"That's Simon?" Durand asked.

Burton nodded, "that is, in fact, Gloria's twin brother Simon. They work together for Malleus. And here we find out that you two talked to Gloria, who is notoriously difficult to find because she has a tendency to wander aimlessly until her brother makes her focus on something, and she just so happened to know the location of the object and the woman we're all looking for. Now, this could all be coincidence, but…"

"I think we're all a bit old to believe in coincidence," Goldman said.

"Agreed," Burton said. She sighed long and loud. "We're going to need to talk to Simon." I could tell from her tone she had hoped not to have to. "That's not going to be easy. Especially considering we really don't have time for it."

"We could leave it, maybe," I said. "Try to put together a team and go after Vandecamp and then deal with this after."

Burton shook her head, "I have this feeling that if we do that, something about all of this," she said, gesturing from me to the floor, "will come back to bite us in the ass. No, they've got some part of the information we need. So, here's what I want," Burton said. She shifted her gaze from me to Goldman who was sitting across from her. "Special Agent Lowe and I need to go get this taken care of. What I'd like for you and Ms. Durand to do while we're doing that is to get our friend Sharkey and a few others on stand-by. We may need them. Also, I'm going to recommend holing up somewhere for a few hours of sleep. I'm guessing from the looks that you haven't gotten a lot recently, am I right?" Goldman begrudgingly nodded. "You have a phone?" Burton asked. Goldman took his phone out and they quickly copied each others' numbers. "When I call," Burton finished, standing up, "you answer." We all stood up after her and walked to the parking lot. "I had an officer drive your car here," Burton said, gesturing to where the big car sat. Goldman visibly relaxed. "I mean it," Burton said as Goldman and Durand walked to their car. "Go get rest." Goldman waved as they pulled away.

"Where to for us?" I asked.

"There's really only one way to get in touch with Simon," Burton said. She reached into her pocket and pulled out what looked like a business card, only it was black instead of the various shades of white that those tend to be. She ripped it in half. Immediately her phone rang. "Hello," she said and waited. "I think it's time we talk," she said. "Good, I'm glad. Where are you?" After a moment she said, "I see. That's fortunate for us, since we happen to be in the same city at the moment. Is there some place we could meet?" She waited a moment, then said, "yes, I'm familiar. That'll do just fine. We'll see you there." She hung up and got into our car. I climbed in beside her.

"Where to?" I asked.

"Isn't it interesting that he just so happened to be in the same city? Even more lucky for us, they happen to have an office in a building not very far from here," Burton said.

"Curiouser and curiouser," I said.

We pulled up to a lonely looking strip mall about ten minutes later. Only one of the offices had a light on inside. Burton opened the door without knocking. A small-ish waiting room with green leather couches and a tiny coffee table with a few old magazines on it.

"Come through, Agents," a voice said. Immediately I felt woozy and put my hand out on the wall to catch myself.

Burton looked at me with a question in her eyes. I nodded in return and she nodded back. We walked through a small divide and around a corner until we came to an office. Standing next to a beat to hell and back cheap old desk was the slender man from the photo. His hair was a bit shorter than it had been in the photo, but other than that, everything was the same, down to the black satin suit vest.

"Please sit," he said.

Burton slid slowly into the chair. I slid into the other one after her, thankful because it stops the room from spinning.

"To what do I owe this pleasure?" Simon asked.

"I need to know why," Burton said, taking the strong-arm role.

"Why what, Special Agent?" Simon asked, hissing more than a little on the letter s. His smile is cold, as well. For a second, I swear he's changing into a giant snake, but it doesn't happen.

"Enough," Burton said. "You and your sister waltzed into headquarters and took this man," she said, gesturing toward me, "obviously under the influence of some glamour. Where did you take him and why?"

Simon made a steeple of his fingers. I've seen people play up the cartoonish villain thing before, but he was fairly obviously taking it to extremes.

He smiled at me, "Were you harmed?"

"I want to know why," Burton repeated a little louder.

"Was he harmed at all?" Simon asked without taking his eyes off mine.

"I said enough, Simon. This can go a helluva lot more ugly than it is right now, and you know it. So let's be civil and cut the bullshit."

"Prophecy, Special Agent Burton."

"Oh, for fuck's sake..." Burton said and twists in her chair as if to leave.

The room goes silent for a moment.

"What prophecy?" I asked.

Simon leaned forward. "Don't," Burton said, but he's already started speaking.

"From time to time, Special Agent, we are alerted to the potential for someone to become very important in events. When we are alerted to such individuals it is customary to pay them a visit—"

"You mean abduct them," Burton said.

"—and to attempt to ascertain why they might be...special."

"Are you saying...are you saying there was some sort of

prophecy about me?" I asked.

Simon sat back in his chair again, and steepled his fingers once more.

"This is horse shit," Burton said. "If that was the case, you would have let me know like you've done in the past."

"You've been party to these...prophecy abductions?" I asked.

She stared at me for a second, then turned her attention back to Simon. "Why didn't you?"

"If our seer is correct, there isn't much time before this particular vision brings itself to fruition," Simon said.

"And let's say I buy this load of shit—what did you find?"

"That information is...proprietary," Simon said, his smile falling away.

Burton looked over toward the door, which is the first time that I've noticed we are not alone. The woman from the picture, Gloria, is standing in the corner of the room. "And if I ask her, I get the same answer?"

Simon said nothing, but I can tell it disturbs him that Burton and I can see his sister. Gloria doesn't move. She might as well be a statue.

"What about me?" I asked. "What if I ask you what you found?"

"Ah," Simon said, his snake-like smile returning. "That is another matter entirely. The subject of the prophecy has every right to ask."

"But you didn't bother to tell me there *was* a prophecy. Burton had to get me here to meet with you. Were you going to tell me?"

Simon looked down at his hands for a moment.

"I see. And why not?" I asked.

"That matters very little now, for here you are." His gestured with his palms open to me as if to present something.

"So tell me—what's the prophecy?"

"Are you saying that you wish for Special Agent Burt—"

"Yes, I'm okay with her hearing. Tell me."

"We were told of his soon to be importance," Simon said.

"I'm not following. Explain," Burton said, lowering her gun slowly.

Simon adjusted his collar, mopped at his brow with his handkerchief. "A low level prophet, though, of course, it seems indelicate to describe anyone in such coarse terms, but you understand I speak to you as a fellow agent," Simon said, nodding. Burton didn't move. "A low level soothsayer, a fortune teller who is not necessarily one of the people we use for delicate or nuanced work, you understand, came to use with information for sale. Her cards, which were fascinating in many ways, being a deck that was long out of print, an heirloom that had been handed to her by her mother's mother who said they'd come from—,"

"The point, please," Burton said.

"Yes," he said, mopping his brow again. "Quite. Well, she informed us of your partner, Special Agent Lowe," he motioned toward me. "She told us that he had come up in multiple forecasts for the future. He was the crux of an upcoming…I struggle to remember her precise phrasing. Quite a lot has happened since then," he said. Really looking at him, I could see that no matter whether he was being genuine or not, his smile would always seem false, oily.

"Do your best," I said.

He nodded toward me, "There was to be, she said, an event coming in which this man," he gestured toward me again, "would serve as the fulcrum, an important point of connection between our world, by which she meant, of course, the world of those who travel the paths of the supernatural, as you call it, Agent Burton, and yours, the world of more mundane concerns. No offense intended," he said.

"None taken," Burton said.

"And so we, being my partner, Gloria, and myself, set about an attempt to discover the whereabouts of Paul James Lowe. He was not an agent who had been, what is that delightful expression you use? 'On our radar'? Wonderful. He had not, so to speak, been on our radar. Finding him was difficult for a time until the tragic news of a year ago."

"The church bombings," I said without meaning to.

"Yes," Simon said, shaking his head. "Such unpleasantness.

However, a boon for us, proving in some ways, my partner Gloria reminded me at the time, the fundamental balanced nature of the universe. Good from bad. Bad from good. Always an equilibrium."

"Alright," Burton said. "So, you found out he was one of us and what, just decided to march into Quantico and take him? You didn't think maybe I was owed a courtesy call?"

"Ah," he said. "This is where I must admit more than a small amount of fault and apologize. You see, my partner, Gloria, is, well, a quixotic being. One moment she is the very soul of contemplation and reflection. A veritable philosopher, you might say. The next, she is all movement and flurry. This is what makes her unique and lovely, a one of a kind among humans. She's often been compared to the Fey, and I would agree. If there were someone who might be a partial-Fey, if such a thing were possible—,"

"Simon," Burton said.

"Yes. Quite. Well, I was preparing to make just such a call when my partner, Gloria, what is the other expression you use? 'Went off half-cocked'? Utterly delightful turn of phrase. She went off half-cocked, as it were, and was already inside the building before I caught up to her. She is ever so fast when she wills it so. I had no choice, then, but to, how did Abner say it so often, 'back her play'? She had decided a course of action and was already so far committed to it that I had no choice but to back her play and hope to make amends later. To wit," he said, gesturing toward himself then spreading his open hands.

Burton seemed to consider it for a moment. Only then did she fully relax and put her gun back in its holster. The tension in the whole room eased. "Okay," she said. "I buy it." She looked over at me, "you okay with this?"

"A prophecy?" I said, rolling my eyes.

"Perhaps that might be too strong a word. A seeing, yes, perhaps that might be a better turning of phrase. Prophecies tend to be about the end of the world, do they not? This might be better categorized as a kind of hint at things to come. And those things, dear Agent Lowe, seem to pivot around you," Simon said.

"So how does he get the memory back?" Burton asked.

"Were it your wish, I could quite simply tell you what transpired," Simon said.

"No," Burton shook her head. "I want it in his words from him."

"Very well. It is my deepest desire to give what you want to you. This will, of course, require that I work my will upon you once more, Agent Lowe. Do I have your consent?" Simon said. He all but winked with delight at the irony of asking now when he hadn't before. I looked at Burton. She nodded.

"Okay," I said. Without breaking eye contact from Burton I said, "anything he does looks even a little twitchy and I want you to give him a couple of new holes to think about." Burton nodded.

"How charming," Simon said, then knelt down next to me. He began chanting something and then put his flat palm on my forehead. Almost instantly I was back in a hazy version of the world. I could hear myself talking, and I said,

I had just put the folder on the top of the done pile when I noticed the bullpen (that's what we call the room with our desks, all us guys—not "officially approved nomenclature" but it keeps up morale so they don't say too much to us) was empty. Clock said 2:14, so that many people out for a long lunch wasn't an option. Don't lose faith in me when I say it was one of those moments where your skin starts to crawl for no real reason.

Two men in black coats walk in. At least, that's what it looked like at first. Turns out, one was a woman, but I didn't see that at all at first. One has on a fedora pulled down low, the other straight black hair that acted like curtains down her face. I'm thinking to myself that there's no way they got past security down in the lobby and reaching for my gun in the top drawer one the man says.

"I would appreciate it if you didn't."

And, look there's a lot about all of this you're not going to believe, but I'm hoping you'll keep an open mind. His eyes meet mine and my hand stops moving. Just like that.

"I'll only need a moment of your time, if you don't mind." The accent is vaguely European, but I couldn't place it. He starts to sit and I'm just about to warn him that there's no chair behind him when he comes to rest in one. I swear on my mother's grave it wasn't there two seconds before. Of course now, these

days, I know what he did, but back then, my jaw hit the floor.

"You are Special Agent Paul Lowe, are you not?" he asks.

"Paul," I say out of habit.

"Ah," he says. He leans back into his chair, making himself more comfortable. "Paul. Of course." He gestures with his left hand and the other man…well, I want to say that he walks to the door, but if I'm honest he drifts. I know how that's going to seem to you but there it is. As if on ice skates the other guy effortlessly drifts to the door and shuts it. The shadows in the room have grown very long and I'm wondering when that happened.

"Special Agent Lowe, I am not a man who likes to hurry things, but creating an opportunity to talk to you is costing my colleague and I quite a bit, so I must be brief."

Again, I'm dumbstruck. Though I desperately want to deny what he's said is what would happen, there's a part of me that is balls to bone convinced that is how it would go down.

"Simon," the person near the door, who I can now hear quite clearly is a woman, says.

"Ah, the chiming of the bells. What is life but a series of unfortunate time limits? It seems, Paul, we are out of time and must play out this scene elsewhere. Kindly take your pen," he said and I found myself picking up the pen, "and write a note to your partner, the lovely Mary Ann Winn, that you've gone for the day and won't be back until the morning." For no reason I could fathom, I found myself writing that exact note, tearing the note off and wheeling over to put it on her keyboard.

"Splendid. Now, if you will?" he said, standing and gesturing toward the door. I stood as well and began to move that direction.

"Coat," the woman near the door said.

"Ah, yes. Mercy me, but where would I be without you? Paul, if you would kindly take a moment and don your coat? You'll likely want your keys, badge, whatever ephemera you usually carry with you home. There's a chap," he said while I put on my coat, slid my weapon into my shoulder holster, and put my badge in my pocket.

"Wonderful. Now, if you'll come with us?" Simon said, again gesturing toward the door.

As we stepped through, rather than entering the outer office with the water cooler and leaking coffee pot from 1974, we emerge into a back alleyway somewhere downtown. I look back and for a second see my desk along with all the others and then, like a slamming door, only a brick wall. The wind has kicked up and Simon adjusts his collar and hat.

"Only a small walk from here, Special Agent Lowe," Simon says and I begin walking without remember wanting to. He falls in to my left, the woman to my right. "You'll of course pardon me for being so rude earlier, beside you is my sister, Gloria, without whom, as you've seen, I am quite useless."

"I greet thee," Gloria says without stopping, her eyes scanning the balconies and fire escapes along the alley.

"Do forgive her—normally she is the very soul of compassion and has a wicked wit, but at the moment she's a bit concerned that we're using the power so out in the open. Doing so tends to invite trouble, you see."

"Thou shouldst be concerned, as well," she said.

"I'll leave such dour contemplations to you, my dear. They suit you better," Simon said.

I don't know how long we walked along that same alleyway, but eventually we came to a door. It resembled the ugly back door of any bar you've ever seen. Sometimes I think there has to be a company that makes them that way because so many of them look the same.

"Ah," Simon says. "We've arrived." He moves around behind me, watching back down the alley, as Gloria says something under her breath and taps the door with her right index finger. The door folds in on itself, like a piece of paper being made into a swan or something. An origami door. Gloria steps through and says, "Clear."

"Ah, magnificent. If you would, please, Paul…?" Simon says, gesturing for me to follow Gloria, which I do without any question though I can't remember giving my legs the order to. Simon then follows us though and the door unfolds back into place. We're left in what could easily be the lobby of any Government building from the 1950s. Drab colors, the smell of floor polish, the echo of men's shoes clomping along the linoleum.

I want to ask where we are, to protest being basically kidnapped, and say more than a few choice words while pulling my gun on them, but I find I can do none of those things. Instead, I can only stare straight ahead and wait.

"Ladies and Gentlement, may I present to you Special Agent Paul James Lowe of the FBI," Simon said. In the darkness around us, I can hear people *talking. I can feel them out there, but I can't focus, even now. "You will recall that he is the subject of the vision we have all become privy to in the last few days. With the permission of the council, my sister and I will now perform a deep look into him to determine what we might expect."*

"Is this necessary?" a voice says. "After all, the vision has been verified."

"Verified, yes," Simon says. "However, as I'm sure we have all become aware, the more information one has when it comes to a vision, no matter the… veracity…of the prediction, the better one can decide if they wish to help it along or forestall it. We know nothing, after all, of Special Agent Paul Lowe other than that his name has come up."

From the darkness a different, deep voice says, "Proceed." Simon affects a kind of bow that seems somewhat insincere even in my shaky state, then turns to me and stares deep into my eyes. He waves his hands, making patterns with his fingers as if signing something for the deaf, all the while chanting something just under his breath. I feel a buzzing in my arms and legs. The room shimmers green and then yellow. Simon steps to my left as his sister steps around my right. She is making the same hand gestures and mumbling the same words. The buzzing grows throughout my body, rising up through my chest and coming into my head. I've also grown very cold. Once it gets into my head I start to panic. What are they doing? What if what they are doing is harming me? I try to resist whatever it is, yelling "no!" inside my head. Simon and his sister are moving faster around and around me, the mumbling going from under their breath to almost a yell. The buzzing grows louder and louder in my head until I can't hear my own voice still screaming "no!" at them. I'm so cold my hands and feet feel as though they are being pricked by thousands of needles.

Suddenly, the two stop, and the buzzing ends abruptly. I want to collapse, but something is holding me up. I'm exhausted and hungry and still very cold. Simon has stopped directly in front of me and his sister comes around from behind. They share a look, then turn to the darkness.

"And?" the deep voice asks.

"There is nothing," the sister says, hanging her head.

"Nothing?" the deep voice asks.

"Nothing," Simon echoes. "He is not in the slightest bit anything more than completely average. There is nothing hidden in him, about him, or around him. I…I confess I am baffled. I have never seen someone less touched by magick in my entire life."

"Then how can…?" the deep voice begins.

"I have no idea," Simon replies. There is the sound of a great number of people whispering in the darkness. The feeling of bodies moving around.

"We will need time to discuss this. Return him and wipe him clean," the deep voice says.

"At once," Simon says. I note there is none of the annoying amusedly superior tone in his voice, now. "Special Agent Paul Lowe, if you will," Simon says, gesturing as though he's showing me out, as though I were merely a guest who had overstayed his welcome. I begin to move, though, one foot in front of the other, as before. They say nothing on the walk back to the building. Gloria makes a few motions with her hands and says a few words as we walk back through the lobby and up the stairs to my floor. Simon makes similar hand gestures and says similar words as we walk into the office, now full of people, none of whom see anything happening. Simon gestures and I hang my coat up on the rack near the door. They walk me to my desk and Simon's sister moves my chair so that, when she makes the motion to do so, I sit down gingerly in it. I watch them walk out. Simon turns just before leaving the doorway and winks at me, then the room swims back into focus and the sounds of the people around me crash in.

I come back out of it and Simon sits back on his heels, lowering his hands.

"There," he said.

"But you said that your…scan or whatever the hell it is you did…you said to the group in that room that I was nothing, that I had no magick."

"And you don't, my dear," Simon said, as if it explained everything.

"But this prophecy still somehow involves me?" I asked.

"Yes. At it's very center. You are the prime mover, yet there is nothing in any way special about you. Don't you find that fascinating?" Simon asked with a smile.

"No," I said. "I don't."

"The foreseeing tells us that events are already building around you and yet there is nothing special about you, magickally. You must understand that to a man like myself, this is a delicious puzzle," Simon said.

"What do you know of Delores Vandecamp?" Burton asked.

Simon stands and goes back to his own chair. As he sat, he sighed heavily. "Nothing more than what we turned over to you. Why, has something more happened with that case?"

"No," Burton said. I almost stopped her but decided to let this play out. "No, I was just asking if there were anything more on your radar with her."

"I would be quite happy to step in and help you if the case is proving too much for you. Humans can sometimes have difficulty when the realms of magick are concerned," Simon said. I wondered if she could hear it, too; he had lost some of his almost-taunting sprightliness.

They were both lying to one another.

"Well, then, since that's all cleared up, we'll be going," Burton said. There was a guarded sense of urgency to her words. I stood up, wobbled a bit, but then regained my footing.

"How much longer will the effects take before they wear off?" I asked.

"It shouldn't be too much longer now," Simon said. Burton and I were almost to the door when Simon called from behind us, "Another group of people is seeking what you seek. They will find it first, but in the process make things far worse. You will have a choice, we are told, and what we worry about it that you will not take the shot."

Burton stopped and turned. "What happens if I don't take the shot?"

His eyes closed and he shook his head.

"Horseshit," Burton said.

His eyes bolted open and he looked at her. "We know this as surely as you know information which comes from your electronic webs. This will happen."

"The fate of the world—"

"We did not say 'the fate of the world.' While this matter is dire, it is not that level of threat. This does impact myriad lives, however. And it all comes down to you," he said, his eyes rolling over to focus on me.

"Next time, I want to know before you step into my building," Burton said, standing. I take that as a cue and stand with her.

"I can, of course, promise nothing, Special Agent Burton. The Fates weave what the Fates will."

"I mean it," she said and turned on her heel. She doesn't slow down at all and for a second I wonder if she's going to run directly into Gloria. At the last possible second, Gloria steps aside and Burton barrels through the door. I follow in her wake.

Once we're both in the car and she's started it and pulled away from the curb, I asked, "What gives?"

"What do you mean, 'what gives'?"

"Granted, I haven't known you that long, but you were genuinely angry at that guy. I thought for a second we were doing the dance, but you were actually furious."

"You can't let that guy sense that he has the upper hand in any way. He's barely human, anymore. I tried being nice once—once—but he nearly...well, it nearly went very badly. So he gets nothing but contempt from me and so far it's worked. But in this case, I actually am angry with him. With them. There are procedures we've worked out and he doesn't get to just decide to waive them."

"Ah, ok," I said.

"And nobody abducts my partner."

"We weren't partners at the time," I said.

"Doesn't matter," she said. "Doesn't matter."

"Okay," I said.

"Yeah," Burton said.

The quiet crept in for a bit, then she said, "you saw him start to change, right?"

"I noticed something. He lost some of his damned eloquence. What happened?"

"He was contemplating disappearing us, or at very least, wiping us clean," Burton said.

"How could you tell?"

"That shift in manner. I've never seen it before. He's never been anything but the condescending prick we talked to for most of that conversation. I'm thinking...I'm sorry, Paul, but I'm thinking that he altered your memory even as you were recovering it."

"What?"

"I think that they *did* find something, but that he kept that from you and from me and I really want to know why," Burton said.

"Well, I'm sorry that this all amounted to nothing," I said.

"On the contrary, we now know a lot. We know that they didn't pass this case off to me because they were swamped. We now know that you figure prominently into this thing, so my decision to bring you in was a good one. And we know that they are also looking for Delores. I think that's what those lies were about." Burton said. "Not to mention, while we were dealing with all of that, this whole thing did give me an idea."

"What's that?" I asked.

"Twins. You saw them in there, Gloria and Simon. They didn't even have to talk to one another they were so tuned in."

"Okay, sure," I said.

"This blade, this thing that Delores is using...it has a kind of twin—the other sword that the group made. I wonder if maybe we might not be able to use that to our advantage," Burton said. "What if, since they are like twins, they can actually communicate in whatever way that happens with one another? What if we could use the sword like a magnet to find the other blade?"

"Okay, so, what...we go back, grab Goldman and Durand and go looking for this other sword?"

"No," Burton said. "I meant what I said—they need to get rest and then get on the horn with their contacts in case this doesn't work. So, we're going to go get Reid and get him to help us find the sword and see what happens."

Burton knocked on the door and then waited. I knew Reid wasn't going to answer. I could tell from the way she was standing she knew it, too. Still—procedure has to be followed. "Vernon Reid, FBI. Open up," she said.

"What constitutes probable cause, here?" I asked.

She looked at me, then back at the door. She knocked again. "Vernon Reid, this is the FBI. Open the door."

"I mean," I whispered, "can we just knock it down? Is that even a good idea?"

"No," she said. "He most likely has at least one boobytrap set up. I know I would."

I looked down at the stone obelisk set just inside the arc of the door. "Betting, then, that isn't just a doorstop?" I asked.

She looked at it, then back at the door. She exhaled. She raised her fist to knock one more time when the door opened. Reid was standing there in a long red bathrobe, his hair wet, with a towel in his hand.

"Special Agent Burton?" Reid asked.

"As it turns out, we're going to need your help again." Reid turned and walked away from the door. Burton and I followed him in.

"What can I help you with?" he asked as he sat down at the dining room table. I stepped to Burton's right between her and the hallway.

"There was a second object that your group created. I want to know more about it," she said.

Reid shook his head. "That was all a long time ago."

"She's killed again," Burton said.

I couldn't shake the feeling we were being watched. I glanced down the hallway, but there was nothing there.

"How is that my fault?" he asked.

"Again, let's not get off on that foot. You told us about how there was an object created before the one Vandecamp has. I need to know about it."

Reid exhaled loudly and shook his head. He leaned forward, planting his elbows on the table. "Like I think I said, it was a sword. I know, that's so hacky, but we all decided together and that's what got the most votes. Now I wouldn't be caught dead doing something so...so..."

"Get on with it, please," Burton said.

"We bought it at the local incense and blacklight place. You know, the headshop that used to be in the mall. The one that called itself 'import gifts' as a cover? We thought that a sword, being basically just an antenna, would be the easiest thing to imbue with power. We were going to start there and spread out to more conventional things later. Maybe bowls that heat themselves or something."

Again, I couldn't shake the feeling we were being watched. I looked down the hallway again. I chalked it up to the fact that he had a mirror sitting at eye level at the end of the hall between the two bedrooms.

"Most of them wanted to go with a samurai sword, but I at least talked them into something less...common." The last word was spit as if it carried poison in it. "We decided on a replica of a typical bastard sword that a knight might have carried during the Crusades. Y'know, the one and a half handers that some of the knights preferred for slashing from horseback. They had one and it was nice enough and within our budget. Remember, we were poor students at the time. Well, sitting right next to it was this other... thing. I don't know how to describe it except that it was like the triskellion only made out of blades. You see something like it in a lot of novel cover paintings these days, but back then it was something new. I don't think that's an accident, by the way."

"What is?" I asked.

"That you're starting to see it show up in people's subconscious more and more. I think that's the object exerting itself into the aether."

Burton nodded. "The guy saw that a few of us were interested and mentioned that he would sell us the pair for a price that was at the outside of our budget, but still doable. It was Delores who seemed to really take a shine to the thing, and we all...well, like I said, everyone was kind of sorry for her being so alone, so we ponied up and bought both objects. The understanding was that we would use the sword the first time since everyone says they're so easy to imbue, then we'd do a working on the other thing, whatever you call it."

"So from jump, the two were linked," Burton said.

Reid shrugged, "I guess. I mean, we didn't work them together or anything."

"You didn't have to. They were purchased together. They were linked from that moment forward," Burton said.

"If you say so. So we took them both home and the next auspicious date we gathered and did the working on the sword," Reid said.

"Describe that to me," Burton said.

"Come on, that's...that's private stuff."

"Describe it," she said.

He exhaled again and it struck me—he wasn't behaving in a penitent fashion so much as he was behaving like a sulking teenager who'd been caught doing something he shouldn't have.

"We knew that to do a working, we were going to have to do the main rite. THE rite, you know? We were talking about who should do it when someone, it may have been Damian, suggested we do series of main rites all linked within the circle."

"An orgy," Burton said.

Reid nodded, "I mean, there's nothing against it in any of the literature, and that much energy would be sure to really drive home whatever we were trying to do. We just needed to figure out how to channel it all in one direction once it really started going."

"So you coupled up, but that left a problem," Burton said.

"Well, two problems. You forget that I was coupled up, and Eric and Damian were fucking, but that left Delores and Alex. I think maybe on some level Damian was hoping they'd fuck and find love, y'know?"

"I'm guessing it didn't work out that way?" I asked.

"It might have. It's just that...how to put this. Delores was always a bit stand-offish, but we all liked her because she was smart and when she did decide to laugh, she had this cutting sense of humor. Like a stand up comedian, y'know? This ability to get right through all the bullshit to the heart of whatever it was. But that night, for some reason, she wasn't just stand offish, she was downright creepy. Alex is a real nice guy. You've met him. Real easy going. But before anything happened, he pulled me aside and said that the way Delores was acting was a real...well, it's not a nice thing to say, but a real fucking bonerkiller. I reminded him that this was official Order business and that we weren't fucking for sport, y'know? I reminded him, too, that he'd have an advantage over the rest of us in that if he wasn't super turned on he could keep control over his head. I was just trying to lighten the mood."

"So what went wrong?" Burton asked.

"Nothing, that night, except this one little thing. I looked up from telling Alex all this just as Delores walked past the doorway. Now, it was the main hallway, and anyone could have walked past, so I don't know, but…"

"You couldn't shake the idea that somehow she'd heard what you'd said," I said.

"Yeah. Anyways, we all stripped down and once we calmed down and got our heads in the game, the whole thing went really well."

"Your Order had way more masculine energy than feminine, though," Burton said.

"Well, from an old way of thinking, maybe. If you go by penis automatically equals masculine energy, then yeah. We were more progressive than that. If you see it the way we saw it, it all balanced out."

Burton's eyebrow arched and I couldn't tell if it was that she didn't buy what he was saying or that he'd just passed some kind of test. I made a note to ask her later.

"So we all got down to business and I'll admit, at first it was hot. Bodies all moving around and whatever. But after a bit it became just energy building and building. We had all agreed ahead of time on the chant and the mental image to hold and so when it got near the time Alex had figured out was the exact moment of the equinox, we all released and focused on the sword at the center of the pictographs in the circle. I know this might sound stupid, but I'm telling you it was so much energy I…well, I could have sworn I saw it. I saw the energy enter into the blade. I wasn't the only one, either."

"So what was the working?" Burton asked.

I could tell Reid was about to object again, so I raised my chin and cocked my own eyebrow. Again, the sulking exhale. "We wanted it to bring light into the world. To bring healing."

"A contrary working?" Burton asked.

"Well, only if you are slavish to the idea that a sword is only an instrument of war. Remember that swords have other meanings, too. Blades can heal just as well as they can harm. That's always been a part of the concept," Reid said. For a second, I could see what his followers saw in him. When he was passionate and engaged in a topic, he seemed taller, smarter—a leader.

"We named it Whiteheart. You should have felt the vibrations that came off of it. It was unreal. It seemed to glow like the moon at night. I wasn't the only one that got caught by the others just standing still in a dark room staring at it. We were all pretty impressed with ourselves."

"Go on," Burton said.

"It had...this'll sound bizarre, too, I know, but it just seemed to give off life. I remember one afternoon, not long after we made it, I was outside just holding it, admiring it in the sunlight, and when I looked down the dead patch in the lawn, you know...one of those brown spots that just never seems to grow no matter how much you water it? That dead patch was not only lush and green, but it had grown two inches just in the hour or so I'd been standing there."

"Tannhäuser effect," Burton whispered to herself.

"What?" Reid asked.

"Nothing. What other effects did you notice from this thing?" Burton asked.

"We didn't really do too many tests or anything. I mean, I suppose, looking back on it, we should have. We're not scientists, though, you know? We just kind of...looked at it a lot. Patted ourselves on the back quite a bit. Eric and Damien said that they thought maybe it made the room warmer, like having an almost-burned-out fire in the fireplace, maybe? I can't really confirm that, though."

"Where is it now?" Burton asked after a moment.

"Why do you need it?" Reid asked.

"They're linked," Burton said.

There was quiet for a moment, then Reid eyes got large, "you think it'll know where it's…it's twin is?"

"It's dark twin, yes," Burton said. "Two brothers, each with the same parents, but with drastically different personalities, will still know a lot about each other. Especially if they are close. These… works…these workings, they are like brothers—alive, on some level sentient, perhaps, but one was loved and given care. The other…" Burton said, but drifted off.

"We…we never thought of it that way," Reid said.

"No," Burton said. "You didn't. There were a number of things you didn't think of. Where is it now?"

Reid thought for a moment, then said, "I don't know exactly where it is, but I have an idea."

"Why would you not know exactly where it is?" I asked.

"It was a long time ago. That was the whole idea, don't you see? To move it, to put it some place where I knew it would be safe and then to forget about it. To forget about the whole fucking thing. All of it," Reid said.

"Bodies thrown into wells have a nasty habit of coming back up out of them," Burton said. I hadn't known her for very long, but from what I'd seen I could tell she was furious. Each comment she made was designed to hurt him. Her level of detachment since I'd met her had bordered on being outright cold, but something about him had gotten under her skin in a big way.

"But what makes you think that Delores hasn't already stolen it? I mean, we were all good at this stuff, but she was really amazing. If the one is linked to the other, and especially if one could pose a threat to the other, don't you think she'd maybe know that, or at least sense it?" Reid asked.

"I do think she senses it," Burton said. "I just think she hasn't found it yet, either. Call it a hunch. I'm guessing that's because one of you had it, then hid it a second place away from the others. And I'm guessing that person is you. Initially it was in Alex's care, yes?"

I watched as Reid's eyes grew larger and larger while she spoke. There was silence and then he said, "How did you—,"

"That's not important right now. I'm guessing, though, that you paid him a visit in the last few weeks because you had a feeling that something was wrong?"

"I didn't know that it was Delores," Reid said.

"Not specifically, no, but you knew that something was wrong and that it might have something to do with the sword. So, you showed up, used some of your own charm magick, your particular gift, and got the sword away from Alex. Then you took it someplace obscure. I'm guessing someplace from your childhood."

Reid sat back in his chair. "How on Earth did you guess that?"

"Charmers, Mr. Reid. They have to appear more than human to the world or the charm won't work. Childhood is when people are at their most vulnerable, when most of the trauma happens. How do you keep the world at arm's length long enough to convince them you're something better than they are, somehow more interesting or powerful than they are? You hide your childhood. If I were going to hide something very important away from the people I'd grown close to, I'd need to take it somewhere they couldn't find it, someplace I'd never told them about. Therefore, someplace from your childhood," Burton said.

I have to admit, even I was stunned.

"So," she finished, "is there a cabin your family used to rent up on a lake somewhere, or maybe a ski lodge that your parents took you to on a mountain somewhere one December, something like that?"

"My mother's home town," he said. In just the short time since we'd walked in, I had watched his expression change from mild contempt to shock and now to awe. I could tell that he knew he'd been bested and that we didn't have to worry about him from that point forward.

"Good," Burton said, her face not changing. "How far away?"

"Just a few hours by car," Reid said. "I can show you."

"I'd appreciate it," Burton said. Reid stood up to gather his things and put on shoes.

I stepped closer to Burton, "Nicely done," I said.

She shrugged. "You see one con artist…" she said. "Okay," she said slightly louder, "let's get on the road."

Once he has us back on the highway headed North, Reid asked, "You're not a hundred percent on this, are you?"

"Excuse me?" Burton asked.

"Something in what you said made me think you're not a hundred percent on this. You think maybe one can find the other, but you don't know."

"Are you sure we need him along for the ride?" I asked Burton.

"Hey," he said from the back seat.

"Yeah, we do. And to answer your question," Burton said into the rearview mirror, "No. I'm not. It's because there's more going on here than just the working. If it were just that, we'd be fine. But something else is going on, too. At some point, either during the working itself or after...somehow...this object became a portal. Whatever was done to it that accomplished that task may have changed its fundamental composition. If so, then it isn't just a twin to...what did you call it, 'Whiteheart'? If it isn't a perfect twin anymore then our chances of using it to find the other one have dropped."

"How do you know it's become a kind of portal?" Reid asked.

"The murders, Goldman's info, and our initial encounter with Delores. Too much power, by which I mean physical strength, and too much agility for someone her age. To do the things she's done to these bodies, she'd have to have been a heavy weightlifter for years and also a world-class gymnast. Since those things aren't true, I'm guessing...but I am fairly sure I'm right...that something is on the other side of this object pouring energy through it," Burton said. "That's why we have to be doubly cautious when we go to bring her in."

"Okay, but I mean, she isn't a ninja, right? She isn't some highly trained assassin, is she?"

"No," Burton said, "but the object is turning her into one. Stop thinking about this blade like you would coffee. It isn't just that it has one property, that it makes someone who holds it stronger or more evil or whatever. It's not just one thing. It's a portal. It is an archway that looks like a blade. And whatever is on the other side of that archway is pouring itself into Delores. We don't have to worry about what training and abilities she had before she came in contact with this thing. We have to try to anticipate what powers and skills the thing on the other side has and how much of those it has been able to transmit into Delores."

"Shit," Reid said.

"Exactly," Burton said.

A few hours later we were pulling into a tiny town up the mountain. The sign said the population wasn't much more than a moderately sized theater would hold. Being summer, there would only be the locals in town, the people who actually called this place home year-round. As we wound around the main road, which curled around the outside of the town, separating it from a beautiful lake, I felt a strange sense of loss. How many of these little towns were actually left in the world for people to grow up in?

"It'll be the first exit," Reid said.

We pulled off into the street that ran through what the people who live there must think of as 'downtown.' The post office, a used musical instrument shop, a tiny bookstore, that kind of thing. Trucks everywhere.

"Stay on this road. It'll lead you all the way out of town to the cross street we want," Reid said.

To the left and right, small groups of people going about their business not knowing anything about a magickal killer on the loose. I thought back to the day before I'd been kidnapped by Simon and his sister. I'd had a meatball sub that day for lunch. I remember that my most pressing thought that day had been whether or not my team, the one I'd worshipped since I was a little boy because it was the one my dad loved and hated all at the same time, would make it to the playoffs this year. Now, here I was, barely a week later, on my way to retrieve a magickal sword to stop a serial killer who was being possessed by a force from another dimension. It almost made me long to go back to fertilizer duty.

"Up here, take the right called 'Lake Road.'" Reid said. Burton nodded and took the turn. Just a few minutes later we were completely out of town, had gone through a tunnel, and were now beside the lake. "Okay, up here, there's another right, take it, and we'll park there. The rest of the way we have to go on foot."

Burton took the turn and we pulled the car into a tiny semi-circle of dirt that lead to a small set of stairs that then tapered off to a gravel pathway down to the beach below. You didn't have to be a mountain goat to get down it, but it wasn't exactly easy. I nearly broke my neck in a slip, but Reid caught me by the arm. Once we were all off the path and on the beach, Reid lead us to a tiny cave about knee height. There was a long chain coming out of the cave that disappeared in the sand.

"You buried it in the sand?" I asked.

Reid shook his head, "No." He reached into the cave with both hands and came out with a rock. The chain was connected to a hook that was embedded in the rock. He took hold of the chain and began to haul on it like a rope. Foot after foot of it came up to him from the sand but eventually it became clear that the chain led off into the water.

"You buried it in the lake?" Burton asked with a grin. "Isn't that a little on the nose?"

Reid didn't say anything. The chain came back with more and more water and muck on it until eventually something came out of the water that shimmered like a pearl. Reid stopped hauling and leaned back against the rock wall panting. He caught my eye and gestured toward it.

Burton and I walked to the edge of the tide and there, lying in the sand, was a sword that looked like it had been made out of pearl and silver. It glowed, even though the sun was out, and it gave off a warmth, the kind of warmth you feel when a beloved parent puts their hand on your chest. I swore I saw grass begin to grow up out of the sand where the sword was lying.

Burton picked it up and for a split second, she seemed taller, her hair caught in a breeze. I followed her back to Reid. She held it out to him to take. He wouldn't take it. "No," he said. "Whatever comes of having that thing, it is all yours."

We climbed back up the pathway and back to the car. Burton walked to the trunk and opened it, but then stopped before putting it in. She was frozen, staring at the sword. A small yellow flower growing out of the hardpacked dirt near her feet seemed to perk up a bit.

"It's…" she said but whatever she was going to say faded off.

I looked at Reid. He raised his eyebrows and stared back at me. Then we both looked at her again. The little flower had grown at least an inch taller.

"It's reaching out to…reaching out to me…" Burton said. The tone in her voice wasn't alarm, but it wasn't relaxed, either. "Not through words but…"

Reid nodded and closed his eyes. "Now you start to see why I knew I had to get it away from people. In some ways, it's just as bad as the other one."

"Burton," I said. She didn't look away from the sword. "Burton," I said again with more force. I might as well not have said anything.

"A golden bough…" Burton whispered. "The white goddess within…"

"Burton!" I yelled and stepped toward her. She looked at me, finally, but for a second her eyes seemed to be made out of pearls. She dropped the sword into the trunk. She cleared her throat and stepped back from the car, shaking her head.

"I felt…" Burton said. She then cleared her throat again and tugged her blazer into place. "I felt it," she said.

"Felt what?" I asked.

"It, the other blade. The dark twin. I felt it," Burton said. "I know where she is."

"Right now? At this very minute you can find her?" I asked.

Burton nodded. "But we have to hurry." She slammed the trunk and was already halfway into the driver's seat. Reid and I barely had enough time to scramble in before she'd started the car and we were on our way.

I pulled out my phone. "Who are you calling?" Burton asked as she accelerated onto the freeway. By the time we were headed in the right direction, she was already ten miles per hour over the speed limit and accelerating. Reid moved from the middle of the back seat to one side and belted himself in.

"Goldman and Durand so that they can meet us wherever you say to go," Burton said.

"There's no time," Burton said.

"It'll take hours to get back to town, even at the speed you're using, how is there not—,"

"She's not back in town. She followed us. She's right here," Burton said, and barely made the next exit with squealing tires.

"Followed us!?" Reid yelled.

"She's here," Burton said, pulling off into an industrial area. "She was going to try to get here ahead of us, wait, and get the sword from us."

"You got all this that clearly?"

"The two objects, they aren't just twins, they are…antennae for one another. Anyone holding the one is immediately linked heart, mind, soul, to the other," Burton said, sliding the car to a stop just outside a run down aircraft hangar.

"We never intended anything like that," Reid said.

"You all never intended any of this. This was all a scam. You were being used," Burton said as she shut off the car. She drew her weapon and got out. I drew my own and got out, motioning for Reid to stay put.

"Okay, so how do we play this? We want her alive, right?" I asked.

"Unbalanced mercy…" Burton mumbled as we advanced on the hangar door.

"What?" I asked.

"Something Crowley wrote. All things have to be in balance. Too much force is evil, which we all kind of know, instinctively… in movies, you always root for the underdog…but, he said that too much mercy actually aids evil. That kind of thing."

"You think we should eliminate her on sight rather than try to bring her in?" I asked.

"I don't think she's going to give us a choice, but I would be lying if I said that I wasn't thinking about it," she said. Burton stopped, rubbed her forehead with the back of her hand, then began to advance on the door again. "We try to take her alive."

Even though I knew she couldn't see, I nodded. Burton was rattled, but still making sense.

The hangar door was opened a bit and we slid inside. Crates stacked in all kinds of places obscured any overall view from where we stood. It was as if someone had designed a maze specifically for this kind of thing.

"Delores Vandecamp, we are Federal Agents! Drop the weapon and come out with your hands up!" Burton yelled into the massive empty of the hangar.

Burton had just motioned for me to go left when a crate near my head exploded. All those days at the academy kicked in and I knelt to get my bearings. I was confused, though; nothing we'd seen so far indicated that Vandecamp had a gun or that she wanted to use them in any way. So who had fired that shotgun slug?

I popped up for a second to see where the sight lines must have been to hit that shot, then knelt again. Another shot went off but didn't hit anywhere near me, so it must have been aimed at Burton. An instructor at the academy had called this part of the process ".45 caliber peek-a-boo."

"Federal Agents! Put down the weapon and come out with your hands up immediately!" I yelled over my shoulder. All I heard in response was laughter. In the heat of the moment, it almost sounded familiar.

I moved around the stack of crates, and then around another, moving my way to where I thought the shots had come from. Just as I circled left around another stack of crates, something hit me from behind hard enough that I went down face first and dropped my gun. I felt the cut on my back. I tried to crawl to my gun but someone put their foot on my shoulder blade and stopped me. I could hear the footsteps move away from me to my left, in the direction I'd last heard Burton.

"Burton!" I finally yelled on my fifth try, "watch out! She's coming your way!"

I struggled for what seemed like years to get to my knees, then halfway to my feet. I leaned against the crate behind me. I put my hand on my lower back where I'd felt the cut but it came away with no blood on it. I struggled over and picked up my gun. Another shotgun blast went off over to my left shoulder, so I started moving that direction. I got about halfway to the far wall when I saw Burton take a slice across the upper arm from Vandecamp's blade. Burton dropped her gun to put a hand on her arm as Delores looked at me. She was blurry, like I couldn't quite make her come into focus. I brought my gun up, but the pain in my lower back made it hard to get into a good firing stance. She was too close to Burton for me to take the shot, so I yelled, "Freeze! Federal Agent!"

I swear Delores smiled and then moved faster than I could blink. I tried to take a shot, but it went wide because Vandecamp was already gone. I get to Burton's side and, leaning against the crates, I grabbed her gun and handed it back to her.

"Who else is in here with her?" I whispered. Burton shrugs. We both leaned against the crates for a moment. That's when we heard Reid yell, "Delores!" Burton closed her eyes and shook her head.

Before we even made it over to where we could see him, we both knew what we'd see. Reid was standing just inside the door with the sword in his hand in what I'm sure he thinks is a ready stance because that's what he's seen in all the movies. Like a nightmare, Delores was on him before Burton or I could even yell for him to watch out. She knocked the sword out of his reach and sliced deep across his chest. Burton brought her gun up and started firing one shot after another rapidly. Again, Delores danced blurrily away as if she was never there. Reid clutched his chest and went down to one knee.

"Ah, Mr. Reid, isn't it?" a chillingly familiar voice said. I moved just a bit.

Just out of arm's reach from Reid stood Simon. In his hand, he held a large gun the type of which I'd seen in history books held by pilgrims, only this one had elaborate writing all up and down the barrel. He brought it up to chest height and a split second before I got my own gun up and was just about to call out for him to freeze, he unloaded the gun and Reid's upper half disappeared. I don't mean that it was turned into bloody pulp by the impact of the shell,

I mean that it completely disappeared.

"This ends now, Simon!" Burton yells. "Hands up, mouth closed, and on your knees." She's got him zeroed in and her hands are rock steady. Still, something about it doesn't feel right. Doesn't feel settled. I raised my own gun to zero in on him, too.

He's not kneeling. Worse, the grin on his face is so snakelike that my stomach tightened into a fist.

He knows something we don't know. I do my best imitation of rushing over to where Reid's lower half has now collapsed and stood in front of the sword. I don't pick it up.

"Burton—," I start to say.

"Now!" Simon yells, turning. For a second I'm stunned at the violence and command in his voice. Then I take off after him, knowing it is already too late. Burton is already three steps ahead of me. We're both running full tilt to get to him, but his head start because of the distance away from us he'd been standing is too great. I can already tell that no matter how fast we run, we will not be able to close the gap.

He makes a motion with his hand and there's a sound as if maybe he's saying something. Just then, he did an incredible pirouette, something you'd see from a world class ballet dancer, and I could see there was something materializing in his hands. Before I could see what it was, there was a sharp sound. My brain was expecting the sound of a bullet, so it takes a second to register that something has happened.

I get that feeling in my gut that I have had a few times before when I've almost been shot. It didn't sound like a bullet, but some part of me knows that I was almost hit with *something*. Belatedly, I ducked to the side, but kept running. Burton and I neared the far wall of the hangar.

We could still hear Simon's footsteps as he runs away, but Burton stopped. I stop next to her, gun drawn, checking the angles. She stoops down and pulls a handkerchief out of her pocket. Lying on the ground in front of her is what looks like a metal stick with swirling patterns all over it.

"What the fuck is that thing!?" I whispered emphatically.

"It...well...it looks like maybe a spellgun," Burton said.

"A what?" Of course I heard her, but I've never heard of something like that.

"A spellgun. Looks like he made it out of an old shotgun, maybe," she said.

I took my jacket off and used it to wrap around the handle of the sword. I picked it up and did another quick sweep of the grounds.

She opened the breach and a spent shell popped out and hit the floor still smoking. Without putting down the weapon, Burton takes a pen out of her jacket pocket and uses it to pick up the shell. On the cartridge is the same pattern of swirls and letters from some other alphabet that I don't recognize.

"What's it written in?" I asked.

"Aklo. Kind of a base language for cultists. Not particularly inventive, but enough spirits and lower haunts know it that you can get your message across to them pretty well," Burton said.

"That's a new one on me," I said. "Any idea what it does or did?"

Burton shook her head. "We're lucky in a way," she said.

"How's that?"

"If he'd had any real skill with charging objects, he'd have used one of the higher languages. Some of those can actually cause physical damage if spoken. This stuff?" she said, setting the rifle and the cartridge down on the floor, "this stuff just sounds terrible. So, either he was in a very big hurry and needed to make something nasty on the fly, or this isn't a skill of his and he had someone else make it for him."

"So why—," I started to say when the wind inside the hangar picked up. Before I could turn more than a few degrees, something hit me in the back. Before I even hit the ground, something else hits me hard in the ribs. From the floor, I saw Burton pick up the rifle and bring it to her shoulder, but something moved so fast it's just a blur and it slams her to the ground as well.

The blur is suddenly filling my entire vision, then solidifies into Delores. She's kneeling in front of me. I can see the blade that we've spent so much time thinking about in her right hand. The expression on her face reminds me of the time I was seven and my best friend Kyle captured a beetle in his front yard. He had it in his hands and while I stood there in awe watching, he flipped it on its back and started to remove one of its legs at a time. I got sick to my stomach, but not from watching what he was doing. It was from the look on his face while he did it; calm, detached, but at the same time with a slight grin at the edge of his mouth. She was looking at me the same way he looked at that bug. She raised the blade up over her head. I knew what was to comes next.

But instead of the pain I expected, I heard a muffled bang. Then there was a strong wind moving over my body toward Delores. Her face went slack as if she was trying to figure something out, and she started to turn. Before she could finish doing so, though, she folded in on herself and disappeared. The wind stopped.

Burton is on knees, the rifle in her hands has smoke coming from the barrel. She then dropped it with a loud clank, and falls onto her hands with a loud exhale.

"What...?" I try to say, but it feels like there is an elephant sitting on my chest.

"Don't...don't try to talk right now. You're...you're hurt." Burton fell on her side and fished her cell phone out of her pocket. I pushed the wrapped sword toward her. With one hand she took it, and with the other she hit one button, waited a second, then said, "My name is Special Agent Miranda Burton, FBI. I need an ambulance to..." but then my eyesight went fuzzy and I faded out.

I come to in a hospital bed. My first thought was a memory from the academy. Our first day learning to breach and secure a room. Dummy rounds and padding, sure, but when one of the trainers got a little overzealous and put me on my back because I didn't clear a corner the way I was supposed to, he stood over me and said to the whole class, "there is no bigger cliché of stupidity in the world than forgetting to clear a corner and then waking up in a hospital bed with your partner sitting beside you telling you what happened after you got your ass handed to you. Don't be that guy,

Lowe."

Here I was waking up in a hospital bed with Burton sitting beside me.

"Shit," I mumbled.

"Try not to move too much. The doctor said it wasn't as bad as it looked initially, but she still recommended that you take it very slowly," Burton said, standing.

"How long?"

"You've been out for about four hours now. Just long enough for a detective from the local PD to come sniffing by and get pretty shirty with me," Burton said.

"Sorry," I said.

"I appreciate it. I was hoping we could do this relatively quietly and then get Delores out without any jurisdiction conversations having to happen. I think we might be able to pull that off still, but he's definitely going to be watching for us. See, they haven't connected all the dead people together in one case, yet, so to them this is still a group of unrelateds. Not Federal, in other words. And I can't show them the evidence we have without blowing the lid off our division."

"So what did you tell him?"

"I said what I always say, that we are here working on a case and that if we need his assistance we'll contact him. Of course, that tends to turn people we might need later pretty hostile. Let's hope he's not one of those," Burton said.

"Goldman and Durand?" I asked.

"I don't know. I didn't want to get in touch with them until I knew more about what was going on with you, and until we'd put a plan together. Him I trust some, but her…"

"Yeah," I said.

"The sword?" I asked.

"Safe," Burton said. I closed my eyes for a second.

"How?" I asked.

Burton shook her head, "I don't know. I'm guessing maybe she was just in too much of a hurry for the blade to pull your blood. Or, at least all of it. I'm guessing you're about a quart low."

I frowned at the terrible joke.

The door to the room opened and a man walked in. At first, I'll be honest, I thought it was movie star John Goodman. I could have sworn it was him. As he got closer to the light, though, I could see that they just looked very similar.

"Jimmy," Burton said.

"Miranda," the new guy said.

"This is my new partner, Paul Lowe. Paul, this is my friend Jimmy. He's a healer."

"Spent some time in Japan. Picked up some things while I was there," Jimmy said to me as he set down the messenger bag he had with him. Strong smells waft from it.

"Jimmy is a Reiki healer, one of the best I've ever come across here in the U.S.," Burton said. "Well, to be fair, at least the best that will take my calls, especially on short notice."

Jimmy looked at the IV going into my arm and the machines surrounding me in disgust. I don't know how, but I can tell he's trying to figure out how to turn them all off without alerting the nurses. "Fucking barbaric," he mumbled.

"I'm going to go get something that passes for food from the cafeteria down stairs. Jimmy, give me a call when you're done, ok?" Burton said. I see her click the lock on her way out.

Jimmy doesn't say anything. He moves a bit away from the bed, closes his eyes, and rests his hands together in front of his chest as if praying. After a few moments he opens his eyes and takes two candles out of his messenger bag. He takes a moment to decide where to place them. He lights each with a long wooden match. The room almost instantly starts to smell like freshly mown grass. He then takes a small stone jar from the bag and opens it. I can't see what's inside but he puts a bit on his left hand and then rubs it into both hands vigorously. The smell is eucalyptus. He stepped to the edge of my bed and said, "I'm going to have to move your gown out of the way to get to you. Just understand that this is for healing. You're safe, and I'm not going to hurt you."

He moves the gown away from my chest and removes the bandage from where one of the deepest cuts is. I'm just about to say something sarcastic to cover the fact that I feel a bit embarrassed and exposed when he places his impossibly warm hands on the cut and the warmth spreads through me. It's one of those moments where you don't realize just how sick and cold you've been until you finally get warm. My whole body relaxed in what felt like the first time ever and I pass out once more.

A few hours later, I woke up to Burton sitting beside my bed again.

"It's about time," she said with a slight grin.

"Oh?" I croaked. I see there's the kind of cup you give toddlers sitting next to my bed. I reach over and take it, gulping water down. I swear I've never been this thirsty in my entire life.

"Slow, or you'll vomit," she said. It's hard, but I do manage to slow down. "Jimmy says he had to work extra hard on those slashes. Not terribly deep, but there was some bad mojo in them, he said."

I set the cup down and put my other hand on my chest. It's rebandaged, but doesn't feel nearly as stiff or as warm to the touch as it did before. The smell of lemongrass hangs in the air. There is no pain in my lower back at all.

"And I used the sword," Burton said.

"You what?" I asked, but then had a coughing fit. Once it had calmed down I asked again.

"The sword. It turns out, it has more than just the Tannhauser effect. It can heal. I don't know that I did it very well, though. I think what Jimmy did probably helped more. Still, though."

"Thank you," I said. Burton nodded.

"Can you feel her?" I asked.

Burton got distant, "Kind of. Not nearly as clear as before. It's like, now that she knows we can look, she's getting more help staying hidden."

"What was that thing?" I asked. It feels like the first time I've talked in years.

"The shotgun? Down and dirty modern magick, that's what. There are some folks out there, and I hate to admit it, but Simon may be one of them, that have figured out that if you can do a working on a sword or knife or arrow, you can do a working on machinery. To be sure, from what I've heard, it takes a sure and steady hand, but it can be done," she said.

"And the shell?"

"I don't know, but I have a pretty good hunch. I think both shells were designed to create a kind of void space on the target once the shell impacted. Or maybe teleport the object away. Either way, that's what happened. Delores was somewhere in front of us hiding. Simon fled to catch our attention. She must have stood up and he hit her with one of the shells that caused her to come out of thin air right behind you. I don't know if that's maybe good luck or if that was the intention, but that's how she got the drop on you like she did. Don't beat yourself up over it," she said. I nodded. "I wish I'd have known more before I used it on her, but I didn't have a choice. As deep as the cuts that hit were, I could tell that next one was going to kill you. So I did what I could."

"Thank you," I said.

She nodded. "I wish there'd been some other choice though. I mean, there she was. Right there. She had the drop on us, sure, but at least she was there in the open. If there had been some way…"

Silence crept in around the edges.

"At any rate, I kept the gun, but without any shells we can't use it as a weapon. I'm going to get it to a psychometrist, though. Has to be one around here somewhere," she said.

"But you can't go through Malleus," I said.

She nodded again, then shook her head with a loud exhale. "Tough to believe. I mean, I knew from jump that Simon wasn't exactly the nicest guy, but to actually be trying to help a criminal?"

"Maybe he's being coerced?"

"Maybe," she said. "Doesn't feel that way, though."

Though I feel fantastic, I suddenly have to cough. It's a loud, wet cough, and it seems to go through my whole body.

"Jimmy says that'll happen. Along with other things. Your body is getting rid of a lot of toxins in the ways that it knows how to. Just hang in there and do what it tells you to do. Lots of water. Don't get too far from a toilet, he says, too," she said. I almost expected a smile, but there isn't one. She wasn't making a joke, just relaying information. "I'm going to go. Doctor will probably release you tomorrow. Jimmy says he thinks that's going to be the case at any rate. I'll see you in the morning." She stood, put on her coat, and walked to the door. With her hand on the handle she said, "I put a uniform outside the door, so let yourself actually relax and sleep. You're as safe as you can be." She walked out. Through the open door I can see the blue of the officer's shirt.

5. Derek Goldman

The car ride from the police station back to the bookstore was a quiet one. I kept expecting that maybe Stacey would try to say something, anything, but she didn't. As soon as I pulled up to door she immediately got out.

"Do you have a key?" I asked. I knew she did but I wanted to say something. To let her know that this wasn't as much of a break as she maybe thought it was. She showed the key to me then closed the car door. I waited for her to get into the store and turn on a light before I pulled away.

I didn't even turn on the radio as I drove back to my place. When I got there and opened the door, it felt like years since I'd been there last. For some reason I thought about the milk and wondered if it had gone off. Then I remembered that all of this had happened in the space of a few days. I closed the door behind me and locked it, then sat down on my couch, keys still in hand, jacket still on. I stared into my empty apartment. I must have fallen asleep like that because the next thing I knew I was waking up, still mostly in the same position, with my skin feeling dried out. I got up, put my jacket on the peg near the door, threw my keys into the bowl next to the door, toed out of my shoes, and stripped off my shirt. I collapsed into bed and, again, fell into dreamless blackness.

I woke to find the house full of light. It was nearly 11. I was still tired, but I made myself get out of bed. I started coffee and waited, staring out the kitchen window. I checked my phone while I waited on the coffee to finish. No calls, the only emails were junk. I sat down at my little café style table with the first cup and turned on the TV to the news. Politics, scandals, something about a YouTube celebrity doing something dumb and shocking. I couldn't focus. My quick estimation was that I'd been out for about 6 hours or so, maybe less.

I called the store. It took four rings, but Stacey did pick up.

"Bitter End books," she said. I smiled because she sounded her usual acidic and slightly bored self.

"How are things this morning?" I asked.

"Good so far," she said. Her voice was a bit more cautious now that she knew it was me on the other end, but I didn't hear any hostility in it. "Jung needs more food."

"I'll pick some up on my way in. Anything else?" I asked.

"Nope," she said.

"Okay. I'm on my way in now," I said and hung up.

Again, I'd only had on the same suit for maybe 36 hours or so, but it felt like I'd been trapped in the same clothes for weeks. The shower felt so good. A fresh shave felt even better. By the time I put on a new suit, it was as if everything that had happened the last two days was all a terrible dream.

I swung by the market on my way in and picked up Jung's food. The sheer mundaneness of the act made me feel fantastic. I pulled up to the bookstore and walked in to find Stacey sitting behind the counter on the store phone and Jung curled at the end of the counter where the sun from the windows was pooled. I stopped for a moment and ran my index finger along the sides of his face, something I'd discovered he loved more than anything else.

"Yeah, so it's been crazy. Look, he just walked in, so let me talk to him and get back to you, but start putting together some stuff now." She hung up.

"Good morning," I said walking past her to put food in Jung's bowl.

"Hi," Stacey said and walked to the door of the office.

As per usual, the cat came running as soon as he heard food hitting the bowl. I shook my head, "convinced you're starving to death, eh?" I asked him. He tucked in to the food and I sat the bag on the counter.

I turned to face Stacey. Neither of us said anything for a moment.

"So," I said.

"Yeah," Stacey said.

"Is there coffee?" I asked.

"Sure," she said, and squeezed past me. I walked back to the front of the store and sat down on one of the stools. After a couple of minutes Stacey came to sit beside me. She handed me a mug and I saw she had one for herself.

"So, look, it's not…" she started then stopped.

"Not that what?" I asked.

She sighed. "It's not that I didn't want to tell you any of that stuff. I just…it's just that you're new in my life. I didn't know if I could trust you with all of it, yet, you know?"

I took a sip, then nodded. "You and me, we have to find a way forward. In a way, Agent Burton's strong-arm tactic was kind of a good thing for us. It ripped the bandage off. Now all this stuff is out in the open."

Stacey nodded and tried to hide her relief.

"Of course, though, you know that we're kind of back to square one in a way, right?" I asked.

She nodded. "Yeah. I thought that was probably going to be the case. Well, I mean, I hoped. You're…you're important to me, Goldman. And I mean that. Not just because you let me stay in your store, but you believe me. When I told you just how messed up this whole thing was, you believed me. That means a lot."

"Okay, so I'm going to ask—is there anything else that, no matter how uncomfortable you might feel about it, you think may be important to the case?" I asked.

She thought for a moment. "No. But, if something does come

up, I swear to you that I will tell you immediately." She made a half-assed Boy Scout honor gesture. I laughed.

"Who was that on the phone?" I asked.

"Well, the last thing that Burton said to us was that she wanted me to start to rally the troops, right? So I was talking to Evan," Stacey said.

"The kid?"

"Look, I know he's young, but you saw—he has skills. Especially if this whole thing involves blades, I think he'll be someone we want to have around. I know Burton will give me shit about it, but there it is," Stacey said.

"And Sharkey?" I asked.

"I don't know what to do about Shark. Taking off like that and leaving us in the wind wasn't too cool."

"No, I didn't think it was, either," I said.

"Still, though; if I'm in a fight, there's no one I want there more than Sharkey."

"By the way, I have to ask…Sharkey as in like the Burt Reynolds movie? Or the Don Knotts TV show?"

"Sharkey would kill me if it came out that I told you, but it's an injoke, kind of," Stacey said.

"What's the joke?" I asked.

"Shark's parents were not only big time hippies, but they were what we'd call foodies these days," she said and smiled as if it explained everything.

My eyes scrunched.

"They were cooks who were particularly interested in learning all the different ways someone makes meat," she said, glancing to the side.

"I'm sorry, I don't…"

"Sharkey's full name is Charcuterie Jones."

I groan. We both laughed.

"Don't ever call Sharkey that, though. The full name? Just don't. You will be killed."

I'm still laughing. Stacey gets serious, though, and her smile fades. "Seriously. Sharkey will kill you."

"Ok," I said. "So, do we call?"

Stacey thinks about it for a second, then nods. "I'll call in a minute."

A companionable silence passed between us. The only sound in the store was the sound of Jung eating.

The phone rang and Stacey picked it up, "Bitter End books."

She looked alarmed, then nodded. "Okay," she said and hung up.

"What's going on?" I asked.

"Burton. She says she's on her way here and to stay put," Stacey said. "She does not sound happy at all."

I could tell we both felt like there was something we ought to be doing but neither of us moved. Burton's car pulled up out front about half an hour later and she walked in. Her shoulder was bandaged, and she looked exhausted. I took my stool to the other side of the counter and she sat down before any of us said anything.

"What's happened?" I asked.

She explained that they had gone to collect the sword we'd been told about. Once there, she'd accidentally touched it and gained a feeling of where Delores was—which had been just outside of town and moving in their direction very quickly. Delores and Burton had the same idea at the same time, it seemed. So, they went to see if they could take Delores in. That's when she backed up and explained that Simon had gotten involved, and that neither he nor Gloria were to be trusted any more. She also explained that in the attempt to bring Delores in, her partner, Lowe, had been badly injured and was in the hospital and that the young man they'd brought along from the original group, a guy named Reid, was now dead.

"And so now, I think I've got a major piece of the puzzle that was bugging me," Burton said. Stacey brought her a mug of coffee, which she gulped.

"What's that?" I asked.

"Well, what's bugged me about this whole case is this—sure, a group of young amateurs...is there any more of this, by the way?" she asked, holding Stacey's empty mug out toward Stacey, who took it. "A group of young amateurs can hit the jackpot and really do some amazing thing. I've seen that. However, this kind of working…these blades…it seems like too much. More than a group of amateurs would be capable of without help. My brain kept coming back to this, wondering if maybe their teacher had been helping them. I had him on my list of people to talk to but just hadn't gotten to him yet." Stacey brought back more coffee and again, Burton downed most of it in one go. "But now, I see that Simon has been manipulating a lot of things. And I think maybe he's been manipulating both sides since before kidnapping Lowe. I think maybe he was manipulating and helping Delores all along."

"Why?" I asked. Stacey brought a full mug of coffee back.

"I don't know. Something to do with this prophecy or whatever. Jesus, I hate prophecy shit." She took the first slug of coffee and sat the mug down hard as if it was punctuation.

Both Stacey and I were taken aback. Burton didn't seem like the kind of person who would cuss lightly.

"I'm sorry your partner is hurt," Stacey said.

"Me, too," Burton responded. "Have you started to get your acquaintances in line? I thought we might need them earlier, but now I'm sure of it."

"I had just started, but yeah, I'll get on that," Stacey said. She picked up the store phone and moved it further down the counter.

Burton stared into space for a minute. "This is going to get ugly, Goldman. I mean ugly. Can I count on you and your partner to help me bring Delores in?"

"Yes," I said.

"Good," Burton said and stood. "I need to crash. Is there a sofa or something?"

I walked her back to the office where the pull out couch was. We got it set up and she collapsed onto it. She was asleep almost instantly. I closed the office door behind me, shooing Jung out as I did.

"Okay," Stacey said after I walked past her. "That's Evan and Shark. I didn't get any explanation but Sharkey did at least sound a little sorry. That's something."

"Do you think they'll both hang with us when this gets rough?"

I asked.

Stacey thought about it for a moment. "I know Evan will. He sees himself as a modern-day Samurai, as you probably put together. He's kind of not wrong about that, either. Sharkey is tough, but a realist. If things start to break against us, there's every chance it'll turn into everyone for themselves, but who knows. Once Burton explains everything, maybe Sharkey will feel some obligation. Plus, you know, there's the other thing."

"What's that?" I asked.

"Two of the women Sharkey used to sleep with will be in one place and in danger. That's sure to get *some* kind of emotion stirred up," Stacey said.

Burton woke up about two hours later. She stumbled out of the office sliding into her coat. "I'm on my way to meet up with a friend of mine who is going to help Paul. I'll be back in about two hours."

"Are you sure you should go anywhere? Maybe you should take some time and just rest," I said.

"No time to rest," Burton said on her way past me. "Vandecamp is still out there." She started her car and was gone a moment later.

Stacey and I picked back up where we'd been. "Renegade Malleus agents? I mean, fuckin A," Stacey said.

"I hope that Burton's plan this next time is better than just 'freeze, Federal Agents.'"

"Yeah," Stacey said. "That didn't seem to work out so good for anyone involved."

A minivan showed up outside in the parking lot and Evan got out. He had a long, skinny leather bag thrown over his shoulder that was almost as tall as he was. The van's driver side window rolled down and Evan leaned in quickly then turned and walked in the door. The van pulled away.

"Evan," I said.

"Goldman," he said. He put his bag gingerly on the counter, then leaned against it. "So, get me up to speed."

I explained the entire situation to him. Stacey broke in occasionally to relate something I'd said back to something they shared in their history together. At the end of it, Evan whistled.

"Wow," was all he said. "Where is this sword?"

"She has it with her, I suppose. I have to be honest, in the moment, I didn't ask. I didn't hear her say anything about moving it, though. Why do you ask?" I asked smirking a bit.

"Well, one, it's me. Swords are kind of my thing. But also, didn't she say that this thing had a...what'd she call it?...Tannhauser effect or something like that?"

"Yeah. I think that was exactly what she said, in fact," Stacey said.

"Well, I mean...if it's making things grow just by being in one place...I wonder if it also has the ability to heal. Like, I wonder if she could use it on her partner," Evan said. "I've heard of that kind of thing before."

"Fuckin A," Stacey said and went to the phone.

"Nice work," I said.

Evan shrugged. "Like I said, it's just kind of what I do. This FBI agent, though...is she going to give me shit about coming along?"

"What, like, 'he's too young' or whatever? I have to be honest, I think she might. We need you, though. I saw you fight, and that was just what you were doing for form. If it comes down to it, and I have a sinking feeling it will, I think it's going to take multiple simultaneous attacks to finally get Delores into custody. That means at least one of us is going to have to go toe to toe with her. I'm thinking that means you."

"Okay," Evan said.

Stacey hung up the phone and came back over to us. "She does still have it. She said thank you, as well. She said she's going to give it a try. Now we just need Sharkey to..." Stacey said. It was at that exact moment that we all heard the heavy motorcycle engine pull up into the parking lot. Sharkey got off and walked inside.

"Shark," Evan said.

"Hey," Sharkey said, walking past him, then "Goldman."

"Let's talk," Stacey said, gesturing back into the office. Sharkey walked back there with her and they shut the door.

"Wow," Evan said.

"What?"

"Sharkey Jones. One of the top knife fighters out there. This is shaping up to be a very interesting day."

"You can say that again," I said.

Eventually Stacey and Sharkey come out of the office. Evan and I had been passing time by playing cards.

"Everything make sense?" I asked.

Sharkey nods. "I'm sorry for bailing on you guys when the Feds showed up. Priors, y'know?"

"It's okay," I said. "I feel like I probably would have done the same were the situation reversed."

The phone rings and Stacey gets it.

"Sharkey," Evan said. "You still got that Benchmade Black Infidel?"

Sharkey smiled. From the right boot came a switchblade. "Wicked," Evan said, his voice full of admiration. "And the Microtech Tachyon 3?" From the other boot came a butterfly knife.

"That was Burton," Stacey said hanging up the phone. "She says we'll all meet up here tomorrow morning. Says that if the sword works, plus the friend she brought in to help, Lowe might be on his feet by then."

"Okay," I said. "Let's order in some food and you guys can all get settled here for the night."

We ordered Chinese because it was the closest place, and Stacey got the office computer to play a bad horror movie off some streaming service she'd hacked. Jung took an immediately liking to Evan, and it seemed as though Sharkey and Stacey were rekindling something. I went to my car and pulled out the sleeping bag I'd been told by my father to always keep in the trunk. It was the only piece of good advice he'd ever given me to date. I left it with Evan, who curled into it and sat his swords next to him within arm's reach. I couldn't help but think how small he looked and then think about what tomorrow might bring for all of us. I left them all that way, went back to my place and collapsed into bed again.

I walked in to the shop the next day to find Burton talking to

Stacey with Sharkey and Evan looking on.

"No, absolutely not," Burton said.

"Why not?" Stacey demanded.

"He's a kid. I'm not going into a shooting situation with a child."

Stacey shook her head, "How long have you been doing this job and you're still seeing with your civilian eyes. Look again—that," Stacey said, pointing at Evan, "is a seasoned veteran swordsman who, if he should happen to need to, can summon the spirit of an ancient samurai to help him for brief periods of time. You're saying that because all of that comes in the shell of a kid you're going to leave that kind of firepower on the sidelines?"

"She has a point," I said. Lowe sat on one of the stools. He still had bandages on, but he looked okay. I nodded to him and he nodded back.

"Fuckin A," Stacey said, seeing me for the first time.

Burton looked at me, then walked over to the boy and stopped. She cocked her head to the side. "Look, I get that you are a powerful warrior in the ring, in competition, but what we're talking about here? This is real. It is likely, given her power level, that Delores is going to kill one of us, maybe more, today, before we can bring her down. A lot of TV shows, they show a couple of minutes of gun fighting and maybe someone takes a shot in the arm. This won't be like that. If everything goes the way we want it to, she's going to be trapped. Back against the wall. Do you know what an animal does when its back is against the wall?"

"They go crazy and swing at everything with all they have," Evan said. "Look, I know when you look at me all you see is a kid. But like Stacey said, this," he said, putting his hand on the handle of his sword, "isn't a steak knife. It's not some cheap knock off that I picked up in the lobby of some Chinese buffet. It's older than you, and it's older than what she's carrying around. Don't make some rule to keep me on the sideline that I'll just have to break. Instead, make me part of the plan. Let me help."

Burton continued to look at him for a minute, then looked at the rest of us and sighed. I looked at our band of misfits standing on that corner, trying to see them as she saw them. Stacey, Sharkey,

Evan, Burton, Lowe, and I. I knew that we weren't all coming back from this. Something in my gut told me.

"Come on," Burton said and we all followed her to the trunk of the cruiser. She opened it and then opened the steel box inside it. Inside the box were handguns, a shotgun, and ammunition. "Goldman? You know how to use one of these?" she said, handing him a nine-millimeter.

"Yes," I replied. He checked slide, then the clip, then racked it.

"Sharkey?" Burton asked.

Sharkey picked up the shotgun and began to load shells into it.

"Ms. Durand," Burton said handing the other nine millimeter to her. "Goldman, will you...?" I pulled Stacey aside to make sure she knew how to work the pistol. She shut the trunk of the cruiser. "Okay," she said. "We're just about to go into a situation that most people train for a year or two before they get it right. You're going to have to adapt faster than that. There is no telling what she's capable of. We've seen her teleport before and there's no reason to assume she won't be able to do it again. We've seen that she has far above regular strength and speed. Do not get anywhere close to her, physically unless you are sure, and I mean *sure* you have the drop on her." The last was aimed at Evan. "I would like to take her alive today, but I am not naïve enough to think that likely. Still, try." Burton paused at that. "Try to stay out of each others' way. If you get into trouble, yell. If you get separated, yell. Clear?"

We all nodded—it just felt wrong to make any noise.

"Okay. Let's go bring her in. For that," Burton said, turning to me, "we're going to need you. The sword leaves me with an impression of where she might be in a broad area. For instance, I know she's here in the city somewhere. It seems like it might be back to the downtown area again. But for anything more precise, Mr. Goldman, we're going to need you."

"But I don't know how..." I started.

"We're going to help you all we can, but you're what we have to work with. So, I'm taking Paul and Ms. Durand in my car, you'll take the others with you. My car will take the lead until we reach the down town area. Then we'll all get out and you will take the lead," Burton said.

"But, again, I don't really know how..." I started.

"No time like the present," Burton said.

We arrived on the same street as we did the last time we came looking for Vandecamp. I pulled my car up to stop just behind Burton's. "So, we're going to do this just out here in broad daylight?" I asked.

"We can't let her keep building strength," Burton said. "You're sure you're in?" Burton asked Lowe quietly.

"You're right. This ends today," Lowe said.

Everyone gathered around me. "Okay," Burton said. "Clear your mind. Just focus on the blade. Finding the blade." She took out a picture someone had sketched of the blade and showed it to me. "Just focus in on finding the blade," Burton said again. She then walked to the trunk of her car and pulled out something wrapped in a jacket. She removed the jacket and for some reason the day seemed a bit brighter. "Focus in on your breathing," she said to me, and put a hand on my shoulder. I felt good, better than I had in a while. The twinge in my right ankle I'd had for years wasn't bothering me so badly. "Focus in on your breathing," she said again. I did.

I pictured the blade. The shininess of it. The somewhat red tint to the steel. The curving of the blades. And just like that, I knew we should head North.

"This way," Burton and I said at the same time, both pointing North.

"That was amazing!" I whispered. She clapped my shoulder twice. "That's never happened before!" I said to Stacey.

"It has," Burton said, leading us up the street. "You just weren't aware of it. You've been lead by it your whole life, today is just the first day you ever focused in on it."

We walked past the building where the first encounter had happened. Though it was daylight out, the day seemed to grow darker as we moved further and further into the rows of abandoned buildings.

"I've never been down here before," Evan said. Though I knew there wasn't, for a split second, I thought I heard an echo of his voice off the surrounding buildings. I felt a deep chill in my bones.

We passed another block of abandoned buildings until we came to the exact center of downtown. I don't know how I knew that's what it was, but I knew it. Burton and I both stopped near a manhole cover. "Okay," Burton said. "I got nothing else. From here, it's all up to—," she was cut off by a thunderclap that made us all crouch and cover our heads. The sky, I noticed, though, was perfectly clear.

For some reason, I knew, *knew*, that it had come from the building just in front of us. This one was in the worst shape of any we'd seen yet, with most of its exterior walls gone. It was just an empty shell of floors. I looked up to the fifth floor and there, leaning out and looking at us, was Delores Vandecamp. She cocked her head to the side, as if we were something to be examined, then leaned back into the building. I pointed up to where she had just been and said, "There." Everyone stood back up and gathered themselves. Like some kind of action movie cliché, we all looked at one another and nodded, then turned and walked into the husk of the building.

"Fifth floor," I said as we marched up the stairs.

"Just like we talked about," Burton said. She stopped and Evan stopped next to her. He held out his hand. She shook her head and reluctantly handed him the sword. Immediately he seemed taller, somehow more handsome. I had to remind myself that I was looking at a boy for a second. The dark, debris-strewn interior of the building seemed to light up for a second.

We made it up the four flights without incident until we came to the fifth floor. Standing there, waiting for us with perfect calm and cool, was Delores. If Whiteheart made Evan seem older, wiser, more radiant, the wicked monstrosity that Delores held in her hand made her seem twisted, grotesque, and she seemed to be vibrating. It was difficult to make my eyes focus in on her.

"Delores Vandecamp, I am a Federal Agent and I want you to surrender the blade and come with me peacefully right now," Burton said. It sounded like the most reasonable thing a person could do.

"And if I don't?" Delores responded. The sound of her voice was like a swarm of angry bees and made me shiver.

"I'm asking you not to make that choice," Burton said.

"Too late," Delores said and just like that, she was in motion. Before any of us could get set up she was among us, the blade swinging. Somehow Evan managed to get his blade up and blocked the incoming cut, but Sharkey isn't quite so lucky. The shotgun Sharkey had been carrying went flying and Sharkey fell. It all happens so quickly I felt numb and unable to do anything but stare. Stacey got the gun she was carrying up and squeezed off a shot. It just so happens that the gun was near Delores' head when it went off and the sound startled her. She ran up the steps behind us to a higher floor.

It took a second, but we all recovered.

"Shit!" Burton yelled.

"Who's that?" I asked pointing to someone lying on the floor over closer to the edge of the building.

Burton looked over and her smile could only be described as vicious. She walked over to the person and we all follow.

Burton tapped the gun against the man's forehead. "Wake up, Simon."

Simon's eyes flutter and then open. They roll from side to side, making him look even more snakelike, which I hadn't thought was possible. "Special Agent Burton," he said, his eyes coming to rest on her and focusing. He was tied up with hundreds of knots all forming a kind of netting running down his body.

"I want to know why," she said.

His too-wide mouth broke into something like a grin and for a second I thought 'she's going to hit him again.' I would have. She only stared at him without moving, though.

"I am unsure as to what you mean to ask me, Special Agent Burton."

"Horseshit. You've been helping this…this creature…the whole time. And I get that from time to time one of you magick types goes off half-cocked and invites something into this dimension on the promise that it'll get you a fancy new car or some other such nonsense, but you? You're not like that. Or, at least I didn't think you were, so out with it."

Simon laughed and tried to move. Only then did he seem to understand exactly how bad his situation was. I could actually see him try to work through what he should do next. It was written in his horrible eyes.

"Come now, Special Agent Burton—isn't this the part that everyone makes fun of? Here at the end I'm supposed to monologue about my grand plan so that the listeners understand it all and then while you're shocked I make a getaway to come back and menace you once more?"

"How do you know I'm not going to shoot you as soon as you get finished with the part that I need to know?"

He laughed again, and again it made my skin crawl.

"The prophecy," Simon said, his eyes rolling toward me.

"What about it?" Burton asked.

"It has all come true, which means that it is very likely that the next part will come true, as well," Simon said. "I had my doubts initially, I confess. I had thought that having someone like you at his side, it was certain that Paul Lowe would survive. How could a stalwart knight such as yourself fail to save the damsel?" He smirked. "And yet, here we are."

"What are you saying...that for your prophecy to happen, Paul has to die?" Burton asked.

"I am saying that so far, Agent Burton, the prophecy might as well have been a checklist. It has been that accurate."

"And?"

"And if it continues to be accurate..." Simon said, letting his words trail off.

"What is the end of the prophecy?" Burton demanded.

"I'm afraid I can't tell you that."

"What can we do to thwart this prophecy?" I asked.

Burton looked at me, then back at Simon. He shook his head slowly. His eyes slid from mine back to hers. "You don't understand, Mr. Goldman. The future is a train, its tracks run true. And, I'll admit, even if I wanted to help you," he said to Burton, "I wouldn't. What we stand to gain is too great a prize."

"The point, Simon."

"Delores VanDecamp is something new. When someone is possessed it is very often against their will. A struggle ensues. Very often the inbound entity is roundly defeated, either by someone from our organization or from the clergy, sometimes both, and it is sent packing. Delores, though, *invited* this entity with such…fervor…that it was scooped somewhat against *its* will. Once it discovered her, a mere mortal, willingly insisting on becoming a portal, it faced a choice—go back to its existence among the stars, drifting endlessly in peace, or a return to the material plane."

"And?"

"Well, a good portion of itself was already here, you see. Pulled by Ms. VanDecamp. Imagine waking one fine morning to find your entire leg already through a portal to another world and that more and more of you was being pulled through all the time. You might face the same choice. Rather than resist, the entity has decided to work with Ms. VanDecamp, thereby increasing its rate of entry. As more an more of it enters her body, she becomes something new. Not quite the entity, but no longer herself. This has happened before, certainly, but not during our modern era."

"And you want, what, to control her?"

"We are beyond that."

"And this prophecy, it told you what happens if the entity is successful?"

Simon's smirk widened.

"There are many ways one can become an immortal. Ms. VanDecamp has chosen a very interesting and quite rare one. There is indeed much we can learn from her and her most unusual… guest. For what it is worth, though, I am sorry about the death of your former partner."

"You sonofa…" I say. "Are you saying…are you saying that you…?"

His eyes never leave hers.

"That you helped her try to kill him just to what…to make *sure* your prophecy happens?" I asked.

She shook her head. "Maybe...maybe we should just gag him now," I said.

"Don't worry. I've got him under control."

I start to explain that I've heard that same line a million times in a million movies just before the bad guy gets away when I saw Simon's eyes unfocus. He whispered something quickly, his mouth forming around the word wrong, somehow, too loose to have formed a word, and he started to laugh.

Burton shook her head and punched him.

"This isn't my first rodeo, moron," she said.

Simon thrashed around at that point. For the first time since I've seen him, he looks worried.

"Everything okay?" Lowe asked as he walks up.

"Where is Gloria?" Simon asked.

"Sharkey," Burton said, "knock him out, please."

Sharkey stepped forward and with one punch, Simon goes unconscious. "Okay," Burton said. "Next time, no waiting for chit chat. We see Vandecamp, we roll in heavy. Got it?" We all nod. "I'm not going to lie, she's gotten even faster than before, and if this asshole doesn't know where his sister is, there's every chance she might be helping Vandecamp. It looks like they're trying to take her in for study, which means she is going to try to interfere. Be on the lookout. There's only one way up there, and no way to get any cover, so hit hard."

We moved up the steps. I kept getting this feeling in the back of my head that telling me she's all the way on the roof. "Roof," I whispered. Burton nodded. We move up the next three floors until we come out on the roof. Again, there was Delores, full of dark buzzing and hard to see. Off to one side stood another woman and I could see that she was already muttering something and moving her hands.

"Go!" Burton yelled. Sharkey, having recovered the shotgun, brought it up and began firing. Stacey started firing as well. Evan took off and did a baseball slide, the sword coming around in an arc. Burton planted herself and started firing at the woman off to the side, who I guessed was Gloria. I fired at Delores.

Vandecamp managed to block Evan's blade with her own and somehow managed to dodge all of the incoming bullets with a move that would easily have won her gold at a gymnastics tournament. She paused for just a second for some reason, though, and two bullets managed to catch her in the arm. She screamed and the sound of it made all of us stop in our tracks. She whirled again, though, and came back at Evan. He had pulled out one of his own swords and was swinging and blocking simultaneously just as she was slicing at him. Though he was not as fast, something about each time the Whiteheart sword connected with the Killraven glave seemed to sap some energy out of her and she slowed down a bit. Unfortunately, his luck couldn't hold up forever and just as I started firing at her again, she landed a cut across his back. It sent him sprawling. To his credit, though, he did not drop either sword. I continued to fire as I moved to him. I glanced over to see that Burton had almost finished subduing the other woman. Unfortunately, my lack of attention for a second left me open and Delores whirled in and sliced me deep across the chest. I spun and went down hard on the concrete. Evan got back up and came at her, but before he could make it, she whirled in next to Lowe. He's stopped firing at Delores to keep a gun trained on Gloria while Burton finished tying her up. Before he can turn to face her, Delores slices him up from his stomach to his chest, then across. As he went down, I could see internal organs through the cuts. Evan yelled and leapt into the air bringing both swords down. Delores managed to parry one away from her, but the Whiteheart sword moved faster than she could, and it knocked the Killraven weapon away from her. It went clanging across the rooftop.

Everyone stopped firing and waited.

Sharkey was already across the roof and had the butterfly knife we'd seen earlier to Delores' throat. Stacey stepped over to the other blade and was about to pick it up when Burton yelled, "Don't!" Stacey immediately froze.

"You will all bow before him when he arrives! He comes! And when he does, your pathetic world will be swept aside for his glorious order!" Delores spat, still struggling though it was clear that without the weapon in her hand, her strength was far less than Sharkey's.

I ran over to Agent Lowe. Burton stood halfway between her partner and Delores. It was clear that for a moment, she didn't know what to do.

"You will all beg to be destroyed when faced with the punishment he has devised for…" Delores continued.

"Fuckin' A, Delores, face it; we have you. Why not just give in so we can help?" Stacey said.

Delores closed her eyes and shook her head slow. "Oh, you don't understand," she said, seemingly coherent again. "You don't have me…I *have you!*" that last coming out as a roar.

I blinked several times to clear my vision because what I'm seeing couldn't be right, but somehow, it was. Delores, who stood about five foot six or so, was now as tall as I am. Sharkey can't hold on to her. Then, in the next second, Delores is easily seven foot tall and heavily muscled. Her face had grown heavy and two huge bottom teeth emerged from her mouth. She finally stopped growing at about eight foot. She flung Sharkey off of her, but luckily enough, Sharkey landed just shy of the lip of the rooftop. Burton was already firing, as was Stacey. I had trouble dealing with what I was seeing. Evan grabbed his swords once more and was already advancing on the monstrosity. Just behind what used to be Delores, the Killraven blade glowed white-hot and what looked like lightning bolts struck out from it hitting what used to be Delores. The bullets have no effect on the thick skin of the monster. The creature punched Stacey who collapsed immediately. It smacked Evan aside, and he hit the concrete hard, going unconscious. The sword slid across the roof and landed at Burton's feet. The monster advanced on her and it was in that moment that I had an idea.

If the object was the portal through which this energy, this monster we faced, was coming, then perhaps it could be destroyed by its light twin.

I dove for the object and, since I was behind the creature as it closed in on Burton, I was able to get to the blade easily. I had no idea what was going to happen if I touched it with my bare skin, but it was clear nothing else we had tried was going to work. I whipped off my coat, though, just in case.

I grabbed the Killraven object, though trying to do so was a lot like trying to hold on to the first fish I had ever caught. Something about it slid and slipped and vibrated so badly that it was extremely difficult to hold on. At every moment, I felt as though I was going to lose it.

"Burton!" I yelled. "Burton! The sword!"

The monster had made it to her and had her by the wrist. It kept her gun from being able to aim.

"Get the sword!" I yelled again.

The monster turned its head to roar at me for just a second, but that was all Burton needed. She dropped to her knees and swept up the sword. Her action made the monster turn its attention on her and as it did, I threw the Killraven blade toward Burton. She understood instantly and sliced through the air.

When the two objects met, the world went quiet, though it was the loudest quiet I had ever heard. Everything seemed to go black and white for a moment, then faded simply to white. I closed my eyelids but the white light went straight through them. Then there was a boom, and I was knocked to the ground. I fought unconsciousness for what seemed like a year, eventually opening my eyes again. I sat up on my elbows.

No one was still standing; everyone had been knocked down.

The monster that had once been Delores Vandecamp was gone, as were the Whiteheart sword and the Killraven glave.

People started to move. Stacey groaned and got to her knees. Sharkey rolled to one side. Evan pushed himself up to standing. Burton sat up and steadied herself with her hands. Only Lowe did not really move. Burton got to her feet and walked to him.

"I can't feel my legs," Lowe said. His legs were bent at obscene angles.

"Okay," Burton said. Stacey went to help Sharkey up. Evan stood, like me, staring at Burton and Lowe.

"It's…" Lowe said.

"Bad. Yeah," Burton nodded and leans in close to him. "Yeah, it's bad. I need you to try to hold on."

In the distance, I could hear the sirens approaching. I knew that they won't make it in time.

"The blue circle…" Lowe coughed a wet cough. Blood flowed out of the side of his mouth.

"Yeah?" Burton said.

"It didn't work…" Lowe said, and coughed again, this time sounding more like an attempt to laugh. Burton laughed too, but her voice wavered at the end.

"I thought…there was supposed to be…some kind of prophecy…" Lowe said. His voice was faltering. He coughed again, this time more blood flowed from his mouth. "Do…do you think there's…some kind of…after…?" Lowe asked but lost consciousness before he finished his sentence.

Burton closed her eyes, then opened them again. Lowe exhaled and I swear, for a second, I could see whatever was him exit. Burton nodded to herself, then stood up. She took off her jacket and laid it over Lowe's head. She looked over toward Gloria with a fury in her eyes I hadn't ever seen her with before. She started to move toward her, but I stepped between them. She looked at me, her eyes shaking with fury. I shook my head once. She stopped then nodded at me.

I walked over to Stacey. She had a shoulder up under Sharkey's arm to keep them both standing.

"You okay?" I asked. She nodded, though I saw her wince with every step they took toward the stairs.

Evan walked over to me, putting his sword away. "I should probably get out of here before…" he said.

I nodded. "Thanks," I said.

He grinned. "Are you kidding? I wouldn't have missed this for the world." As the sirens closed in on us, he moved past Stacey and Sharkey quickly down the stairs.

I walked back to Burton. She was standing at the lip of the roof staring at the police cruisers that were just pulling up outside.

"What a mess," I said.

"Yeah," she said, "but I can get it taken care of."

We both watched as the cops started entering the building below.

The director looked at Burton, then back at me. She sighed, then said, "Her methods are too unorthodox, even for us. Consider, Mr. Goldman, that she lied to you, manipulated you into taking this case, left out critical details that would have helped you along the way, and all to protect her own ego. No. No, while she is a gifted young woman, I'm afraid there is no way we could accept her. The original judgment stands."

"And if we find her snooping around either Malleus or FBI affairs in the future?" Burton asked.

"How you deal with her impeding your affairs is, of course, up to you," the director said. I couldn't help but feel a shiver at the last part.

"I'll warn her," I said.

"Please do," the director said. She smiled but I could tell there was no actual good feeling behind it. Not toward Stacey.

Burton turned and walked out the door. I followed. Once we were out of the building, I asked, "Okay with you if I tell her myself?" Burton nodded and gestured to the car. I nodded back, then walked across the parking lot to where Stacey was sitting on a bus stop bench. "Hey," I said as I sat down.

"Hey yourself," she said with a grin. "Congratulations," she said.

"Thanks. I still don't know if I'll make it through the academy unscathed, especially at my age, but we'll see. Burton says she's made certain people along the way aware that they should be 'highly motivated,' her words, to…help me along." I laughed.

"And me?" Stacey asked.

I tried so many different combinations of words in my head to see if there was some way to make this sting less but found none. In that second, though, I realized that she was a strong person, that I'd seen her go through so much and still be okay. So I decided to treat her like an adult. "I'm sorry," I said. "They said no."

She nodded, then looked away. After a few minutes, she turned back to me and said, "Okay."

"The director was very specific in her warning, too. You need to steer clear of all of this," I said. "There was a barely veiled threat to it."

She nodded but said nothing. "And Burton?"

"The same," I said.

She nodded once more.

"I'm really sorry, for what it's worth. I know you were just trying to do what you felt was right to help."

Stacey stood. "Bureaucracy," she said. "They'd never understand. To them, all of this is just rules, jurisdictions, code violations." She scuffed at the cement with the toe of her boot. "You'll help Burton with that, right? Make her see?"

"I will do my level best," I said. "In the meantime, I've been thinking about it, and I want to give you something." I pulled out my key ring and slid two of them off. I held them out to her in my palm.

"What is this?" she asked.

"I'm not going to have much need of it, and it wasn't in my care for very long, true, but I can't bear the idea of selling it off to some shmuck who is just going to turn it into some copy making franchise or, worse, a coffee house." I said. I gestured toward her again with my open palm. "Will you take it?"

She stepped closer but didn't reach out for the keys yet.

"I don't have any money," she said. "And I don't think there's any way I could get a loan."

"Do you have a dollar?" I asked. "And a pen?"

She fished in her pocket and found two singles. Then fished into a jacket pocket and found a pen with no cap. She handed that to me and I laughed. I pulled out a slip of paper that was in my pocket. It turned out to be a receipt for coffee from earlier. I shook my head. On the back of it I wrote, "I hereby sell the book store located at..." and I filled in the address and the name of the place, "to one Stacey Durand for the price of $2 and no cents on this the..." and I filled in the date. I wrapped the receipt around the keys and handed it to her. She gave me the two ones. I tried to hand back the pen, but she said, "Keep it. As a memento of this auspicious occasion."

"I'm going to make changes, you know. Hold open ceremonies in the back. Hire kids from the LGBT shelter…you can't come back and say you don't like it. The store is mine, now."

I smiled. "I wouldn't have it any other way. With all that's going on, I don't know if I'll make it back to town…I was wondering… will you take care of Jung for me, too?"

She nodded.

"Remember; he prefers salmon to whitefish, but any fish to chicken," I said.

"I know," Stacey said.

I looked back toward Burton and the car. She wasn't looking at me, but I could tell, even from this distance, she was anxious to get going. "I should go," I said. We both stood.

"Take care of yourself, Goldman," Stacey said, holding out her hand.

I shook it, "You, too." I pulled her in for a hug. I was surprised that she let me. Then we pulled apart, turned, and walked away.

When I got into the car, Burton asked, "Everything okay?"

"Yeah," I said. "You know, I really think it will be."

"Where to?" I asked as I got into the car.

"Well, we've been asked to give testimony at the trial of Simon and his sister before the Malleus tribunal. That's in about an hour or so," Burton said.

"Think there'll be trouble?" I asked.

"I don't think so. They'll pull their memories and there's really no way around that. Plus, we'll be there to make sure we get our part told correctly."

I nodded. She started the car and we pulled out into traffic.

"So, is there?" I asked.

"Is there what?" Burton asked, putting on her sunglasses.

"Right before he died, Paul—he asked if you thought there was an after."

Burton doesn't say anything. I can see myself reflected in her glasses.

"So, do you?" I asked.

"I think any answer I give would be missing the point," she said, and we pulled out onto the freeway.